Langdown Manor

SUE REID

LANGDOWN MANOR

SCHOLASTIC

For Morag

While some events described and some of the characters in this book may be based on actual historical events and real people, this story is a work of fiction.

Scholastic Children's Books
Euston House, 24 Eversholt Street,
London, NW1 1DB, UK

A division of Scholastic Ltd
London ~ New York ~ Toronto ~ Sydney ~ Auckland
Mexico City ~ New Delhi ~ Hong Kong

Published in the UK by Scholastic Ltd, 2012

ISBN 978 1407 13477 2

Printed and bound in the UK by CPI Group (UK) Ltd, Croydon, CR0 4YY

2 4 6 8 10 9 7 5 3 1

Upstairs

The carriage stopped. I had arrived, I thought. I was here, at Langdown Manor, and there was nothing I could do about it. I hadn't wanted to come here, and as I stared out of the carriage window at the plain facade of grey stone, I felt as if the house didn't want me there either.

I'd said the name of the house that was to be my home many times. It was as if I needed to say it to believe in it. Even after I'd waved Father farewell, I couldn't truly believe I was leaving him and the only home I'd ever known. But now I was here I had to. For the hundredth time I wished Father had not sent me to England to live with my mother's sister and her family. Family I had never met – and never wanted to. But Father gave me no choice. He had taken my hands in his and held them tightly. 'A young lady needs a lady's example,' he had said. 'Now that your mother has died, there is no one to give you that. You will like it,' he had added, as if to convince himself. He didn't convince me. 'You have cousins. Your aunt hopes you will be a companion for her eldest daughter.'

So I was to be the companion of a girl I had never met?

'You are going,' he'd said.

The footman who had met me at the railway station came round to open the door. The swaying of the carriage had made me feel slightly sick, and I stumbled as I stepped down, my feet almost as unsteady on the firm ground as they had been when I'd stepped ashore at Dover. The footman escorted me up the steps to the great front door. While we waited for it to be opened I looked again at the house. I had an uneasy feeling that I was being watched. I wondered how my relations felt about my coming to live with them. Father had said that Aunt had written back to him at once, but he hadn't shown me the letter.

An old man opened the door. 'I am his lordship's butler,' he said. 'Welcome to Langdown Manor, miss.' He bowed his head slightly. I couldn't tell what he was thinking. His face might have been carved out of stone.

He stood back and I walked ahead of him into the hall. 'Wait here, miss,' he said. 'I will inform her ladyship of your arrival.' He disappeared through one of the many doorways that led off the hall. I wondered what lay behind them. The hall itself was hushed and quiet as if no one ever used it. I had only seen three servants and yet surely a house as big as this must need hundreds to run it. I thrust my gloved hands back into my muff – it was almost as cold inside as it was outside. At one end of the hall was an enormous fireplace, but no fire had been lit in the grate, and there was no sign that there had ever been one. Maybe people in England didn't feel the cold. After only a day in this drab grey country I was already beginning to feel that I would never get used to it. India seemed a million miles away. I gazed upwards. An oak staircase swept upstairs. The wall was lined with portraits. Haughty-looking men and women stared back at me from behind the frames. My ancestors, I thought, then corrected myself. No, these were my uncle's ancestors, not mine. I didn't like the way they were staring at me. They made me feel like an unwelcome intruder. How was I ever going to get used to living in a mansion like this? I had lived in a bungalow. You could almost have fitted the whole of it into this one room. I didn't know what to expect, or even how to behave. Everything was going to be different, from the weather to the food. I knew a little about both now – and I didn't think much of them.

A gust of icy air blew past me into the hall. I looked round to see that the footman had nudged open the door and was manoeuvring my trunk inside. It was the same trunk Mother had brought out to India many years ago, before I was born. All my worldly possessions were inside that trunk – well, all that I'd managed to cram in. My old ayah had said that I should leave some behind, to make sure I'd come back. She hadn't needed to say that. I knew I'd go back one day. I knew I'd hate England. Mother had, and I was like her, everybody said. I'd found the trunk in Mother's room, hidden under the bed, a few days after she had died. I'd never seen it before.

The words 'Penelope Fitzsimmons, Bombay, India' were scrawled in thick black ink on a label that was as mottled as an old person's skin. Mother's name and mine. The clasps were rusty, but to my surprise they'd clicked back easily, as if the trunk had been opened many times. The day after Mother had died I'd opened her wardrobe and buried my head in her gowns to breathe in her smell. But the things in the trunk hadn't smelled like Mother – they'd smelled musty and old, not like Mother at all. I hadn't known what to expect, but it hadn't been this – these yellowing mysterious things. A lacy veil was attached to a plume of three feathers. The feathers flew up into the air when I touched them – like drifting snow, or how I imagine snow. I've never seen it. I'd felt as if I was gazing into a secret world, one Mother had kept locked away in her trunk. I'd never seen Mother wear any of these things, but they must have held some meaning for her for her to have kept them.

Right at the bottom I'd found a thick bundle of yellowing envelopes bound in red ribbon. I'd picked them up curiously, then put them down again. I hadn't wanted to read them – then. I'd shut the lid with a bang. I couldn't think why Mother had kept these things – why would she want to be reminded about a past I felt sure she'd hated? My ayah of course took them out before she packed the trunk for me. I found them discarded in a box. I couldn't bear to think what would happen to them if they were left behind, so I'd slipped what I could fit into the trunk before it was locked.

The butler reappeared out of the gloom. 'Follow me, miss,' he said. He led me up to a door and knocked. I felt my heart thump. Behind that door were the relations I'd never met. What would they be like? What would they think of me? Had Father told them anything about me? He had told me hardly anything about them.

'Miss Penelope, your ladyship,' the butler said, announcing me. It made me start to hear him say my name. Few people call me by it. Those who know and love me always call me Polly.

Three heads had turned at my entrance. Three pairs of eyes swept over me. The younger girl smiled, the elder merely stared. What my aunt thought, it was hard to tell. She had the kind of face that was able to conceal what she felt. It wasn't the welcome I'd expected. I was beginning to feel that I had been catapulted into the wrong family – *'will someone please explain who this girl is and why she is here'* – when my aunt stood up. 'Forgive me, my dear,' she said. 'I hadn't expected that you would look so like your mother.' I couldn't tell if this pleased or pained her. 'But then you will know that, of course,' she added. I shook my head. No, I'd never seen a photograph of Mother at my age. She had never shown me one. So far as I knew she hadn't had one. 'Come with me,' Aunt said. She led me over to a small table, on which was an array of silver-framed photographs. She picked one up and handed it to me. I felt as if I were looking into a mirror.

The same defiant eyes and obstinate chin. (That was how Father described them!)

'The similarity between you is very striking,' Aunt said. She hesitated. 'I grieve for your loss,' she said. 'I was very fond of your mother.' That should have drawn me closer to her, but somehow it didn't. I put the photograph down hastily. It had unnerved me to see how alike we were. I felt sad, too. All that was left of Mother was photographs like this, the few things of hers I had, and my memories.

'Now you must meet your cousins. Arabella,' Aunt said, beckoning forward the elder of the two girls, who was sitting on one of the spindly chairs that scattered the room. If I was the mirror of my mother, Arabella was like hers, magnified many times over. Her eyes were cold and watchful. I was suddenly reminded of a snake my ayah had found on the veranda outside our bungalow. We had eyed each other warily until Father had removed it. He'd told me it would only injure me if it felt frightened or threatened. In India I had dealt with snakes by keeping my distance. I'd never thought I'd have to live with one.

'Arabella has been looking forward to having a companion her own age,' Aunt added.

Didn't Aunt have eyes in her head? Couldn't she see how Arabella was looking at me – as if I were a curiosity that had been dug up and should have been left where it was.

Her greeting didn't make me feel any better. 'Welcome,

cousin Penelope,' she said. The words seemed to slide through her lips in spite of herself. 'What a pretty gown, cousin,' she added. 'Is it an Indian fashion?'

If I hadn't already guessed what sort of girl she was I'd have known then. It's the sort of thing girls say when they want to put you down. There was nothing wrong with my gown, except that it was too thin. No one seemed to have thought when they packed for me that England was a colder country than India. Aunt didn't appear to have noticed any sarcasm in her daughter's remark. 'It is indeed. But maybe a trifle thin for our climate. Have you nothing warmer that you can wear?' *A wrap that had once been Mother's.* It was worn and the colours had faded in the sun. I could imagine Arabella's face if I put that on.

'Then come and sit by the fire,' Aunt said when I was silent. 'Tomorrow, I will look over your gowns. We may be able to find some of Arabella's that will fit you.' I wasn't at all sure that I wanted to be clad in Arabella's cast-offs. Nor could I imagine myself in pink! I sat down on one of the spindly chairs by the fire. My youngest cousin – who Aunt introduced as Clementine – sat down next to me. Her face, I was relieved to see, was as open and friendly as Arabella's was closed and watchful. There was another cousin, George, who was at university, Aunt told me. And my uncle was in town, but would return in time for dinner. 'Now we will have tea,' Aunt said. She got up and tugged the bellrope by the door. 'We were waiting for you, my dear,' she explained. The footman who came answered the bell so promptly I felt sure he'd been listening. He didn't look at me. His face was as expressionless as a sheet of clean paper.

'You may bring in the tea now, Robert,' Aunt said.

She drew her chair closer to me. There was so much she wanted to ask me, she said, but her questions were oddly impersonal. What had my journey been like? Had the sea been rough? She was sorry that the train had been delayed – but not once did she ask about Father, or my life in India. I felt as if a door was swinging shut. Behind it was my past life. It was as if Aunt felt about India as I felt sure Mother had about England.

The footman brought in the tea, setting down cups and plates on little tables next to us. Clementine liked a lot of milk and sugar in her tea. I took neither.

Clementine stared. 'Don't you like milk?' she said.

'Not in tea,' I said.

'Is that an Indian thing?' she asked curiously.

I was about to answer when Aunt cut in. 'Even in England, we don't always take milk in our tea. You know that, Clementine,' she said briskly. Even the word India wasn't allowed to sully Aunt's lips.

A silence fell. Anything I wanted to talk about seemed to be forbidden. I tried to hide my yawns – I hadn't had a proper night's sleep since I had left home.

'Perhaps you would like to rest,' Aunt said, when I'd given up trying. 'You must be tired. You've had a very long journey. I will send Baxter to you to help you unpack and to attend to you. She is not a trained lady's maid, but very willing. I'm sure you will find her satisfactory. Arabella, perhaps you will show Penelope to her room. I am sure you girls have much to talk about.' She smiled indulgently. Why did grown-ups think that all you had to do was throw girls together for them to make friends? I had more in common with Clementine, who asked if I had ever ridden an elephant and who has promised to take me to the stables.

We walked upstairs in silence. I'm sure we were both wishing that I'd never come.

'This is your room,' Arabella said, opening a door into a large chamber that overlooked the park. A fire had been lit, but a howling gale blew through this room, too. Pieces of yellowing newspaper were stuck in the gaps between the windows and the frames, but it sounded from their constant rattling as if someone was trying to climb in. I saw a damp patch on the ceiling. Old wallpaper had peeled away like skin in places. I began to see that the grandeur that had so impressed me when I'd arrived at the house was merely a facade. Underneath it, cracks were growing and spreading. Chairs wobbled, paintwork peeled and water poured down from leaky gutters – as if the whole edifice was being propped up when perhaps it should be quietly allowed to crumble. It was as if I was looking in on a dying world, in which people like my relations would soon have no place. But in the meantime appearances were to be kept up, the rot ignored until it was no longer possible to do so.

Arabella loitered about, casting curious glances at my trunk, which had been put down at the foot of my bed – a huge four-poster. Tired red hangings lifted slightly in the gale. What did she think I kept in it? A collection of elephant tusks? My pet snake? I had no intention of opening it until she had gone. I couldn't think why she stayed – we had nothing to say to each other. At last she gave up and left me to dress. Dinner was not till eight. In two hours' time. How long did it take to change a gown? I crawled on to the bed and thought longingly of the cosy bungalow I'd left. How would I stand this cold and draughty place? Misery tugged at me – a nagging ache. Why had Father sent me away to live in this family where I was not wanted? Where I did not belong and never would? Rain had begun to patter against the window. I would *never* get used to this place, *never*. I pulled the hangings shut around me.

Downstairs

'Get that darn creature out of here!' Cook bellowed. 'As if I hadn't enough to do.' I leapt back hastily as a cat tore past. I'd picked the wrong time to come down to the kitchen! There hadn't been a right time, mind, not since Emma had left.

'Sorry, Jess!' I leaned back as Maddie pushed past me and grabbed the cat, sticking out her tongue at Cook's back. We grinned at each other. 'Come on you, out you go,' she said, opening the door and releasing the cat. It arched its back and rubbed itself against her legs, but she shut the door on it firmly. 'She always complains, but it's me and Maisie who have all the extra work,' she grumbled. I went with her into the scullery. A huge pile of dishes filled the sink. 'Look at them!' Maddie said. She turned on the tap furiously. I jumped aside as the water spurted out. 'And it's not even my job!'

I smiled wryly. I had more than enough to do myself. Yesterday I'd been summoned to the housekeeper's room and told that I, Jess Baxter, was to attend on her ladyship's niece until a proper lady's maid was hired. Mrs Smithson had made it sound like an honour, but to me it was just one more chore to add to all the others – and an unwelcome one at that. I didn't want anything to do with the family upstairs. Upstairs I was just a servant; downstairs I felt that I had a place in the world, even if Mr Barrett made it plain to us lower servants just what *that* was.

Maddie moved aside for me, and I held the vase I'd brought down from the hall under the tap. The flowers had begun to wilt, but the fresh water would revive them. 'When's the new scullery maid arriving?' I said, running water into the vase. 'She should have been here by now, shouldn't she?' I turned off the tap and gave the vase a wipe.

'She should have,' Maddie said, going back to the sink. She picked up a pot and began to scrub it. 'But she wasn't in the wagon sent to fetch her.'

'What?' I exclaimed. 'Where is she then?'

'Beats me,' Maddie shrugged. 'All I know is we're still one pair of hands short. Cook says it wouldn't have happened if she'd been allowed to choose her staff.'

'She's got a point,' I said. I felt sorry for Maddie. Emma, the scullery maid, had been given notice and had left the same day. We'd never found out why. In the month since then Maddie and Maisie had had to share the scullerying work on top of their own duties in the kitchen. Ivy Harte, the new scullery maid, we'd been told, was the daughter of an old friend of a lady's maid who had once worked in service at Langdown Manor. Ivy, though, had never worked in service before and it seemed wasn't about to now either.

'Wotcha, Maddie.' A head poked round the scullery door – it was that cheeky young footman, Robert. 'Make us a cup of tea, love,' he said to Maddie, giving me a wink.

'Can't you see I've enough to do,' Maddie protested. She began to scrub furiously, head bent down over the sink, but the cheek that I could see had turned pink. She'd never admit it, but Maddie had a soft spot for Robert. I knew that she was wasting her time, but I hadn't the heart to tell her. I liked Maddie, but we weren't close. Sarah was my best friend at Langdown. We had known each other nearly all our lives, and had begun service at Langdown the same day. It had been lucky for us, we'd agreed, that they'd needed two housemaids.

'Then I'll just have to ask my favourite housemaid.' I felt Robert's arm come round my waist. He gave me a squeeze.

'Leave off, Robert,' I said, wriggling out of his grasp, 'or I'll drop her ladyship's precious vase and then where will I be?' But in spite of myself I was smiling. Robert made me laugh.

I put down the vase. Robert sauntered past me into the kitchen and sat down. 'Heard the latest?' he called back, stretching out his long legs under the table. You could depend on Robert for gossip. He knew it all – upstairs and down.

'As if we got time for gossip,' Cook said, coming to the scullery door, and wiping her floury hands on her apron. 'Maddie, what do you think you're doing? Leave those pots for now. There's all them vegetables to chop still. Oh, and while you're about it, make Robert that cuppa.' Even Cook had a soft spot in her thorny old heart for Robert. ''Urry up,' she called as she sailed back to her kingdom. 'We 'aven't all night now – and we're still a pair of hands short.'

'She doesn't have to tell me,' grumbled Maddie as we walked together back down the passage. She went over to the range and picked up the teapot. I hung round the door watching while she poured tea into a mug. I didn't go in – it was too hot and steamy in there for me. I don't know how the kitchen staff stand it. 'There,' she said, setting it down on the table in front of Robert.

'Thanks, Maddie,' Robert said, wrapping both hands around the mug. 'It was perishing on that box – had to sit there nearly half an hour. Her ladyship's niece's train was late. Points failure.'

'I know,' I said. I felt I was living on borrowed time. Every time a bell rang to summon a servant my stomach plummeted southwards, thinking it was for me. I knew that I'd be sent for soon – and I was dreading it.

'No,' he said. 'That's not what I was going to tell you. It's young Ivy.' He grinned. 'You have a treat in store.' He put down his mug and rubbed his hands together.

'Yes, we know, she's not coming,' Maddie grumbled.

'Oh yes, she is. She's here.'

'What!' Maddie and I exclaimed together.

'Yes, she's here all right.' Robert grinned. 'But wait – you haven't heard the best of it. She went to the front door.'

'No!' We gasped as one.

'Oh, yes,' said Robert. 'Old Man B didn't know what had hit him when he opened it. I was in the hall, see, saw it all. "I'm the new scullery maid," she says. "What do you think you're doing here then, servants round the back," he replies. What does young Ivy do? Drops her box at his feet. "I've carried this all the way from the village. I can't carry it no more."'

'She never!' said Maisie, who had come in from the still room.

'Oh yes, Maisie, love,' said Robert. 'You should have seen Mr B's face,' he went on. 'I thought he'd send her packing, but his soft heart got the better of him and he got young Sam to bring in the box for her. But round the back she went.'

'Why didn't she take the wagon sent to meet her?' I exclaimed.

'That was what Mr B said. "No one told me about a wagon," she said. "Do you think I'd walk if I could ride?"'

'Well, I never,' I said. 'Got a tongue on her.' Maddie, Maisie and I shared a glance. I think we were all wishing we'd seen Mr B's face. None of us liked him. He liked to lord it over us. I'd like to have seen him discomfited for once.

Cook shook her head. 'Gone to the front door? I don't know. When I was a girl...'

'Servants knew their place,' Maddie and I mouthed silently at each other. We giggled, taking care that Cook couldn't see.

'...servants knew their place. What's the world coming to?'

Cook went on, 'So, as it seems that everyone knows more about the whereabouts of my staff than I do, perhaps you could tell me where the lass is now, Robert?'

'With Mrs Smithson, getting a proper wigging, no doubt,' said Robert, grinning. I smiled. I couldn't imagine that she would. Mrs Smithson was the kindest of the housekeepers I'd worked under. Not that there had been many. This was only my second job since I'd begun in service three years ago. Mrs Smithson was probably the only member of staff who liked Mr Barrett. I could never understand what she saw in him, but the gossip was that once they retired they'd marry. I hoped for her sake Mrs S would realize her mistake before she let the old misery take her down the aisle.

Cook snorted, slapping down a handful of dough with floury hands on the table. She began to roll it out. 'She should have let me choose my maid. What does her highness know about scullerying? One day I'll 'and in my notice and then they'll be sorry.'

I smiled to myself. No one took much notice of Cook's threats – Maddie had told me that she made them around once a week.

'Well, we'll have to hope for the best, I dare say.' She turned round. Her eyes fell on a big basket of fruit and vegetables. 'Maddie, what are you thinking!' she roared. 'I need those vegetables washed and scraped – now! Or there'll be no dinner – upstairs or down.'

'Sorry, Cook,' Maddie murmured. 'Jess, give us a hand, will you?'

I put down the vase, and took hold of one handle of the basket. 'What have you got in here?' I gasped, as we lifted it up. It felt like we were lugging a crate of bricks. How many vegetables could one household eat? We staggered into the back kitchen. I put the basket down heavily. Too heavily. Some of the potatoes bounced out and rolled across the floor. Maddie bent down wearily to pick them up.

'I don't care what that girl's like,' she muttered. 'I just hope she starts soon, or they'll find themselves looking for another kitchen maid, too.' She pushed some stray wisps of hair back under her cap.

I helped her sort the vegetables into heaps. Brussels. Carrots. Potatoes. Parsnips. Greens. Then I picked up the vase again and made my way to the stairs that led from the basement up to the hall. I was halfway along the passage when I heard a sudden exclamation.

'I beg your pardon, your ladyship.' It was Cook's voice. She sounded furious. I nipped back down the passage and poked my head round the door to see who she was talking to. Standing by the kitchen table I saw a girl half my size. My mouth dropped open. 'Is this her?'

'It's her,' Cook said grimly. 'And I hope she's not started as she means to go on. "Mrs Smithson says, go to the kitchen for a plate of something," she says to me. And me with the dinner still to cook!' Robert was still sitting at the table. He grinned, as if he was enjoying the joke. Cook glared at him. 'Robert, if you've finished your tea, get back where you belong. And you, girl,' Cook's voice snapped like a whip. 'Sit down. Arms like sticks,' I heard her mutter as she went back to the range. 'They'll be sending me children next. What was Mrs Smithson thinking of?'

The girl pulled out a chair and sat down. She looked like she'd blow away in a draught. 'Get that down you, girl,' Cook said, ladling meaty broth from the stewpot into a bowl and setting it down in front of Ivy. 'And when you've done,' she went on, 'Maisie here will help you carry your box upstairs.'

'I can manage,' the girl said. 'I'm stronger than I look. I carried my box all the way here, didn't I?' She began to spoon up the broth as if she was half starved.

I gasped. 'Listen to the cheek on her!'

Cook was shaking her head. 'I'll let it by as you're new, but don't you ever speak to me like that again.'

The girl nodded, but there was a defiant flush to her face. She pushed aside her plate and stood up. 'I'm ready now.'

'Maisie,' said Cook, 'take Ivy upstairs and show her where she'll be sleeping. Then you,' she said to Ivy, 'get changed and you can make a start on the pots in the scullery. Maddie will show you what to do. You do know what a pot looks like?' she added sarcastically.

Ivy opened her mouth to speak, but had enough sense

this time to close it again. The look on her face said it all though. *You want me to start tonight?* I slipped away before the storm broke behind me. Sarah was upstairs checking the fires and I'd the beds to turn down and then there'd be her ladyship's niece to attend to. Mrs Smithson hadn't told me a lot about her and all I knew was that she'd come all the way from India. My mind switched to young Ivy. We didn't know a lot about her either. But if this afternoon was anything to go by, I didn't see her lasting long.

UPSTAIRS

'Wake up, miss.'

'Leave me be,' I murmured. My head felt heavy with sleep.

'I must ask you to get up, miss.' I felt a hand touch my shoulder. I shook it away in surprise. What did my ayah think she was doing? She'd never laid a finger on me before. I was missy sahib and she did what I ordered – not the other way around.

'Leave me, Shamala. I'll call you if I want you,' I said.

'I don't know who Sh-Shamla is, miss, but I have to get you up and dressed. Dinner's in half an hour.' It didn't sound like Shamala. I rolled over and opened my eyes. I was still drowsily expecting to see an Indian face peering anxiously at me from behind a mosquito net. Instead I found myself staring into the face of a girl I'd never seen before. She was looking at me nervously – as if she wasn't sure what I'd do or say next.

'Who are you?' I demanded.

'Baxter, miss.' She bobbed a curtsy. 'Her ladyship's asked me to attend on you.'

'Baxter's an odd name,' I commented.

'It's a common enough name in England, miss.'

I felt my head begin to clear. Of course, I was in England now.

'What's your first name?' I asked.

The maid looked awkward. 'You should call me Baxter, miss.'

'Well, leave me, Baxter,' I said dismissively. 'I don't need you.' The maid gaped at me as if I had been rude. I couldn't think why. She was a servant. She had to do what I said.

'I must ask you to get up, miss. It's half-past seven and her ladyship expects you downstairs.'

In India servants did what they were told. In England, it seemed, it was different. It was one more thing I was going to have to get used to.

I sat up and swung my legs wearily to the floor.

'Begging your pardon, miss, but you'll need to change.'

Did I? I looked down at myself. My gown was crumpled from lying on it. I sighed. All my clothes were still in my trunk, and it was locked. I took the key off the chain I wore around my neck and slipped off the bed. I unlocked the trunk and began to burrow down inside it.

'Miss, you don't need to do that. I'll unpack for you!' Baxter exclaimed.

'No!' I didn't want her to unpack. I didn't want anyone rifling through Mother's things. They were precious.

Baxter looked confused. 'But, miss…'

'I must take a few things out first,' I said, fingers diving beneath my clothes searching for where the letters and Mother's things were tucked away – the long white kid gloves, the jewels, ribbons, sashes and silk scarves.

As I stood up again I saw Baxter's face reflected in the mirror. She looked upset, and I felt that I'd offended her. She was younger than I'd thought at first, around the same age as me. It was the hair scraped back under the white cap that made her seem older.

I took the precious bundle and laid the garments carefully in one of the drawers in the dressing table. When she'd finished unpacking, I'd put them back in the trunk and lock it again. No one but me was allowed to touch Mother's things.

'Now you may unpack,' I said, standing aside.

Baxter bent down and began to lift out my gowns. 'Bit thin, aren't they, miss?' she commented. Then she went pink, as if she'd said something she shouldn't have. 'Sorry, miss.'

'I've just come from India, which is a much hotter country than this,' I said. I sat down on the bed and pulled a blanket round me. Why hadn't anyone told me how cold England was? A gale was still blowing in the room.

'And they'll need pressing, too, miss,' Baxter carried on as if I hadn't spoken. 'Tell me which one you want to wear tonight and I'll tidy it up for you.'

What does it matter what I wear?

'I don't care,' I said.

Baxter chose to ignore my tone. 'Then how about this one? It's very pretty.' She held up a violet silk gown. 'I think it would look very nice on you.'

'Mother liked it,' I said. I'd worn it on her birthday, a few weeks before she'd been taken ill. I hadn't worn it since. I felt my eyes fill. I turned my face away so that Baxter wouldn't see.

'Then I think you should wear it. She'd be proud of you.'

'Mother is dead,' I said abruptly. 'That's why I had to come here.' Hadn't anyone told her anything about me? It was as if my past was something to be ashamed of.

'I'm sorry,' she said. I could hear pity for me in her voice. I didn't want her pity. I angrily rubbed away the tears that had filled my eyes. 'Let me run you a bath,' she said. 'You'll feel better for it. And the dress will be ready for you when you get out.'

At least the bath water was hot. I turned on the hot tap and let it run until the room filled with steam. Lying back in the water, the hot steam swirling about me, I could almost pretend I was home in India. But the cold felt so much worse when I got out.

The dress was lying on the bed when I got back. Baxter helped me into it.

'Turn round,' she said, 'and I'll tie the sash for you.' As I turned round, I caught a glimpse of myself in the dressing-table mirror. I didn't like what I saw – a scowling face beneath tousled dark hair that looked as if I'd been dragging my fingers through it.

'Your hair's in need of a brush,' Baxter said.

'My ayah used to brush it for me,' I said. 'One hundred brushes every night.'

'What's an ayah, miss?' Baxter said.

'It's what we call a nurse in India,' I told her.

'Bit old for a nurse, aren't you?' She went pink again. 'I'm sorry, miss, I shouldn't have said that. I expect it's different in India.'

'It is – very different.'

She picked up the brush and began to draw it through my hair. 'You have lovely dark hair,' she said. 'You'll be putting it up soon, won't you? Miss Arabella is coming out this year. I expect you'll come out with her.' She said it as if it was something to look forward to.

I pulled a face. It was bad enough that I had to come out into society at all. But to come out at the side of the queen of vipers? I felt I'd sooner jump off the roof.

Baxter had observed my distaste. 'What! Surely you want to be a young lady? There'll be parties, and dances, and balls. You'll go to London too – for the season.'

I didn't want to go to London for the season. I didn't care if I never had one.

'There,' Baxter said. She laid down the hairbrush on the dressing table. My hair lay thick and glossy over my shoulders. I squared them. I'd meet my uncle this evening, and I wasn't looking forward to that. I'd had quite enough of my new family already. Three was more than enough when one of them was Arabella.

Somewhere far below a gong boomed. 'That's a gong, miss – it's to let you know it's time for dinner,' said Baxter.

I know what a gong is. We're not savages in India!

She lifted my hair up and tied it with a ribbon. She gave me a quick appraising glance. 'You're ready, Miss Penelope.'

I didn't feel ready. I felt as if I was about to be ravaged by lions.

They were waiting for me when I went down. They were talking quietly, their backs to me. About me, no doubt. I felt lonely suddenly, an outsider looking in on a happy family group.

'Ah, here she is,' said Aunt, turning round. She sized me up with a swift glance. I couldn't tell what she thought. Arabella said nothing.

Uncle's greeting was warmer. 'Welcome, my dear,' he said giving me a kiss. He smelt like Father; cigar on his breath. He gave me his arm to escort me into the dining room. It was a heavy dark room with red-flocked wallpaper and wooden panelling. In the middle of the room was a huge table, set for four. Uncle handed me to my seat, opposite Arabella, a mass of pink ribbons and lace. She glared at me – it was like a fuchsia glowering at a tulip. Uncle took his seat at the head of the table. Aunt was seated about a mile away at the other end. Silent footmen appeared and disappeared by my side, dishes came and went, my glass was filled and refilled. I felt as if I was living a dream. None of it felt real. Any moment now I was sure I would wake up and find myself at home, hear the patter of bare feet, as servants brought in the evening meal, the wail of the muezzin, calling the faithful to prayer, heat stinging my eyelids.

'Do you hunt?' asked Uncle stabbing at a piece of meat on his plate as if it was a tiger in a pit.

'My dear, what a question. How can a lady hunt, riding side-saddle?' Aunt exclaimed.

'Many ladies hunt, seated side-saddle. It is becoming quite the fashion,' Uncle said. He smiled at me.

I smiled back. I had found an ally in my uncle.

'I do hunt,' I said. 'Father hunts tigers in India. He shoots them from the back of an elephant. He made me a necklace of tiger teeth.' There, I had got them both in. India and Father. I saw Aunt frown. Arabella wrinkled up her nose in distaste. But Uncle chuckled.

'Does he, by jove,' he said, laying down his knife and fork. 'We can only offer foxes here, I'm afraid.'

I laughed dutifully. 'He shoots other wild beasts, too. India is full of them,' I said.

The silence round the table warned me that I was on dangerous ground, but nothing would induce me to get off it again. I would not be diverted. I would talk about my home and family whether they liked it or not. I could not brush away the past, however much Aunt wished it.

'We must find a good mount for you,' said Uncle breaking the silence.

'Clementine said she would take me to the stables tomorrow,' I said.

'She can take you in the afternoon,' Aunt decreed, 'when she has her afternoon walk. In the morning I must look over your gowns.' No one had remarked on the gown I was wearing, and I felt it was time they did.

'Do you like my gown?' I said. 'It was Mother's favourite.' It was the only reason I had brought it to England. I was glad Baxter had suggested that I wear it. Wearing it made me feel closer to Mother somehow.

'It is very pretty,' said Aunt at last. 'But it would be more suitable in summer.'

'In India it is suitable all year round,' I said trying to draw the conversation back to India. I knew I was being difficult, but I couldn't help myself. Arabella's cold stares provoked me. I would never fit in here. Never. And if they found me difficult how did they think I found them? My coming here had been a mistake, and the sooner they realized it the sooner they'd send me home again.

'Tomorrow we will see if any of Arabella's old gowns will fit you,' Aunt said.

I'd sooner go naked.

'But we will of course have new gowns made for you, too,' she added, seeing my expression.

Arabella perked up. 'You promised me a new gown, too, Mother,' she said.

Gowns! Gowns! Gowns! Was that *all* my cousin cared about? I concentrated on my meal. I have a hearty appetite and I was hungry. I ignored the disdainful glances Arabella cast at me. *Even if a lady is hungry, she should never show it.* But I was very sure I wasn't a lady, and just as sure I'd never be one.

Downstairs

'She never!' gasped Sarah. Her big eyes grew huge. 'Fancy you letting her talk to you like that!'

'What choice did I have?' I said, shrugging.

'Well I can tell you I'd not want to be a maid in India,' Sarah said, 'if that's how they talk to their servants.'

'And then there are all the diseases.'

'Snakes.'

'Ugh!'

I was sitting in my favourite room – the maids' sitting room – my friends curled up on the sofa next to me. There was always a scramble for it. Bits were bursting out of the arms and the back was worn dark and shiny, but it was the only comfortable seat there was. A fire had been lit in the grate and we'd dragged the sofa up close to it. I could hear a voice singing in the scullery. Young Ivy was still there, up to her elbows in soapsuds. She could sing, I thought. I smiled wryly when I thought of the entrance she had made earlier.

Here we could say what we liked, safe from the watchful eyes and ears of the upper servants. They never came in here. Barrett ruled the servants' hall and you didn't dare talk about your betters there. Not that we thought the family upstairs was better than us. Only different.

I drew up my knees under me. 'She's all right, I suppose,' I said grudgingly. 'She's just not used to our ways. Actually, I feel a bit sorry for her.'

'I can't think why,' said Sarah. 'She's rich, isn't she? She'll never have to work, like the rest of us.'

'But she's no older than me and she's come all that way to live with a family she doesn't know.' My dad would never send me halfway round the world to live with strangers. Sometimes I just don't understand posh people.

'It's Miss Arabella I feel sorry for,' Sarah said, as if I hadn't spoken.

'You feel sorry for Arabella!' I looked at her in astonishment. 'Whatever for?'

'She's the young lady of the house, isn't she? She's coming out this year. Now she's got to share her big moment with a cousin she doesn't know. I wouldn't like that.'

How did Sarah learn all this?

'She's a haughty creature, that Miss Arabella,' said Maisie. 'Gives you the run around. Will do her good.'

'Miss Clementine is quite different,' put in Ellen. 'Lovely manners. Such a sweet child.'

'She'll change. Arabella was sweet at that age,' said Maddie. Sarah and I exchanged a glance. We didn't agree. We all loved little Miss Clemmie. I couldn't imagine her ever changing.

But Maddie knew the family better than we did. She'd been here longer than all the rest of us.

'She asked me to put aside some carrots for the horses,' said Maisie. 'She told me she's taking Miss Penelope to the stables tomorrow. Apparently Miss Penelope loves riding.'

I saw Sarah blush. You only had to say the word 'stable' or 'horse' to Sarah for her to blush. I knew that it was Fred, one of the stable hands, that she was thinking of. They'd known each other almost since childhood – like Sarah and me – and everyone knew that they were hoping to marry, when they could afford to.

I smiled looking around at my friends. I wished I didn't have to attend on Miss Penelope. I'd been much happier when I was just a housemaid. The work was hard, and the hours long, but there wasn't so much of that bowing and scraping I hated so much. 'Yes, Miss Penelope. No, Miss Penelope.' And most of all I hated being called Baxter! But you had to put up with it, Mam had told me. I'd not wanted to go into service, but I'd had no choice. Maybe there were other choices for girls now, but I didn't know how to use a typewriter and I'd never want to work in a factory. But Miss Penelope had even less choice than I had. She'd been shunted off halfway round the world, and all that she had to look forward to was marriage or being a spinster. I wouldn't want to change places with her even if I could.

Robert's head appeared round the door. 'Didn't you hear

the bell, Jess? Miss Penelope's maid is expected upstairs. Time for bye-byes.'

I groaned and climbed off the sofa. And that was the other thing I didn't like about my new position. My life at the end of a bellrope.

'So the life of a lady's maid is not all it's cracked up to be then?' said Sarah. I shook my head vigorously.

'But at least there isn't so much cleaning. Just think of all the extra housework Ellen and me have to do now.'

'I know, it isn't fair.' But it wasn't my fault. I hadn't asked to do this job. Roll on the day when Miss Penelope came out and had a proper lady's maid to look after her.

UPSTAIRS

'Tum tucked in. Tum *and* behind tucked in, Miss Penelope,' Madame said.

I wobbled downwards once again. Rising was even worse. In a few months' time I'd be doing this in front of the King and Queen. How would I ever manage it in a corset?

I scowled. It was a stupid way to spend a morning. But I had only myself to blame. Rashly I'd told Aunt my age – nearly eighteen – and she had decided that Arabella and I would come out together. Now I had to polish up all the accomplishments expected of a young lady – how to curtsy and climb in and out of a carriage gracefully. Aunt was to arrange for some dancing lessons for Arabella and me, and I was to practise the piano daily – one hand at a time until I could manage both together.

I glanced at the window. Outside clouds were gathering – a forerunner of rain to come.

We had begun the day sorting through my gowns. Out of fashion or too thin for the English climate, Aunt had pronounced. She'd made me climb in and out of gowns that Arabella had grown out of, which Aunt said would do nicely until new gowns could be made for me. Baxter had crawled on hands and knees around my ankles, taking in a tuck here, unpicking a hem there. Arabella and I grew in different directions.

All my protests were ignored as I was hustled into a pink gown.

'You look lovely,' said my aunt. Baxter pulled in the fabric at my waist. Her eyes met mine. Her lips were twitching.

So now I was a figure of fun, too. I'd make sure to tear it the first time I wore it.

'*Please* pay attention, Miss Penelope. We have a lot of catching up to do.' I jerked myself back to the present. A despairing note had crept into Madame's voice.

'Remember what I told you. We are backing out of the royal presence.' I saw her glance at her watch. Did she find this as tedious as I did? I reversed, wondering how I was to do this without tripping over my train. 'Hold out your arm, Miss Penelope,' Madame sighed. 'The Lord Chamberlain will throw your train over your arm before you walk backwards. Watch and learn, Miss Penelope. Watch and learn.' It was her favourite mantra. I marched backwards, arm stuck out. I must look ridiculous. I glanced at Arabella. Her face was like stone. I'd more easily get a smile out of a statue. 'Much better, Miss Penelope,' Madame cooed. 'Perhaps we should stop now, when we are doing so well. Tomorrow we will practise getting in and out of a carriage like a lady.'

If I hadn't killed myself first.

I'd arranged to join Clemmie and her governess in the hall at three for Clemmie to take me to the stables. It was in the house that I felt my worst, I decided. I'd be myself again after a good gallop.

I was in the hall before the clock struck three, dressed for riding in habit, bowler and veil. I didn't have to wait long for Clemmie. She clattered downstairs, promptly followed by Miss Dunn, her governess. She wasn't in riding clothes. I saw her stare at mine. I was wearing my white habit, and I shone like a beacon. Like my gowns it was more suited to the tropics than to this cold country. 'It's what we wear to ride in India,' I told her. I twirled so that the habit flared out, like an apron, which was what it was. 'It's a lot safer than an ordinary habit if you fall,' I explained, lifting it to show her. 'It won't get caught on the saddle.'

'Oh, how clever!' said Clemmie clapping her hands. Miss Dunn had caught sight of a petticoat. She blushed. How unladylike!

'But aren't you going to ride?' I said to Clemmie.

'Not today,' she said, giving Miss Dunn a furious look. She whispered in my ear. 'She says it's too cold.'

'Miss Clementine has a weak chest,' Miss Dunn explained, wrapping a thick scarf around Clemmie's neck.

'Oh,' I said, not sure what to say.

'It's all right,' said Clemmie. 'They say I'll grow out of it, but in the meantime they make an awful fuss.' She glared at Miss Dunn. But even when she glowers Clemmie's face is so sweet you can't help smiling.

The stables were tucked away to the side of the house, beyond a huddle of other outbuildings. The wind whipped my face. Baxter had assured me it was a fine day when she'd pulled back the curtains that morning. In England that seems to mean that it isn't actually raining.

Clemmie opened the gate into the yard. Two men were washing their arms in a bucket of soapy water. They threw me a curious look, then touched their caps when they saw who I was with. I looked past them to see a boy leading a horse up to a stall. Her flanks were steaming as if she had been ridden hard. I caught a glimpse of a white star on her forehead. I watched while the boy sponged her down and threw a blanket over her back. He was whistling. The tune was oddly familiar. I tried to remember why, and then I did. Father used to hum it sometimes when he'd thought that Mother wasn't listening. It used to irritate Mother, but I liked it. It was comforting to hear it now. It made Langdown seem a little less strange.

'Hello, Fred!' Clemmie shouted. She seized my arm, pulling me along with her.

'Miss Clementine, Miss Penelope!' expostulated Miss Dunn, lifting her gown in one hand to hasten after us. 'Remember who you are. A young lady does not shout and she does not run.'

The lad had straightened up at the sound of Clemmie's voice. 'Good afternoon.' He bent his head politely, pushing back a strand of auburn hair that had fallen into his eyes. His hand was very white for someone who worked outside all day, and there were little freckles on his arm. He looked up and caught me staring. I blushed and looked away.

'I've brought my cousin Penelope to see the stables,' explained Clemmie. 'Her father hunts tigers in India! Will you find her a horse to ride?'

'A mount for a lady whose father hunts tigers,' said the boy. He leaned back against the stall and stared appraisingly at me – as if he approved. I felt myself blush again. 'I have the mount for you, miss,' he said. 'Right here. Follow me, miss.'

He opened the door to the stall he'd been leaning against and I followed him in. 'This is the horse for you, Miss Penelope,' he said, slapping a horse on its side. It was the horse I'd seen him lead back into the yard. She whinnied, turning her black-brown head towards me. It was quite dark in the stall, but even in that dim light I could see the milky-white star blazed on her forehead. I fell in love with her at once.

'She's beautiful,' I murmured, putting out my hand to stroke her nose. She stamped her foot and shook my hand away to nuzzle my palm. I saw Fred smile. 'What is it?' I said.

'I can see you like horses,' he replied. 'You can always tell. Something about the way you touch them.'

I smiled back. 'What's her name?' I asked.

'Starshine,' he said.

I laughed. 'Of course.' Fred was easy to talk to, I thought. I found it hard to remember that he was a servant.

I ran a hand down the horse's nose and touched the star. 'Hello, Starshine, I'm Polly,' I said. The name slipped out automatically.

Fred looked perplexed. 'Polly is a sort of nickname,' I explained. 'It's what my friends call me. Father said Penelope was too grand a name for a tomboy like me. So I became Polly. And you and I,' I turned back to Starshine, 'are going to be friends, aren't we?' I stroked her mane. 'Fred, would you saddle her for me, so that I can ride her?'

'What now, miss? I'm afraid that's not possible. I've already taken her out this afternoon.'

'Well, can I ride another horse then?' I asked.

He shook his head. 'I'm sorry, miss, I've had no instructions from the house that any of you young ladies are to ride this afternoon.'

'Does that matter?' I exclaimed.

'I'm afraid it does,' he said.

I felt like crying with frustration. I'd put on my riding habit for nothing. All day I'd been looking forward to a ride. All Aunt ever did was put obstacles in my way. *Yes, you may go to the stables, so long as you only look at the horses.* I couldn't even try appealing to her. She, Uncle and Arabella had gone out for a drive in the carriage and wouldn't be back until tea. It would be dark by then. I stalked away angrily, but I wasn't watching where I was going. Halfway across the yard I heard a shout and felt a hand grab my wrist, and pull me backwards. I tried to shake it off, but the grip was too firm.

'Sorry, about that, miss,' Fred said breathlessly, releasing my wrist. 'But I had to stop you before you stepped under that horse's hooves. Didn't you see her?' He nodded his head. A few feet away, a young horse was walking round and round, dragging at her halter, fighting a lad for it. 'That filly is a wild one, you never know where she will put her hooves next,' he said.

I felt a bit shaken, but I laughed. 'Thank you, Fred,' I said.

'She's his lordship's latest purchase,' Fred said, admiringly. 'But she needs a bit of handling. Nervous. His lordship hopes to race her at Ascot later this year.' He hesitated. 'Well, if you're all right, miss, that lad needs help.' He touched his cap and ran up to the boy's side. I watched as they struggled with the horse. She was putting up quite a fight. I felt I knew how she felt.

I went to find Clemmie. She was leaning over the edge of a stall, talking to her pony and stroking its nose. Miss Dunn was standing well back, glancing around nervously, as if afraid that a passing horse would kick her. 'Has Fred found you a horse to ride?' Clemmie asked. Neither of them had seen my narrow escape.

'He has,' I said. 'Her name is Starshine. She's beautiful. But I can't take her out today,' I said crossly, 'or any other horse.' I still felt sore. Why hadn't Aunt thought I might actually want to ride?

'Never mind, we'll go out tomorrow,' declared Clemmie. 'It will be fun, won't it, riding together. Usually Fred or one of the other stable boys takes me out. Arabella won't – she doesn't like horses.'

That didn't surprise me. I couldn't imagine Arabella on a horse. And at least, I thought as we walked back to the house, there was one place at the manor where I could avoid her. That would be bound to please Arabella as much as me. I couldn't imagine that Arabella and I would ever be friends.

I glanced back before we turned round the side of the house. A girl in maid's uniform was opening the gate to the stables. I wondered what she was doing there. The girl must have felt my look because she turned round and stared back. I suddenly had the oddest feeling – that she knew who I was and she'd rather she didn't. I told myself that I was being ridiculous. She was just curious to see what I was like. And why not? Everyone else was.

I found it hard to get to sleep that night. The windows rattled, and the rich dinner lay on my stomach. If only I'd been able to ride… I pulled back one of the hangings round the bed and slid to the floor. I padded in my bare feet to the window and slipped behind the curtains. Outside the rain clouds had begun to clear and the moon was as round and ripe as a plum, riding the night sky. The stars seemed to go on for ever. As I stared at them, I imagined Father doing the same. It made me feel closer to him – almost as if he was in the next room rather than thousands of miles away. He used to tell me to look at the stars when he was away from home. *The same stars shine over us, wherever we are*, he had told me. It used to comfort me. I liked to think of him looking up at the stars, like me. But in India now it would almost be dawn. I turned away from the window and slipped back into bed, burrowing down under the bedclothes. As I lay there I thought about Starshine and the filly who was to be tamed and the boy who loved horses like me. Tomorrow I would see them again.

Downstairs

'I saw her,' Sarah said. Her voice, coming so unexpectedly in the dark, made me jump. I'd thought she was asleep, not lying awake, counting sheep, unable to sleep, like me.

'Who?' I said sleepily. I didn't want to talk. I was trying to get to sleep.

'Why, Miss Penelope, of course.'

'Oh, her,' I said. I'd spent the afternoon altering Miss Arabella's gowns to fit Miss Penelope. None of them suited her. The pink one was hideous. I'd found it hard to hide what I thought, as I'd crawled round her feet tacking up hems – the two girls weren't at all the same shape – Miss Penelope went in where Miss Arabella went out – but I felt sorry for her. I wouldn't want to be her, even if it did mean I'd never have to work again.

'Yes, she'd been to the stables. I saw her when I went to see Fred.'

'Oh?' She hadn't asked for her riding habit to be put out.

'What do you think of her now?' Sarah said. She sounded if she had something on her mind.

I wasn't sure what to say. I felt as if I was feeling my

way along a dark tunnel without a light to guide me. I had my own opinions, but now that I was attending on Miss Penelope I felt uneasy sharing them. I'd already said more than I'd meant to yesterday. Yet Sarah was my best friend. I didn't want to have secrets from her.

'Don't you have any opinion?' Sarah sounded almost aggrieved.

'Well, I spent a lot of time today altering gowns to fit her, but we didn't talk much. I don't know that she's happy here though.'

Even saying that felt like a betrayal. I couldn't understand myself. I hadn't broken a confidence. But Miss Penelope had told me that her mother had died and it was that I think made her seem more like a real person to me, not just one of the family I had to wait on. But Sarah was my friend. My first loyalty should be to her. I felt uncomfortable. I didn't know where I belonged any more. I wasn't an upper servant, nor was I strictly simply a lower servant now that I was waiting on Miss Penelope.

Sarah was silent, as if she knew how I felt, and didn't like it.

I tried to change the subject. 'So how was your day? Did you see Fred?'

'Yes, I saw Fred – and he told me that he'd found Miss Penelope a horse to ride and he was sure she was a game one. More than I've learned from you!'

'He shouldn't go gossiping,' I said – more sharply than I'd intended. But hadn't I done just that, yesterday in the maids' sitting room?

'He's my sweetheart, Jess. He can say what he likes to me!'

I felt the reproof. *But I can't to you, not now.*

'Sarah, I—'

'You don't talk to me like you did,' Sarah interrupted. 'You don't even sound like you. You sound … like … like an upper servant.' She made it sound like an insult.

I could hear snores from the bed by the window. Good. Ellen was fast asleep. One less person I could offend then.

'That's unkind of you, Sarah,' I said. 'Anyway, I'm not, not really.' I was neither one thing nor the other. It hadn't been my choice.

'I know, I'm sorry, Jess.'

'What's bothering you, Sarah?' I might not be able to see her face in the dark, but I knew Sarah too well for her to be able to hide how she felt from me.

'I can't quite explain, but … I suppose I just didn't like the way Fred spoke about Miss Penelope. And I'll tell you something else, Jess.' Sarah spoke as if it was an effort, as if she'd rather not have to say what she was about to say. As if speaking her fears aloud would make them real. Though what fears she could have I couldn't imagine. But she had them all right; I could hear it in her voice. 'He called her Polly,' she said in a rush.

'He must have made a mistake.'

'So you think that's all it is?' I could hear how desperately she wanted to be reassured.

''Course, Sarah, what else could it be? Polly. Penelope. They don't even sound the same,' I said. I felt a bit confused. I didn't understand how it mattered. I propped myself up on an elbow and faced the dark outline I could see in the bed next to mine.

'What if it's not a mistake? What if it's … what if he likes her?' Sarah sounded miserable. So that was what this was all about.

'Because he couldn't remember her name? Now you're being daft!'

'No, because of what he said earlier. Oh, I don't know. She's pretty, and she likes horses.' I heard a sob.

'Sarah! Fred's a stable hand and Miss Penelope is her ladyship's niece. What could there possibly be between them?' I couldn't believe my ears. None of what Sarah was saying made any sense.

Sarah gave another sob. It was too much for me. I hated it when anyone cried, especially if it was my best friend.

I got out of bed and tiptoed over to Sarah's. The floor was icy. A fire was only lit in our bedroom if one of us was sick. I hopped from foot to foot. 'Can I get in?' I said. Sarah sniffed. I took that as a yes and slipped in beside her.

'Your toes are cold,' she said. I drew them up under my nightgown. Sarah was still sniffing.

'Where's your hanky?' I said. I felt like her mother.

'I don't know,' Sarah said.

'Have mine then.' I held it out to her. Sarah could never find her handkerchief. Her fingers took it from me.

'Thanks, Jess,' she said, wiping her eyes.

'Sarah,' I said. 'Miss Penelope is lonely here, she's far away from her family, she likes horses and she chatted to one of the boys who looks after them. And that's all. What more could there possibly be between his lordship's niece and a stable hand?' How many times did I have to say it?

'Nothing – but you can't help your feelings, can you?'

'I'm sure you're wrong. They've only just met. You read too many romances, Sarah. Fred cares about you. You've known each other ever so long; he'd not throw you over for a girl he's just met. It wouldn't enter his head. But you need to save up to have a home of your own. It'll take time, maybe a long time. I know it's hard. You've just got to be patient a while longer.'

Hard or not I envied her. I even envied her distress. I wanted there to be someone to cry into my pillow about. I wanted to have someone to think about and plan a life with. But who'd want me, with my homely face? I didn't see them queuing up.

'Thanks, Jess, I feel a lot better.' Sarah handed me back my hanky.

'Keep it,' I said, pushing it back to her.

'Night, Jess.'

'Night, Sarah.' I made a dash for my bed and pulled the bedclothes up to my chin.

As I lay there trying to sleep I thought about what Sarah had told me. About Fred mixing up the names. What if Miss Penelope *was* also known as Polly? I'd feel a bit hurt, even though that was silly. I didn't want to be in her confidence. I didn't want anything to spoil my friendship with Sarah. I was glad Sarah had confided in me. She was my friend – my best friend – not Miss Penelope or whatever she chose to call herself. She belonged upstairs. I was downstairs. There was a line drawn between the two. It was invisible but we all knew it was there. Upstairs and downstairs. No one could cross it. Sarah would feel a lot better if she could just remember that.

Upstairs

I was awake in the morning even before I heard Baxter's knock. I'd drawn back the hangings round my bed and run to the window, pulling aside a curtain to see what the day was like. It wasn't raining, but a thin fog clung to the trees like a shroud. It would soon lift, I told myself, slipping back between the sheets. I told Baxter to lay out my riding habit and hat. She gave me an odd look. 'What? You're not thinking of riding today, are you? In this fog, miss? You'll lose your way.'

I'd never do anything in this country if I worried about the weather. It was always either too wet or too cold.

'I'll ask one of the stable hands to take me out,' I said. 'And Clemmie said she'd ride with me.'

Baxter didn't say anything, but I felt sure that she disapproved. Not that it was her business to approve or disapprove. This afternoon, whatever the weather was like, I would be on the back of my horse, galloping across the park. The thought lifted my spirits. I was even able to smile at Arabella at breakfast. She must have forgotten who I was because she actually smiled back.

I asked Aunt if I might ride. She frowned, looking out of the window. 'I am not sure it would be advisable in this fog,' she said.

'But it might lift,' I said stubbornly.

The look Aunt gave me felt like a reproof. 'Let us see, Penelope.'

'One of the lads will accompany them,' Uncle said. 'She will be quite safe.' I could have kissed him. He gave me a wink, then attacked his plate of kedgeree with gusto. Never have I seen anyone eat so much. If horses were Uncle's first love, food was his second.

Clemmie and I arranged to meet at the stables at two. As soon as lunch was over I ran up the stairs two at a time. Baxter helped me put up my hair into a net and adjust my veil. Thin fingers of chilly sunshine were poking through the fog as I made my way to the stable block. I felt as if the sun had come out just for me. For the first time since I'd arrived in England I felt almost happy.

Starshine was already saddled and bridled when I reached the yard. I picked up my habit with one hand and ran up to her. Clemmie had been down to the kitchens and brought me a carrot for her. Starshine took it off my hand in one bite. I rumpled her mane. Fred was helping Clemmie up on to her pony.

'Good afternoon, miss,' he said, coming up to me next. He touched his cap.

'Starshine's been looking forward to her ride,' he said. He bent down to adjust the stirrup for me. 'Up you get, miss.'

I gave him my cane, and he helped me up. I hoicked my right leg over the forked pommel that was attached to the saddle, my left sliding underneath. I reached down for my cane, then watched as Fred climbed up on to his horse. I liked the easy way he swung himself into the saddle. I hadn't ridden astride since I'd sat behind Father when I was little. Aunt would have a fit if I suggested anything so unladylike.

He led us out of the yard at a slow walk, the horses' hooves ringing on stone. I was longing for a gallop. The fog was really lifting now, and I yearned to give Starshine her head.

'Have you been round the park yet, miss?' Fred said, twisting round in his saddle to me. I shook my head.

'That's what we'll do then,' he said. 'It's too big to see it all in one day, but we can make a start. There's no better way to see the park than from the back of a horse.'

He pointed his whip. 'We'll ride down to the bottom of the drive, then left to the copse and round the back of the hill. Then back to the yard.' He turned back again. 'Follow me,' he called.

We broke into a gentle trot. As I rose up and down in the saddle I began to feel impatient. At this pace it would be dark before we'd got halfway round the park. I might as well be in the yard, trotting round on the end of a lead.

I urged Starshine forward. 'Keep close to me, Miss Penelope,' Fred said as I edged ahead.

'You don't need to worry about me,' I called back. 'I've been riding since I was a child. I know how to gallop side-saddle.' I felt that he was assessing my horsemanship. I'd show him that he had nothing to worry about.

'Not today, Miss Penelope. You've never been out on Starshine before. And it wouldn't be safe, not in this weather. Fog can come down fast in these parts.' He was being as fussy as an old woman. I was perfectly safe. I urged Starshine into a canter.

'Miss Penelope!' I heard Fred's voice call behind me. I took no notice. With another mere touch we were off, galloping across the parkland. For the first time since I'd put foot on English soil I felt free. Starshine's mane was streaming out behind her, her hooves thundering under her. I felt jubilant. This must be what it felt like to fly. My hands were tight on the reins as we swept past the great oak trees, down to the first field, where I headed her round, before turning in a wide loop and round and back.

I could hear hooves galloping after me. I didn't need to look round, I knew who it was. But he couldn't catch up with me. I was too far ahead. I pulled on the reins to bring Starshine to a halt. Fred galloped up to me. I smiled but he didn't smile back.

'What did you think you were doing?' He was practically shouting. 'Never do that again.'

How dare he talk to me like that? I pulled on the rein to turn Starshine's head around, away from him. 'I can look after myself.'

He leaned across and grabbed the reins. 'No, you can't.'

I tried to grab them back. But he was too strong for me.

'I'm taking you back to the yard,' he said. 'Now. I can trust Starshine, but I can't trust you.'

What had he said? I tossed my head haughtily.

'I have to make sure you're safe!' Exasperation burst out of him. 'What would her ladyship say if anything happened to you?'

'She'd probably be relieved,' I said.

He stared at me as if I were a spoilt child.

Clemmie trotted up to us. Her eyes were round and scared. 'What happened?' she cried. 'Did Starshine bolt?'

I shook my head. 'We're going back, *he* says.' I jerked my head at Fred. I didn't try to hide my fury. Clemmie looked startled. Her eyes turned from Fred to me. Fred was looking as if he might explode.

In single file we trotted back to the stable yard – Fred in front, Clemmie at the rear, me between them like a prisoner.

When we reached the yard I didn't wait for Fred to help me down. I ignored the hand he held out to me.

'I can manage on my own,' I said, sliding down Starshine's back.

I stroked Starshine's soft nose. 'Goodbye,' I said. 'I'm not sure when I'll be back.' I said it loudly so that Fred would hear. If he did, he made no sign. I shrugged my shoulders. What did I care what he thought anyway? I stalked away, leaving him to help Clemmie down.

In my chamber I saw that a gown had been laid out for me – pressed and freshly ironed – another one of Arabella's despised cast-offs. I looked at it in distaste. I didn't want to wear anything that had been on my cousin's back. I pulled off my hat and habit, shook out my hair and flung myself on the bed face down. Everything felt hateful. I was still lying there when I heard the gong sound. Four o'clock. It was nearly time for tea. Baxter would be up soon to help me dress. I didn't want to see her either. I didn't want to see any of them. I wanted to go home, feel the Indian sun on my face, sit with Father on our balcony and watch the evening sun go down behind the hills. I felt tears begin to trickle down my face. I ignored the knock at the door. I heard Baxter enter, heard her move about the room, picking up discarded clothes, folding them and putting them away. I heard the rustle of her skirt as she came up close to the bed.

'Are you ill, Miss Penelope?' she asked.

'Go away,' I muttered into the pillow.

'Miss Penelope,' she said. 'I must help you dress now. You can't go down to tea like that. What would her ladyship think?' Her voice was gentle. And it was as if she'd touched a spring inside me – everything that I'd been feeling poured out.

I hardly knew what I was saying or how much she could hear – my face was still pressed into the pillow. But somewhere in the tumble of words she must have heard how much I hated living at Langdown, how I missed my father, how they hated me and I them and how I would never fit in here. Never. Ever.

'Miss Penelope, don't take on so. You'll get used to us in time.' I felt as if I could hear a smile in her voice. Was she laughing at me? I turned my furious face to hers. It must have looked awful, all red and tear-stained, for she looked startled.

'It can't be easy for you,' she said. She wasn't any older than me, but she sounded like a grown-up and me like a child. Which was how I was behaving. She fetched me a flannel and I wiped my eyes.

'It takes time to get used to a strange place and new people,' she said. 'I remember when I first began in service. I was only fourteen. I'm seventeen now. I thought I'd never get used to it. I was a long way from home, too. My family might as well have been in India for the amount I saw of them. You'll see your father again soon. He'll come and visit you, of course he will.'

I shook my head dolefully. 'No he won't. They'll not let him. They never even talk about him,' I said. 'Every time I try to talk about home, Aunt stops me. I am sure that she hates India. She hates Father, too. I know she blames him for Mother's death.' I don't know what made me confide in this servant girl. But I had to talk to someone.

'Maybe she finds it painful to talk about,' said Baxter. 'Families are funny things. They'll need time to get used to you, too, you know.' I was silent. I didn't agree. They weren't even trying to understand me.

'How was your ride?' she asked me. 'You were looking forward to it, weren't you?' I winced and turned my face away. She'd unwittingly touched a sore place. I was wishing that I hadn't lost my temper. I'd found a refuge in the stables and I'd spoilt it.

'I'll never ride here again,' I said at last.

She looked perplexed.

'Fred won't want to take me out,' I said. 'I ... I...'

How could I tell her what an idiot I'd been? I flushed.

'Oh miss, don't you worry about him. You can ride whenever you want. One of the other lads will take you out.'

It was true. I could ride whenever I wanted. But I didn't want anyone else to take me out. I'd felt comfortable with Fred. But I could never tell Baxter that. What would she think – her ladyship's niece more at home with a stable lad than her cousins. But it was true. I'd felt more at ease with Fred than with anyone else at Langdown, except Clemmie, and Clemmie was a child. We shared something special – Fred and me – a love of horses. Now that refuge had been roughly torn away – and by my own two stupid hands. 'I can't trust you,' he'd said. I sighed and got up and let Baxter help me dress, then she fetched a comb to tease the tangles from my hair. Now I had to face the family. What would Aunt say when she learned how I'd behaved today? My legs felt like jelly as I walked downstairs.

Downstairs

'Who do you think you are?' Ivy stood at the end of the table, staring down her nose at us. 'The front door for the h'gentry h'only. H'servants round the back. How many times do I have to tell you?' I was laughing so hard I was crying. It was Barrett to a tee. The way he held his head, the barely concealed contempt for us lower servants in his eyes. How did she do it? Even Sarah smiled, though I noticed how her eyes kept sliding to the door. She'd left her seat by my side and now was sitting facing me – all the better to see who was coming in and out.

I shifted my attention back to Ivy. I didn't want to miss a single minute of her performance. I couldn't believe the change in her. You'd never have known it was the same little shrimp who'd sat huddled at the table, scooping up her broth as if she was starving. She was small still, but when she performed for us she seemed to grow taller. Some words I'd heard somewhere once popped into my mind. *All the world's a stage*. I wasn't sure what it meant, but all the world was Ivy's stage. I hoped I'd never fall out with her. I could imagine how she might mimic me.

I heard a chair scrape as someone sat down and looked round to see that Maddie had shifted up next to me. 'Isn't she a card,' I said.

'Should be on the stage,' Maisie on my other side said. Maddie merely grunted, drumming her fingers on the table. She wasn't smiling. I felt sure I knew why. When the upper servants had departed to eat their sweet in Mrs Smithson's parlour, it had left a spare seat next to her, but Robert hadn't taken it. There were plenty of spare seats at the table now. The upper servants always left, halfway through the meal, to eat their sweet and gossip in Mrs Smithson's sitting room. If I was a proper lady's maid, that's where I'd be now, too. But I was glad I was still able to sit with my friends. The other lot didn't have half as much fun as we did.

Across from me Sarah was pretending to eat, pushing her pudding round her plate. Fred hadn't come by for dinner. He often didn't but today I wished he had. I'd thought I'd reassured Sarah but it hadn't lasted. I'd never seen her so jumpy. I scooped up the last of the rice pudding Maddie had made for us. It was delicious. Sarah didn't know what she was missing. At the head of the table, Ivy was now pretending to be Mrs Smithson. I felt a bit sorry that she'd picked her. I liked Mrs S, but Ivy couldn't, judging from the performance she was giving. Maybe she had had a proper wigging the day she'd arrived. Or maybe she just hated authority. She rolled her eyes and clasped her hands together. 'Oh Mr Barrett, sir, you are so 'andsome… You make me skin go all goosey.'

Robert guffawed.

'Can't think what they find so funny,' muttered Maddie, pushing back her chair. By they I knew she meant Robert. She reached for Sarah's plate, which was barely touched. 'Didn't you like it?' she asked. She sounded hurt but Sarah didn't answer. She was gazing at the door – all smiles. I didn't need to look at it to know that Fred had come in. He was leaning against the doorjamb, arms folded. Sarah got up and slipped round the table to join him. She looked up at him and he looked down at her. They were looking at each other as if they were the only people in the room. I was relieved, but it made me feel lonely too. If I dropped down dead in front of them now they wouldn't notice.

Maddie and Maisie were making their way down the table, stacking plates and glasses. 'I'll have your plate, Robert,' Maddie said, leaning in close to him in a desperate bid to draw his attention away from Ivy. 'Robert,' she said again, loudly when he didn't respond. I felt myself cringe. Couldn't she see that she was wasting her time? Even if she had got up and danced on the table, Robert wouldn't notice. If only she would find someone else. Jim now, the second footman, was blushing as Maddie leaned across the table. But Jim blushed if a girl even looked at him.

Robert pushed the plate over to her, but his eyes never

left Ivy. A flush crept up Maddie's face. She slammed down the plates, and turned to Ivy, who was still prancing up and down at the end of the table. 'Ivy!' she exploded. 'How about mimicking a scullery maid and helping us clear the table.'

'Yes, 'm, right away, 'm,' Ivy said, casting her eyes down, and bobbing a curtsy.

It had been a mistake for Maddie to show her temper. Robert got up and so did all the other lads. As they strolled out, Maddie's face went redder still. Ivy had mocked her in front of everyone and she wouldn't forget that. 'And I want those pots scoured proper today, then you're to help Maisie with the vegetables and there's the floor to clean. It wasn't cleaned proper this morning. Chop chop.' Maddie was practically shoving Ivy towards the scullery now.

I got up too, and made my way along the passage to the maids' sitting room. I could hear from the clatter in the scullery as I passed it that Ivy was hard at work. She was singing, loudly, a little ditty that made me smile. 'Upstairs and downstairs and all the in-betweeny stairs.'

I made myself comfortable in a corner of the sofa. I had work of my own to do; a bit of sewing to finish on one of Miss Penelope's gowns. I picked up the needle, but even though it was only early afternoon I felt my eyelids droop. What with all the extra work on top of my usual chores I never got enough sleep. I laid the needle down and shut my eyes.

'Jess!' It was Sarah's voice. She shook my shoulder. 'What are you doing, sleeping in the afternoon?'

So it was all right to wake me then?

I rubbed my eyes and peered sleepily at her. 'What is it?' I said. 'Has Miss Penelope rung for me?'

Sarah looked guilty. 'N-o,' she said.

'Wish you'd left me to sleep then,' I muttered. I picked up the needle again.

Sarah had curled up in the other corner of the sofa. 'Oh, Jess.' She moved a bit closer to me.

'What is it?' I asked grumpily. I wasn't pleased that she'd woken me up. Didn't she know how tired I was every day, and I wasn't sleeping well at night either.

'Fred's worried,' she said. 'He says that Miss Penelope is a handful, worse than his lordship's new horse.' Sarah looked desperate. 'He says he came down on her a bit hard. Now he's afraid she'll complain. Jess, what if he loses his place?'

'He won't, silly,' I said.

'He might if she complains,' Sarah said darkly.

'She won't do that,' I said biting the end off a piece of thread.

Sarah leapt on my words eagerly. 'How do you know?'

I could have bitten my stupid tongue in two.

But her big eyes were fastened on me. I couldn't let her down. 'Oh, I don't know,' I muttered. 'It's just a feeling I have.' I couldn't explain how I knew. I just did.

'She told you what happened then?' Sarah probed.

I hated this. This probing and questioning. I felt as if I was being pulled between the two of them, and I didn't like it. 'No, she hasn't, but I know she's upset.' I'd already said more than I'd meant to. If only Sarah understood how difficult this was for me.

'Upset?' Sarah pounced. 'Why should she be upset?'

I wanted to crawl away somewhere. Whatever I said it would be the wrong thing.

'Look,' I said at last. 'Let's just say I have a hunch that there's nothing to worry about.'

To my relief that seemed to satisfy her. I saw a smile peep at me, as if what I'd said had made the sun come out. 'Feeling hungry now?' I asked. 'You didn't eat much dinner. Maddie was upset you didn't finish her rice pudding!'

'I wasn't hungry then,' Sarah mumbled. Her face had flushed pink. How often I'd wished I had someone of my own, but I wouldn't want to be as much in love as Sarah was. Never ever.

Upstairs

I walked into the stable yard. It was three days since I'd been there. For three days I'd grabbed at any excuse to avoid it. Yesterday I'd shown unusual enthusiasm for piano practice. The day before the weather had been on my side. It wasn't on my side now. The sun was shining. It was a beautiful winter's day. I tried to reason with myself: I had a choice. I could remain cooped up and miserable in the house, or brave the stables. No report of my bad behaviour had reached Aunt. Clemmie had even told everyone that she had seen me gallop side-saddle. I'd thought that Aunt would faint! But Uncle had chuckled and said he hoped I'd join them the next time the Hunt met at Langdown. If I was to do that, I had to get into the saddle again. I'd have felt better if I'd had Clemmie, an ally, by my side. But Clemmie had gone to a party at a neighbour's, and wouldn't be back till dark.

I unlocked the catch on the stable gate. The door to Starshine's stall was open. As I walked up to it, I could hear Fred's voice inside, coaxing Starshine out. I wanted to turn and run, but I was too late. Fred had seen me. My cheeks spread with an enormous blush. He touched his cap.

'Good afternoon, Miss Penelope,' he said. I bowed my head slightly. I'd told myself that if I saw him I'd be polite but distant. I felt my colour begin to subside. Starshine was already saddled and bridled and Fred helped me up. Neither of us said a word. Good. Then we had both reached the same conclusion. We both wanted to get the ride over as soon as possible. Tomorrow Jem could take me out. I couldn't think why I hadn't asked for him today. I patted Starshine's mane. I had to admit that I had missed her.

Fred swung himself up on to his horse, and we left the yard at a walk. I kept how I felt about that to myself. Today I would do exactly as he said. He would have no cause to complain. But almost as soon as we had left the yard, Fred rode up to my side. He cleared his throat and I felt suddenly nervous. I pulled on Starshine's rein and waited.

'I've got something to say, Miss Penelope. I hope you won't mind, but I wanted to say I'm sorry about the other day.' His face looked really anxious. 'I came down on you too hard. I was out of order.' I had wanted to leave the memory of that ride buried but now he'd raised it I had to respond – somehow.

'I'm sorry, too,' I mumbled. 'It wasn't fair on you, or Starshine.' As soon as I'd said the words, I felt better as if the big weight that had been lying on me had rolled away. I hadn't been looking at him, but now I raised my eyes to his. He looked enormously relieved – as if he had been really afraid what I might say. When it was me who had been afraid what he would say! I felt a grin spread over my face. I'd been stupid. I'd got into a state about nothing. We walked on in silence.

'You're a good horsewoman,' Fred said suddenly. 'You can tell by how someone handles a horse. Good hands.' We fell into a trot. His praise pleased me. He had good hands too, I thought. His horse knew exactly what he wanted. He barely touched the reins, guiding him with his knees. 'Fancy a canter?' he asked. I nodded. 'We'll go down to the copse and round by Emmett's farm,' he said, pointing his whip to the valley below the ridge of the hill. Emmett's was the estate's dairy farm, he told me, which supplied the estate with milk and freshly churned butter.

Fred kept a half eye on me as we rode. Whose fault was it if he didn't trust me? But I soon forgot him in the excitement of cantering across the fields. Starshine knew exactly what I wanted to do. I had never ridden a horse that was so easy to handle. She was the gentlest creature, too. I'd take her out every day now, even if…

A loud clang rang through the air. Rooks rose cawing like a black cloud from the trees. I felt Starshine tremble. Then almost before I knew what was happening she put her head down and bolted forward. I grabbed at the reins and pulled on them as hard as I could but I couldn't hold her. She was terrified – far too terrified to stop. Behind me I heard Fred shout. Starshine was galloping towards the copse. We had nearly reached it when I saw the tangle of brambles and branches and how thick and close together they grew. If I let Starshine ride into that I'd be torn to pieces. I made one last desperate tug at the reins. It was no good. 'I can't hold her!' I cried desperately. I had to make myself fall. There was nothing for it. I gritted my teeth, and, gripping the saddle with both hands, twisted myself right round to the side, hauling my right leg over the pommel and pulling my left foot free of the stirrup. I tried not to think about what I was going to do. It had been raining so the ground wasn't hard, but it was still going to hurt. I shut my eyes and gripping the pommel pushed myself over the side. The world seemed to rock sideways as I fell. I gasped as I hit the ground, my shoulder and knee taking most of the impact. It hurt more than I'd expected. I rolled over and over, curling into myself before I came to a halt. I kept my eyes shut, feeling my breath come in tight gasps before moving slightly, untwisting my skirts and gently flexing my legs and arms to see that they still worked. I heard Fred call, heard steps run up to me.

'Miss Penelope!' His voice was close by my ear. I opened my eyes. He was crouching next to me, a lock of hair dangling over his forehead. I saw him peer anxiously into my face. 'Are you all right? You took quite a tumble.'

'I couldn't hold her. It wasn't my fault. It was that noise. It startled Starshine. I had to let go.'

'I know,' Fred said. 'I heard it, too. It must have been the blacksmith. I've never heard him strike the anvil like that before. I only just managed to hold Nimbus.'

Then you're a better horseman than me, I thought. I tried to move again.

'Don't move,' he said. 'Lie quietly. I'll be right back.' I turned my head then and saw that Starshine was trotting towards us. Fred coaxed her to him gently, patting her back to calm her before tethering her reins loosely to his horse. I saw her lower her head to crop the grass. I smiled.

'She's all right?' I said as Fred came up to me.

'She's fine,' he said. 'But what about you?' A frown wrinkled his forehead. 'Can you move?'

'I can move my legs and arms,' I said. I touched the side I'd fallen on gingerly. It ached, but it was only bruised, nothing more.

'It was lucky you rolled off sideways, not backwards,' he said. 'Can you try to sit up? I'll help you.' He put an arm behind me and I carefully manoeuvred myself into a sitting position. His arm still held me and I leaned back into it. It felt warm and comforting. I glanced up and saw Fred looking at me, a peculiar expression on his face. I felt myself blush and shifted slightly away from him.

'I'm all right now,' I said. He took his arm away.

'You've some grass and leaves on you,' he said.

'Oh,' I said. I looked down at myself. I was muddy too, on

the side I'd fallen. I put a hand to my head to right my hat and veil, tucking stray hairs in behind my ears. Fred was still watching me. My face felt hot.

'There's still some grass on you, miss,' he said. *Oh, so that was why he was looking at me. I was a mess.* 'On your back,' he said. 'Here, let me.' I felt his fingers on my back, gently but firmly brushing away the grass. 'I'm not hurting you, am I?' he asked.

'No,' I said. I liked the feel of his hand on my back. I was sorry when he took it away.

'There,' he said. 'You look better now.'

'I think I could stand if you helped me,' I said. He held out a hand to pull me up. I wobbled and reached for him.

'Steady,' he said, putting an arm round me. I leaned back against it again, It felt strong and comforting, but I made myself push it away. I was determined to get straight back up on my horse. Father had taught me to face my fears. Not that I had any real fears about Starshine. She turned her head to me and gave a soft whinny. It was like a signal.

'Are you sure you are all right?' Fred asked.

'I'm fine. Just a few bruises. See.' I walked unaided over to Starshine. It hurt, but I hid how much. He'd never let me up, if he knew. 'You'll need to help me,' I said.

He shook his head. 'You're not getting up on Starshine now.'

'I've got to get back somehow,' I said.

'That was a nasty fall,' he said. 'You can ride back behind me on Nimbus. There's room for both of us.'

He held out his hand. I was tempted to take it but I had to get back on to Starshine. 'I'm only bruised. Help me up, Fred.'

He smiled. 'Only if you'll let me lead you back.'

I didn't answer. I wanted to finish our ride, but if I told Fred that now he might refuse to help me. 'Are you going to help me, or do I have to do it myself?' I leaned forward to grasp the pommel. I put one foot in the stirrup. I'd meant what I'd said. Fred had folded his arms and was grinning as he watched me. He didn't believe me. Very well. I bunched up my skirt and tried to pull up my other leg, wincing as I did it.

'No!' he exclaimed. 'You can't get up on your own. You know you can't. Let me.' He bent down to help me and I settled myself back in the saddle. Starshine was still contentedly munching the grass. She didn't seem to mind me on her back. I leaned forward to try and untie the reins that tethered our horses together. Fred saw and shook his head. 'I should take you home,' he said.

Home, I thought. I looked back at the house. I had no wish to return to Langdown. Here I felt at home. There, I did not.

'No,' he said again. But I sensed that his resolve was weakening.

'Let's ride,' I said, looking down at him. 'Please!'

'Yes, let's,' he said, looking back up at me.

He untied the reins that still tied Starshine to Nimbus. 'Keep close beside me,' he said, swinging himself up into the saddle. 'Then if Starshine bolts again…'

'She won't,' I said.

He grinned. 'Are you always so sure?'

'Always,' I said.

I felt so peaceful, riding by his side. We rode across fields that I hadn't even known belonged to the estate.

'I hadn't realized it was so large,' I said.

He shrugged. 'It's not that big. Only a few hundred acres.'

I was used to a much bigger country, but it sounded a lot for one man to own. We passed near a farmhouse. It looked snug and cosy.

'It looks nice,' I said. 'I'd far rather live there than at the manor.'

'That's the estate's dairy farm,' Fred said. 'I grew up on a farm like that.' I couldn't have hidden my surprise very well for he grinned and said, 'Didn't think I was a farmer's son, did you?'

'I hadn't thought about it,' I said. I wondered what had made him leave a farm to go into service.

'I didn't want to go into service,' he said, as if he'd guessed what I was thinking. 'But Father died and Mam couldn't afford to keep the farm on. I was lucky I knew enough about horses to get the job here.'

'You won't always be in service then?'

Fred shrugged. 'Mam needs what money I can send her. And here I'm one less mouth for her to feed.' His eyes strayed over the countryside.

So, I thought, you're a captive here like me. It made me feel as if there was a bond between us. Neither of us wanted to be at Langdown. I was pleased that he'd confided in me. I felt as though we had stepped over the invisible barrier that had separated us. We rode in silence while I thought what to say.

'But you love horses, don't you?'

'Horses, yes, all animals. But I'd like to have my own little patch of land, grow things…' He swung round in the saddle: 'Tell me about India.'

'Well, it's hot,' I said, 'and it smells.' We both burst out laughing.

'You love it though, don't you. I can tell,' he said. 'Will you go back there one day?'

'I hope so – one day. But I don't know when that will be.' When I've learned to be a young lady, I thought to myself. And I didn't want to be a young lady. There had to be more to life than that.

I looked around me, at the fields that stretched for mile after mile. In spring the trees would be in leaf, and birds would build nests in the hedgerows. I would ride every day over these fields. It wasn't enough.

I was sorry when the house came into view. We were

trotting, but as we got nearer Fred slowed us to a walk. I was glad. I didn't want the ride to end, ever.

'Tomorrow?' I said as we clattered into the yard.

'Tomorrow,' he said, as he helped me down. I lingered as he led Starshine into her stall. I leaned against the wall and watched as he began to rub her down. I'd liked to have stayed there in the stall, breathing in the smell of horse and dung and hay. When I left I felt as if I'd left a part of me behind – there, in the stall with him and Starshine. Tomorrow, he'd said. Tomorrow.

Downstairs

'How many more?' Ivy grumbled, arms up to her elbows in soapsuds. She looked over at the pile of dirty pans heaped up beside the sink. 'Every time I wash one someone brings me another. Cook must have used every pot in the kitchen to cook their dinner today.'

'Wait till there's a house party,' I said, turning on the tap to fill the kettle. 'You'll learn what hard work is then.'

Ivy groaned. 'Shall I kill myself now, or later?'

I grinned. Sarah, Ellen and I had just finished upstairs – going from one bedroom to the next, closing curtains, picking up clothes, turning down the bedcovers and laying out nightclothes. Her duties over, Sarah had disappeared to find Fred. Ellen was in the servants' hall, picking out a tune on the piano. My duties weren't over yet. I still had Miss Penelope's bottle to fill. Then there was the mending to do and her riding habit to brush. The skirt looked like she'd been rolling in mud.

I'd been shocked to see Miss Penelope's bruises – all down one side. But she had seemed cheerful in spite of her fall and had made me promise not to tell anyone. They'd only fuss, she'd said. I just hoped she wouldn't fall again, and hurt herself badly, or I'd feel guilty that I'd kept her secret to myself.

I took the kettle back to the kitchen and put it on the range to heat. Maddie was scrubbing the table. While I waited for the kettle to boil I pulled up a chair near her and stretched out my legs. By night time they were always aching. I seemed to be upstairs and down all day.

Robert pushed open the door with a foot. 'More dishes for young Ivy,' he announced, putting down a tray.

'Take that tray away,' said Maddie, her cheeks a bit pink. 'Those dishes aren't for Ivy and you know it.'

'Aw, don't scold,' said Robert. He put an arm round her and gave her a squeeze. He winked across her at me.

'Leave go,' Maddie said, blushing.

Robert lifted both hands up. 'All right, all right.' He sauntered down the passage, whistling. A moment later I heard Ivy laugh, then Robert's voice. They suited each other, I thought, show-offs both.

Maddie's lips set in a thin line. 'He's everyone's best friend, isn't he?'

'He is,' I said, lamely, not sure what else I could say. The kettle had begun to sing. I got up to fill the bottle.

Sarah was in the maids' sitting room when I came back downstairs, Miss Penelope's riding habit in my hands. I was surprised to see her.

'You're back early,' I began, then immediately wished I could bite out my tongue. But Sarah just smiled.

'Fred had extra work to do this evening,' she said, drawing up her knees under her. 'It's the Langdown Meet soon. There's always a lot to do.' She looked at the habit lying on my knee. 'What's that?' she said, though I knew she knew very well what it was.

'It's a riding habit,' I said, sounding as casual as I could. 'Miss Penelope got it dirty out riding today.' I picked up the brush, praying that it would be an end to her questions. Sarah just nodded.

I stretched out my legs to the fire. It had burned down, and there wasn't much heat in it. But compared to our bedrooms, it was a furnace in there. I began to brush the habit, enjoying the companionable silence that had fallen between us. Sitting there together, I felt almost as I had before Miss Penelope and Ivy had come to disrupt our lives. I'd felt comfortable then – a lowly housemaid, but one with a real place in the world.

It wasn't peaceful for long. A barely stifled giggle outside made me and Sarah look up. We both knew who it was. A moment later Ivy bounced into the room. She flopped down on the sofa next to us. 'All finished then, Ivy?' I said tartly.

'Near enough,' she said. She curled up in a corner of the sofa. 'Just need to rest my legs a mo. Ooh, they ache.' She gave a grimace and began to rub them.

Sarah and I looked at each other. Did she think we were stupid? We knew she'd been out in the corridor and we knew with whom.

'It'll be the staff ball in a few weeks' time,' I said. 'Have you got anything to wear, Ivy?'

'Staff ball?' She looked blankly at us.

'Yes,' I said. 'The family throws a huge party for their staff and tenants before they go to London for the season. There'll be dancing—'

'—and entertainment,' Sarah said, looking at me, the temptation to tease Ivy getting too much for her. I felt my lips twitch.

Ivy's eyes gleamed. 'That'll be me then, won't it?'

If Ivy's head got any bigger she'd not get it through the door.

'You'll not be short of partners,' Sarah said, catching my eye again.

'You mean 'im, do you? Whatsisname? Robert?' Ivy looked bored. 'I can do better than 'im.'

'How much better?' Sarah said.

'That'd be saying. But he's not what I'm after.'

She only wanted an audience, I thought. But I didn't feel like indulging her – not tonight. I turned back to the habit, and picked up the brush I'd put down.

But Ivy hadn't finished.

'I never was meant to be in service, you know,' she said.

'No?' Sarah said. We exchanged a glance.

'I had expectations.'

'Really?' said Sarah, innocently. 'What sort?'

I felt a giggle rise and looked away.

'Oh,' Ivy said, giving an airy wave of her arm. 'We were rich, but we lost all our money when Father died. My life would have been very different if he hadn't. Father never wanted me to go into service.'

I couldn't resist it.

'So you belong upstairs, do you, Ivy?' I said.

I heard Sarah stifle a snort. Ivy didn't seem to hear or if she did, she took no notice.

'Well, we'd had servants of our own, you know,' she said.

'A butler and your own personal lady's maid, I suppose,' said Sarah. I stuffed my face in the habit. It was too much.

Ivy was a performer. You never knew when she was being Ivy, or pretending to be someone else. 'There's no accounting for fortune,' I said when I was able to speak again.

'You what?' Ivy looked perplexed.

Let her chew on it, I thought, picking up the habit. I'd had enough of the game, besides I had things to do. I got up and Sarah got up, too.

'I'll come with you, Jess.'

We were barely outside the sitting room, when we collapsed in giggles. 'Does she really think we'd swallow all that?' I exclaimed.

'I suppose they could have had an odd job man for the heavy work and a girl come in to help her mam.'

'Just added a bit of garnish to the facts,' I said.

We laughed.

As we passed the scullery I saw a pile of pans still unwashed by the sink. 'She won't last long,' Sarah said, nodding at them.

'I know someone who won't be sorry,' I said.

Sarah nudged me. 'Sssh. Look.'

'What?'

'Maddie,' she hissed.

The kitchen door was open. Maddie was marching down the passage towards the scullery. She swept past us without a glance. 'Ivy'll catch it,' Sarah murmured, 'when Maddie sees those dirty pans.'

We were halfway up the stairs when a shout of fury reached us. 'You're right, she won't last long,' I said. But I'd be sorry. Ivy made me laugh.

Upstairs

'Tomorrow,' he'd said. Tomorrow. It was tomorrow now. For once at Langdown I had something to look forward to. I opened my eyes. Baxter was drawing the curtains. Outside, rain was sliding down the windows.

At lunchtime it was still raining. Winter rain in England had one thing in common with sunshine in India – both went on for ever. There'd be no riding today. I looked despairingly out of the window. As a footman put my pudding in front of me, Aunt gave a little cough to draw my attention back to the table. She had an invitation, she announced, that would cheer us up. Nothing could do that, I thought, gazing bleakly at my plate.

'Lady Whichcombe would like you to meet her daughter,' Aunt said. Arabella and I were both invited to a tea party at Whichcombe Park. I glanced at Arabella. She who was usually so careful to hide her feelings could scarcely conceal her disgust. I felt I'd sooner jump into a nest of snakes than spend an afternoon with Arabella's friends. But as soon as the meal was over we were bundled into the carriage that was to take us to Whichcombe Park.

A bevy of girls was waiting to meet me there. They gathered around me, quizzing me as girls do to find out whether I'd 'do' or not. 'What does your father do?' one asked languidly, raising her perfectly kept hand to her perfectly kept hair. I could tell from the glances they gave each other that they already knew. Arabella had primed them. The correct answer in this company was that he did nothing. My answer was the wrong one.

'He is a tea planter, in India,' I said.

'How very … unusual,' one remarked barely able to conceal her disdain. The girls moved closer to each other. I did not do. I would not be allowed into their club. Now they were free to tear me to pieces.

'That's a pretty gown,' one of the girls said. She exchanged a glance with another girl, who took up the cue. 'It reminds me of yours, Arabella,' she said.

'That's because it is mine,' Arabella giggled. A titter rippled through the group. *Arabella's cousin doesn't have a gown fit to wear. She has to borrow her cousin's clothes.* I couldn't take them all on. I moved away before they did. But as I took shelter in another corner, pretending to admire a painting, to my surprise I saw one of the girls leave the group and walk over to me.

'Don't mind them,' she said. 'Not all English girls are hateful snobs.'

She told me that her name was Flo, and that she was

staying at the park while her parents were away. 'Mother thinks it is nice for me to have the company of other girls. She doesn't realize how I detest them,' she said, nodding at Arabella's friends. We sat down next to each other, while the footman handed round plates of tiny buttered scones and dainty cakes. 'Will you be coming out this year?' she asked.

I pulled a face. 'I'm afraid I will,' I said.

My reaction seemed to surprise her. 'Don't you want to?' she said.

'No, I don't.'

'But it should be lots of fun,' she urged. 'Parties and balls and races at Ascot and Goodwood, sailing at Cowes.'

'But we'll just be watching, won't we? I'd rather take part.'

The vipers had collected in another part of the room. One glanced round and whispered to her friends. Their giggles were audible. I must have spoken loud enough for them to hear. I ignored them. Now that I had an ally, I could afford to.

'I suppose we will.' She leaned towards me. 'Will you be presented at Court?'

'Aunt would like me to be.' *I wouldn't be, if it were up to me.*

'Oh good,' she said. 'Then we will see each other when you come to London.' She pulled her chair closer to me and whispered, 'Don't tell anyone, but I'm dreading it. I've been practising how to curtsy for nearly a year and I still cannot rise without wobbling.'

'Neither can I,' I said.

'I've even had dreams in which I trip over my train and fall at the King's feet.'

'Down, down, down,' I mimicked Madame's voice. 'Hold the pose. Now – fall over.'

Flo laughed. 'I usually do!'

I laughed with her. But I kept to myself that I found the whole thing rather silly. I didn't think she'd feel the same.

In spite of Flo I was almost relieved when the carriage came to collect us. One viper was better than a whole nest. We rode back in silence. Arabella didn't make any attempt to talk to me, and I didn't want to talk to her. I leaned against the cushioned back and kept my eyes fixed on the window. Why did she resent me so much? The dislike we felt for each other seemed to grow and grow until I felt as if there was hardly enough room in the carriage for both of us. As the carriage swung through the lodge gates and began to ascend the drive I felt more and more depressed. The lights had been turned on in the house. It should have been welcoming, but it wasn't. They felt like little eyes, mocking me. *Here you are, unwelcome one.* The carriage stopped and I felt it shake slightly as the footman who'd escorted us jumped down. He opened the door for us, holding up an umbrella to shelter us from the rain, though it was hardly raining at all by then. Arabella got out first and I stood to follow her. The footman took my hand and I stepped out. On the bottom step I hesitated. I didn't want to follow Arabella in. I didn't want to be within a hundred miles of her. Arabella had done her best to wreck the afternoon. I'll go to the stables, I thought. I hadn't been able to ride, but I could still go to the stables. If I hurried, I might be in time to say goodnight to Starshine before the stalls were locked for the night. I felt the misery begin to slip off me. I felt at home at the stables, which I never did in the house. The footman was still standing there patiently, the umbrella held over my head. I didn't want him to see me run round to the stables. I had to think of a way to get rid of him. 'Don't wait for me,' I said. 'I think I dropped my bracelet round here earlier. I'll stay outside and look for it.' I bent down, and poked at the gravel, pretending to search for it.

'I'll help you, miss.'

'There's no need. I'm sure I'll find it soon.' *Go, please go.*

'Very good, miss.' He folded the umbrella. The crunch of his footsteps on the gravel grew fainter. He must have thought me mad.

I waited until the carriage had gone. Then I walked round to the stables. It was nearly dark but there was plenty of light from the house to help me find my way – not that I needed it. I knew the way so well now that I could have found it in the dark if I'd had to. At the gate I ducked down quickly – the coachman was in the yard talking to one of the grooms. I waited until I heard him say goodnight and slipped back out of sight as he came up to let himself out of the gate. When

I could no longer see him, I crept back again. The yard was empty now. The horses had been bolted in for the night, and lights had come on in some of the rooms up above the stables. What did I think I was I doing? I was about to turn away when a lantern flashed full in my face. I blinked.

'Miss Penelope! What are you doing here?' It was Fred. He looked astonished. 'I thought we had an intruder,' he said, lowering the lantern.

I certainly felt like one the way he was looking at me.

I felt an idiot, too. I wanted to explain, but I couldn't think what to say. He'd think me mad. I winced, imagining him talking about me to the servants. What would they say? What would *he* say? 'That Miss Penelope, she's a rum one. I found her hanging around the stables in the dark. I don't know why.'

I couldn't think why now either. Some stupid idea I'd had about it feeling like home. It didn't feel like home now.

'I'm sorry,' I said. 'I don't know what I'm doing here either.' I turned to go.

'No, wait,' he said. 'I'm sorry. I didn't mean to startle you. We have to be careful,' he explained. 'These horses are valuable.'

He had lifted the lantern up a little. 'Is something wrong?' he said.

I may as well tell him the truth. 'Fred, I've had an awful afternoon,' I said simply. 'I couldn't bear to go back into the house. I just didn't know where else to go.' I looked at him pleadingly. He was silent. Had I made an awful mistake? What made me feel I could trust this boy that I hardly knew?

He was looking steadily at me, but the hand that was holding the lantern was trembling.

I felt myself shiver. He leaned forward and I felt his hand touch my arm. It was the lightest softest touch, but I felt the warmth from it run all through me. 'You're cold,' he said. 'You'll catch a chill. Here. Put this on.' He took off his jacket and draped it gently over my shoulders. We neither of us spoke; we just stood there quietly together. I felt comfort slowly seep into me. I felt as if I could have stood there with him for ever, but at the house I knew that they'd be wondering where I was. Reluctantly I slipped off the jacket and handed it back to him.

'Thank you,' I said.

'For what?' he said, putting it back on.

Surely he knew. For being there, for being a friend. For making some little part of Langdown feel like home.

'Will you be riding tomorrow?' he asked. He hadn't been looking at me, but now he raised his eyes and looked full into mine. I felt dizzy. I felt as if I could hardly breathe. Happiness flooded through me.

'Do you need to ask?' I whispered.

UPSTAIRS

I stood in the middle of the room, watching as bolt after bolt of creamy white fabric was unrolled and laid on the bed for my inspection. They all looked the same to me, but Madame said they were ivory, cream and lily of the valley. Aunt told me to choose my favourite. I picked the first one Madame had unrolled. I didn't care which I wore. I didn't want to be presented. I didn't want to go to Court. And I most certainly did not want to be a young lady.

But in a few weeks' time this fabric would be draped around me – my presentation gown. In it I was to emerge like a butterfly from a chrysalis – a young lady.

Arabella was being fitted for her gown, too. She flitted from one fabric to another as a moth hovers round a candle, unable to make up her mind. I wanted to cry with impatience. How long did it take to choose a fabric? Aunt wanted us to match each other. But we'd never do that.

Outside, rain had begun to fall. But I was sure that Fred would be wondering where I was. I'd said I'd see him today. 'Aunt,' I said, striving to keep the impatience out of my voice. 'I was to have gone riding this afternoon.'

'In this rain?' she said, lifting her eyebrows.

They were expecting me, I told her.

'Not in this rain,' she said firmly.

It was still raining when at last I was free to go. But I wasn't going to let that stop me. Fred was expecting me. Sam, the hall boy, let me out. He yawned. It was the hour the servants had off.

I ran round the house to the stable yard. I kept my head down. The rain was coming down harder now. The door to Starshine's stall was open. I ran up to it. Fred was bent over inside, shirt-sleeves rolled up to his elbows, forking out the old hay and muck. He put down the fork and wiped his forehead, his back still to me. 'Hello, Fred,' I said. I saw him start, as if he hadn't expected me. He turned round slowly, raising his eyes to mine.

'I didn't think you'd come,' he said. *I'm glad you did*, his eyes said. A flush spread over his face. 'Hot work,' he said, nodding at the fork.

I felt shy. 'I had to see Starshine,' I said.

And you, my eyes said.

I felt Starshine's nose nuzzle my arm. She gave a whinny. I was neglecting her. I hid my hot face in her mane, pretending that it was for her alone I'd come.

Fred picked up the fork and began to rake the hay. 'Didn't have a chance to do this earlier,' he said. He was looking anywhere but at me. Then he put down the fork, leaning it against the side of the stall. 'You must be cold,' he said.

'And look, you're wet!' he exclaimed as if he'd only just noticed. 'Here.' He tramped over to the wall and unhooked his jacket off a nail. 'Put this on if you're staying.'

Please stay, his eyes said.

I'm staying, mine said. He put the jacket round my shoulders. His hands rested there. I felt them tremble.

'Polly,' he said softly. He had never called me that before. I looked up. His eyes were gazing into mine. I felt as if I was standing too close to a fire. I looked away.

'Polly,' he whispered again. I raised my eyes to his. I felt as if his hand was holding my heart, squeezing it tight. This time I didn't look away.

He bent his head to mine. Our lips met.

How warm they felt against mine. Warm and sweet and soft. I had never kissed a boy before. I felt dizzy.

I felt his hands drop to my waist. He pulled me close to him. His heart was beating rapidly against mine. My head was resting against his shoulder. 'Polly,' he murmured. 'Oh, Poll.' Then he held me away from him and we looked at each other. I gave a little shiver. 'Are you still cold?' he said. He slipped the jacket off my shoulders. 'Put it on properly, it will keep you warm.' I slipped my arms into the sleeves of his jacket. It was too big for me, and the sleeves hung down over my hands. I saw him smile. 'It doesn't fit very well,' he said. I snuggled into it.

'It fits very well,' I said. I smiled.

He touched my cheek softly. 'You have a dimple here, when you smile. Right there. It's nice.'

I took his hand and held it to my lips.

'Oh, Polly,' he said. It was his arms I could feel round me now, his breath warm against my cheek. I felt as if the world was vanishing around me. There was only Fred and me. I could have stood there with him for ever. Nothing else mattered.

I felt his hands slacken suddenly. I moved closer, but he pulled away.

'Poll,' he said. 'We shouldn't do this. I'm sorry... I don't know what came over me. You... I...' He swallowed.

'I'm not sorry,' I said. 'I'm glad.'

'Oh Poll,' he said. 'Don't you see? You're a young lady and I...' His foot kicked the wall angrily.

I leaned my head against the rough wood of the stall.

'I don't care,' I said stubbornly.

'You should,' he said.

'Fred—' I began. How could I tell him how happy he had made me? He couldn't take that away from me now. He just couldn't. I wouldn't let him.

'Fred!' a voice bellowed from the yard. 'How much longer are you going to be mucking out that hoss? There's the yard to sweep still, and then the carriage wheels need oiling. Her ladyship needs it for a drive tomorrow.'

'I should go,' I said. I slipped my arms reluctantly out of the jacket and handed it to him. Our fingers touched.

'I'll see you tomorrow,' I said. He dug the fork into the hay. He didn't answer. He didn't look round.

I felt as if I was floating as I ran back to the house. I floated up the steps and into the hall. I floated towards the staircase. Halfway up I nearly floated into Arabella. She reared back, gazing at me as if I was some frightful apparition.

'Penelope!' she exclaimed. 'Your hair!'

It was dripping on to the carpet. I hadn't noticed.

'What of it?' I said.

'It's wet.'

She sniffed suspiciously.

'You smell of the stable,' she said wrinkling up her nose. I couldn't think how she knew. She never went there.

I felt myself blush. 'I've been to see my horse.'

She looked at me as if I was mad.

'In this weather? Couldn't you have taken an umbrella?'

'I didn't think.'

She pursed up her lips. 'It isn't ladylike.'

What was?

'You shouldn't spend so much time with servants. It upsets them.'

'Why not? Clemmie does,' I said. I'd seen her slip through the door that led to the servants' quarters in the basement. She had tea down there too sometimes.

'Clemmie's a child. Anyway, she grew up with servants.'

And I hadn't? Where did she think I'd lived before I came

to Langdown? In a hovel? 'Arabella,' I said, 'if you'd made any effort to be my friend, maybe I wouldn't need to seek the company of servants and animals. Now, if you will excuse me! I must dry my hair.' I elbowed past her, up the stairs.

I walked quickly, half afraid I'd hear her slippered feet patter after me. But she didn't try to follow me. I reached my room, and flung myself on the bed. I lay on my back and stared up at the ceiling. The damp patch seemed to have grown bigger. I shut my eyes so that I could shut it out, shut out Arabella's sneering face, shut out everything but Fred – and the memory of what had happened between us. Had he truly kissed me? Had I really kissed him back? I tried to remember how his lips had felt, on mine.

My wet hair soaking into my gown. I sat up. There were damp patches on the bed where I'd lain. I looked at them in dismay. Baxter would be along soon to close the curtains and light the fire. What would she think when she saw them? I grabbed a towel and began to rub my hair. I still felt as if I was hovering above the ground. Outside it was almost too dark now to see. Langdown, Arabella, suddenly it all felt unreal. I thought of Fred, sweeping out the yard, oiling the wheels on Aunt's carriage. The kisses we'd shared. *That* was real.

Tomorrow, I thought. Tomorrow.

Upstairs

'Closer!' Madame urged us. 'Closer.' We were practising our new dance steps, prancing across the ballroom floor, holding each other at arm's length. 'Young ladies, you do not attend this morning. Neither of you.' Her reproof slid off me. My feet felt as if they were dancing several inches off the floor. I was holding Arabella as far from me as I could, our fingers barely touching. We had ignored each other since our encounter on the stairs the previous afternoon. But now I reached out to pull Arabella towards me. She leaned away. 'We may as well do as she asks,' I hissed, 'or we'll be here all day.'

'You wouldn't like that, would you?' she said slyly. What lay behind those eyes? She didn't know, did she, how could she know? What had she said to me on the stairs? My heart had been so full of Fred I'd barely taken it in. Now I remembered. *You shouldn't spend so much time with servants.* Panic rose inside me. I fought it down. Surely even Arabella wouldn't suspect that I had fallen for one of her father's stable hands? I felt her hand tighten on my waist. My slippered toe edged towards hers. I yearned to send her sprawling across the polished floor.

'Heads up, ladies. Look at your partner. Keep your heads level.'

I kept my head level, but nothing would induce me to look into those cold grey eyes. I grasped Arabella firmly round the waist for one final twirl. It took her by surprise. She stumbled and spun away from me across the ballroom floor. 'Oh dear,' I said as she grabbed at a chair to right herself. 'Are you all right?' I ran to her side.

'I can do very well without your help,' she hissed.

'I think maybe that is enough for today,' Madame said despairingly.

At lunch I saw that an extra place had been laid at the table. Cousin George was expected home that day, though he hadn't telephoned to say when. 'He will have to wait till we get back if he wants to be fetched from the station,' Aunt said as we rose from the table. 'I will not postpone our drive.' The coachman doubled as chauffeur – when Aunt could be persuaded to be driven in the motor – and he could not be in two places at once.

'How like the boy not to think of others,' Uncle growled, wiping his mouth with his napkin.

I was to have accompanied them, but I'd pleaded a headache when I'd learned Arabella was to be in the party. Nothing would induce me to spend any more time in my cousin's company than I had to. Aunt said I looked tired, and suggested a rest. I was tired – I had hardly slept at all the previous night. But I had no intention of resting. As soon as I saw the carriage depart, I hurried upstairs to put on my riding clothes. I'd not told Baxter to put them out, but they were pressed and clean. I pulled a coat on over my riding habit in case I met a servant and ran to the top of the stairs. I was about to descend when I heard voices below. Peering over the banister I could see Clemmie and Miss Dunn standing in the hall, in their hats and coats. I had forgotten that Clemmie had stayed behind. I crouched down, in case they looked up and saw me while I debated what to do. But there really was only one thing I could do – return to my room and wait till they came back from their walk. Cursing my luck, I made my way wearily back to my room, and sat down on my bed. I picked up a book, then threw it aside. I didn't want to read. Precious minutes were slipping by – minutes I'd thought to spend with Fred. I got up again. I couldn't sit there all afternoon. I opened the door and looked out. No one was about. I went back to the stairs and ran softly down. If Clemmie and Miss Dunn did return and see me I'd simply tell them that my headache had gone, and I'd come outside for some fresh air.

I was halfway along the gravel path that led round the house to the outbuildings when I heard a motor horn toot. A pink two-seater motor car was sweeping up the drive. The driver waved. He had seen me. Fate it seemed was against me today. The motor car came to a halt and a man in goggles jumped out. The engine was still running.

He bounded up to me. 'Cousin Penelope,' he said, pulling off his goggles. He bowed. I stared. Cousin George, I thought. But how did he know who I was? The faint shadow of a moustache clung to his upper lip.

'Don't look so startled,' my cousin chuckled, pulling off his driving gloves. 'If I'm not mistaken, that's a riding habit you have on under that coat. You see I know all about you. Very fetching, too.'

My mouth had dropped open. I must have looked anything but fetching.

He laughed. 'There's no mystery,' he said. 'I've seen a photograph of your mother. You're the spitting image of her. Now,' he said. 'Allow me to introduce myself properly. I'm your cousin George.' His eyes twinkled. 'And this,' he said, nodding at the motor, 'is my beloved motor car. Isn't she a beauty?' He gazed at it proudly. 'Come and have a look.'

We walked over to the car.

'Are the family at home?' he asked me.

'Only Clemmie,' I said. 'Everyone else has gone out in the carriage.'

'And you seized the opportunity to have a ride while they were away?'

I blushed.

He smiled. 'Your secret's safe with me,' he said.

We reached the car. 'It is beautiful,' I said, running a hand over the pink shining metal.

George opened the door. 'Why don't you hop in?' he said. 'I'll take you for a spin.'

I stared at him.

'Wouldn't you like a ride?'

Yes, I would. I was on my way to the stables for just that purpose.

'Come on,' he said, patting the side of the car.

I would have to postpone my ride, but it wouldn't be for long.

'A short one then,' I said.

'A very short one,' George said.

I climbed in and settled down on the brown leather seat next to my cousin. There didn't seem to be anything else I could do. Besides, I was eager to see what it would be like. I'd never been for a drive in a car like this before.

'We won't be long,' he said. 'I promise. You'll still have time for a ride on a gee-gee afterwards.'

He let out the clutch. 'Make sure you hold on to your hat,' he said. I jumped as the engine began to throb. Forgetting my hat I clung with both hands to the edges of my seat. George laughed, looking round at me. 'Quite different to riding a horse, isn't it?'

I laughed. The way the car was behaving, it didn't feel that different. 'How fast can it go?' I asked.

'This beauty?' said George. 'She can reach a speed of 45 miles per hour. Not as fast as a galloping horse, I know, but she does have certain advantages that a horse doesn't have.

And believe me, it won't be long before the motor car will be able to go a lot faster than a horse. Cars, Penelope, are the future.' He was very sure of himself, I thought.

'Do you ride, too?' I asked as he put a foot down on the accelerator. 'On horseback I mean.' The car began to glide forwards.

'Of course,' he said. 'I'll be at the Langdown Meet. Will you be joining us?'

'Need you ask?' I said.

He laughed. 'I thought so.' We were going faster now. The wind rushed past my ears. 'Like it?' he shouted.

'Love it!' I shouted back.

'Better hold on to your hat!' George bawled. Too late. I watched helplessly as the wind grabbed it and spun it away. He laughed and I joined in. I'd pick it up later. He put his foot down again. The dial on the dashboard began to climb. 'Let's see how fast she'll go, shall we?' he said.

And then – I wasn't sure what happened, but I heard him curse, and the wheel spun fast in his hands. We swerved violently to one side. I heard a horse's startled whinny. Where had that horse come from? I looked round to see that a carriage had turned into the drive. As we careered past, only just missing it, I caught a glimpse of Aunt's shocked face peering out at us. Then we were bumping over the grass. 'Hold tight!' George shouted, flinging out an arm in front of me. The car rocked over to one side, and I felt a sharp pain zigzag up my arm as I was flung against the edge of the seat. My heart was racing. A dull pain pulsed in my shoulder. I tried to take deep breaths. 'Sorry about that,' said George quietly. 'Are you all right?' I nodded. My shoulder was throbbing, but I didn't mind the pain. I was furious with myself for letting myself be persuaded into that car. I'd ruined the afternoon that I'd hoped to spend with Fred, and I had only myself to blame.

'Young fool!' I looked round to see that the carriage door had opened. Uncle was striding towards us.

'Cripes, I'm for it now,' George murmured.

So was I. I put my head in my hands and groaned. What would Uncle say when he saw what I was wearing?

He reached the car.

'Young fool!' he said again. 'Don't you have eyes in your head? You could have had us all killed.' The fury in his eyes encompassed me.

'Get out of that motor,' he said. George climbed out obediently like a naughty schoolboy. I wished I could crawl away into a hole. 'Are you all right, Penelope?' Uncle asked, turning to me. I nodded and he opened the door for me, holding out his hand to help me out. His eyes took in my riding habit, my hatless head, my hair standing up like a brush. 'You have recovered from your headache, I see?' he said dryly. I felt myself flush. He shook his head – I could see that he was disappointed in me. 'George, help your cousin to the house,' he said. 'I will see you both in the drawing room.'

George gave me his arm. 'I am so sorry,' he said. Not half as sorry as I was. We made our way slowly up to the house. What would Aunt say when she saw me? Oh why oh why had I ever got into that car?

Uncle leaned against the mantelpiece and lit a cigar. George and I were sitting on chairs facing him. I felt like a pupil awaiting the schoolmaster's scolding. My cup of tea was abandoned on a table to my side. I felt my arm throb, but its steady ache helped distract me. Uncle pulled on his cigar. He looked at George. 'Explain that – toy – outside if you'd be so good.' George stared past him into the fireplace.

'Dash it, Pater. A chap must cut some sort of a figure at university, you know.'

'So long as that chap can pay for it,' said Uncle, knocking cigar ash into the grate. Aunt hated Uncle doing this, but now she said nothing. Uncle was so angry, not noisily angry any more, but quiet, which was more frightening.

'Pater, I've put down one payment…'

'You weren't thinking of presenting me with a bill for the remainder, were you, George? You already have a very generous allowance,' Uncle said.

'Please, Pater, not in front of the girls!' George pleaded, casting a glance at Arabella and Clemmie. Arabella sat stony-faced. Clemmie was looking as if she'd burst into tears.

'I think they should hear this,' said Uncle. 'After all, the more you fritter away the less there'll be for your sisters' dowries.'

But I didn't need to hear it, I thought. I shifted uncomfortably on my seat. George's extravagance and my cousins' dowries had nothing to do with me. Father sent me an allowance each month, but I had no idea what provision if any had been made for my marriage. *If* I married…

'Father!' George pleaded again.

'As I said, you have a generous allowance,' Uncle said calmly. 'Do you see this house? There is death-watch beetle in one wing and the roof leaks. If you wish to inherit a home rather than a mountain of debt you will need to learn to moderate your spending – and the sooner the better.

'Nor will I tolerate such reckless behaviour,' Uncle carried on. 'You could both have been killed. We could all have been killed!' His voice had begun to rise. A vein bulged in his neck.

For some time now I had felt Aunt's eye on me and now she rose. *You deal with George and I will deal with Penelope.*

'I don't think Penelope needs to hear this. Come, Penelope.' I'd anticipated a scolding, but at least it would be in private. I followed her into the morning room. Aunt sat down behind the huge desk. I stood in front of it, hands clasped nervously together. I felt like a servant who has not given satisfaction and is expecting dismissal. There was a big bronze paperweight on the desk. I fixed my eyes on it.

'Sit down,' Aunt said, gesturing to a chair. I sat.

'Are you all right, Penelope? You didn't hurt yourself, did you?'

Only my shoulder, but if I tell you that you'll never let me out of the house again.

'I blame George for what happened, but I am disappointed in you, too. You did not tell me the truth, did you? You didn't have a headache, and I see that you are in your riding habit. I had expected better, Penelope.'

I made up my mind to apologize. 'I'm sorry, Aunt.'

She sighed.

'We haven't got off to a very good start, have we, Penelope?'

I kept my eyes on the paperweight.

'Look at me while I am talking, Penelope.' I forced myself to look up. Her eyes were the colour of the sea on a cold day. 'I know you miss your home. I fully expected it would be hard for you to adjust.'

You don't know how hard.

'I am sure our life here is very different to what you're used to...'

Why must she talk as if she'd rescued me from an Indian slum?

'...which is why I have made allowances... But...'

It was coming – she would say that I was an ungrateful minx and that she was going to send me home. I felt my palms grow sweaty. Once I'd have been overjoyed. I'd have leaped over the desk and kissed her. But not now.

'...if by this behaviour you think that I will send you

home, I am afraid I must disappoint you. I would be letting my sister down.'

What? I jerked my head up and looked her full in the face. What was she talking about? How could she even think such a thing?

'I hope what I tell you now will not hurt you, Penelope, but I think it is important that you know the truth. My parents did not approve of the match your mother made and forbade all contact with your parents. But I wrote to her, against their wishes. I would not abandon my sister.'

The letters, I thought. The letters Mother had kept hidden in the trunk, and which now lay in a thick bundle locked in a dressing case. 'And when I learned that it was her wish that you come here, I agreed. I felt I could not go against her dying wish. It was some small amend I could make her.'

Lies, lies, lies. It was all lies. What *had* Father written in his letter to my aunt?

'Mother was sick. She didn't know what she was doing,' I muttered.

Aunt looked angry, but she made an effort to control herself. It was almost the only time I'd seen any strong emotion on that impassive face. 'I cannot help what you think,' she said at last calmly, 'but I can assure you that she wanted the best for you. She did not want you to make the same mistake she had.'

I felt my throat tighten. How could she say such a thing?

How *could* she? 'Mother and Father loved each other very much,' I said.

'Love is not always enough,' Aunt said gently. 'Your mother left behind the comforts she was used to for a dangerous uncertain life. A life cruelly cut short.'

But it was the life she had chosen. And I would make my own choices, too.

'Let us start again, Penelope. Soon you will come out into society.' It felt like a sentence hanging over my head. Aunt was smiling now as if she had handed me a present. I gave the kind of smile I did when I was given a present I didn't want.

'I can never replace your mother, Penelope. But I want to be your friend,' she said.

No, you don't. You want to squash the life out of me. But I won't let you. You'll fail just as your parents did with Mother.

I turned my eyes from her and looked away, out of the window. The morning room was at the front of the house and I had a clear view of the drive. George's car was limping up it. Two boys stood behind it, leaning into it to push it along.

'Ah, the car,' I heard Aunt say. Her gaze had followed mine. 'Perhaps we should talk about that, too.'

I wasn't listening. My eyes were still fixed on the car. A third boy, in the driving seat, turned round to say something to the other two, his hand still on the steering wheel. I felt as if something had hit me hard in the chest. It was Fred.

'Penelope! Did you hear what I was saying?'

Something about the car? I dragged my eyes away from the window.

'I must ask you to give me your word that you will never go out in the car alone with George again. He's a good boy, but reckless, and I could never forgive myself if any harm came to you.' She hesitated. 'It is perhaps fortunate that the car is to be sold as soon as it has been repaired.'

I hate her! She has asked for my word, but she still cannot trust me.

I clenched my hands behind my back. 'I promise,' I muttered.

'Let us put all this behind us now, Penelope,' Aunt said. She stood up and I stood up, too. She proceeded past me into the hall. I'd forgotten that I'd hurt my shoulder, but now I felt it throb. Baxter would run me a bath. Warm water would soothe it. As I made my way to the stairs, I glanced out of the hall window. I could see the wheel marks left by George's car in the gravel. So, I thought, the car was to be sold. Even elder sons it seemed didn't always get their own way. If only I had not got into that car. If only I'd gone downstairs a few minutes earlier… But in spite of everything I still had something precious and no one – not even Aunt – could take it away from me.

Downstairs

You can't keep secret what's going on upstairs. Sometimes I wonder if they realize just how much we know. To them we scarcely exist, it's like we're invisible. It's only when we fail in our duties that they seem to notice us at all. Even then it's not us they see, it's the inconvenience we cause them they notice. A spilt cup of tea. *Look at the mess you've made. The gown I want to wear has a tear in it. How come it wasn't mended in time? Oh I know I didn't tell you I wanted to wear it until you came to dress me, but you should just have known.*

Usually it's Robert who is the first to know what's going on. He knew all right, but so did we! The young master had taken Miss Penelope out for a drive in his new motor car and nearly collided with his lordship's carriage. We shouldn't have been upstairs, but the family being out we'd taken the opportunity to nip up and finish the chores that should have been done earlier – now I'm waiting on Miss P there's always too much to do. Ellen had burst into the library where Sarah was polishing the floor and told her. Then Sarah had run along to the study where I was dusting to tell me. We crowded together at one of the big windows in the drawing room to get a proper look. The motor car had tipped almost over on to its side, but we knew they were all right when his lordship went over to the motor and helped them out. He looked furious, waving his arms and shouting, but he was too far away for us to hear what he was saying. We were still standing there gawping when the carriage was close enough to the house for us to see the coachman's face. If we could see them, then they could see us! We fairly leapt downstairs – it's the eighth deadly sin for a maid to be seen upstairs by the family, unless they've asked for us.

'What luck the car didn't hit the carriage,' Maddie said as we gathered round the table later. 'I don't like to think what might have happened.' She was gazing at Robert as if he'd been exposed to the most terrible danger. Robert had been riding on the box.

'It very nearly did,' Robert said. 'Sid pulled up those horses so tight, I nearly fell off! Would you have minded if I had?' I heard him murmur to Ivy, who was peeling vegetables by his side.

'It would have broken my heart,' she said. She winked at me, earning me a scowl from Maddie. Often now I feel as if I am walking on glass. I'm fast becoming no one's friend. Maddie sees even a friendly wink from Ivy as an insult, and Sarah sees my silence on the topic of Miss P as disloyalty. Not for the first time I found myself wishing that Ivy and Miss P had never come to the manor. Between the pair of them they'd managed to turn our household upside down.

'He's downright irresponsible, that Mr George,' said Cook, shaking her head.

'Tsk tsk, Mrs Venning,' said Mr Barrett. We all jumped – none of us had known he was there. I hate the way Mr B creeps up on us. Robert says he has soft soles made specially for his shoes so we can't hear him. He says one day he'll tie bells to them so we'll always know where he is.

'I can't help it, Mr Barrett,' Cook said. 'I have to say what I think. Mr George has always been like that. A worry to his parents. And goodness knows how much that motor cost.'

Mr B shook his head. 'It's none of our business,' he said. 'Robert!' he barked.

'Yes, Mr Barrett.' Robert jumped to attention.

'You're needed upstairs. The family have finished tea.'

'Very good, Mr Barrett!'

Mr B crept back to his lair, the butler's pantry. Everyone began to relax again. Robert slouched back in his chair.

'I'd love to ride in that motor.' Maisie looked dreamy.

'What – be driven by Mr George? You'd end up in the ditch!' Robert scoffed.

'It's a lovely colour that motor,' Ellen said. 'I've never been in a motor car.'

'I'd rather drive it,' said Ivy.

'With me beside you,' said Robert, trying to put an arm round her.

She pushed it away. 'We'll 'ave to see, won't we,' she said. 'I 'ad my mind on a gentleman.'

'You don't want to bother with them.' Robert leaned over and whispered something in her ear. She giggled. Maddie was pretending she hadn't noticed, but her face had come out into red blotches as it always did when she was upset. Poor Maddie. I kept my eyes fixed on the range. The stewpot was bubbling away nicely, coming up to the boil – just like the atmosphere in that kitchen.

It was Cook who boiled over first. 'Robert!' she exploded. 'Let Ivy get on with her work now. And you heard what Mr Barrett said. And you run along now, too, Jess. I want everyone out of the kitchen who hasn't got a job to do here.'

'Ta ta, all,' Robert said, pulling on his white gloves and standing up lazily.

'I'll see you later, Ivy,' he called back, as he strolled to the door. I could have slapped him. They were heartless, the pair of them. Neither of them thought of poor Maddie's feelings. Ivy was just enjoying herself, but Maddie's heart was near breaking. Couldn't they at least wait till she was out of the room?

I made up my mind to say something to her. But before I could do that I had my own jobs to do – run Miss P's bath and press her evening gown. Later I'd brush down her riding habit – I couldn't think why she'd put that on.

The chores done I nipped downstairs again. For once I found Ivy where she should be – in the scullery.

I went up to the sink and ran water into a glass. I was just wondering how best to broach the subject when Ivy said, 'I expect you think I'm rather fast.'

I hadn't expected that. I fumbled for something to say.

'I'd be careful with young Robert,' I said cautiously. 'He's a bit of a lady's man.'

'You don't have to tell me that,' said Ivy with feeling. 'Puts that Maddie's nose out of joint and she takes it out on me. Anyway I have no plans in that direction as you know.'

'Then leave him alone!' I exclaimed. 'You encourage him. You know you do!'

'I like an audience, that's all,' said Ivy stubbornly. 'I thought you'd 'ave worked that out by now.'

I glanced back down the passage. The kitchen door was open and I could see Maddie bent over the table, her back to us, stirring something in a bowl. Cook was absorbed over the range. I hopped up on to the counter by the sink.

'What made you choose service, Ivy?' I asked.

'Choose?' she snorted. 'Does anyone choose service? I needed a roof over my head – fast. Mam married again and my stepfather and I don't see eye to eye. He's mean. Can't think what Mam sees in him.

'Remember the day I came here? When I got here I was told a wagon had been sent to pick me up. Mam wrote later that it turned up but he never told me. But I don't mean to stay in service. As soon as I've enough saved up to rent a room, I'm off out of here.'

'To do what?' I asked, legs swinging.

Ivy reached for another pan. 'Cor, these are murder on my hands. Look at them.' She held them out to me. Her fingers were red and cracked. 'I want to go on the stage,' she said, 'if anyone will have me, hands like these!'

'The stage!' I gasped. 'It's not respectable.'

Ivy didn't seem to have heard me. A dreamy look had come into her eyes. 'One day it'll be me up there, and her ladyship and the whole lot of them stuck-up lords and ladies, down below, watching me,' she said. 'Me, Jess. Me – Ivy Harte.' She thumped her chest. Soapy water ran down her front.

I gave her a disbelieving look. 'Her ladyship wouldn't go to one of those places,' I said.

''Course she would. She does. All them posh people do.'

I knew nothing about the stage, except that respectable girls didn't go on it. That's what I'd been brought up to think. But sometimes when I spoke to Ivy I felt as if the world I knew was tottering. Ivy challenged everyone and everything. It made me feel uncomfortable, and I wanted to feel safe.

I knew one thing – Langdown Manor wasn't big enough for her. It was big enough for me.

'One day half London will be eating out of my hand – the posh half,' Ivy said.

She wasn't lacking in self-belief.

I shook my head.

'Jess,' said Ivy, patiently, as if she was talking to a child who was a bit slow. 'Things are changing for girls, you know. The world's opening up. Besides, acting and singing is what I'm good at. If I can't make it on the stage here, I'll go abroad.' It felt funny to hear little Ivy talk like that, but she knew a lot about things I didn't. 'What about you, Jess?' she said suddenly, swivelling round to me. 'What do you want to do? Surely you don't mean to stay in service all your life?'

The question took me by surprise. I thought for a moment. What did I want? Same as most girls really. Get married, have a family of my own. But I couldn't see that happening.

'Do you want to be a proper lady's maid?' Ivy said.

I shook my head vigorously 'No. Never.'

'You'd get to travel.'

'And be at my mistress's beck and call every blessed minute of every blessed day! No fear.'

She gave a wry smile. 'It's the worst thing about being in service, isn't it? All that kowtowing. "Yes, sir, no sir." Even down here. We all 'ave to know our place, don't we? That Mr Barrett!' She snorted.

I smiled. I knew what she meant.

'Well, what about a job in a factory, or a shop. Or,' she swivelled round again, 'you could learn to type, and work as a secretary.'

'What – me?' I couldn't see it somehow.

She shrugged, and turned back to the pans. 'You should have more faith in yourself, Jess.'

I slipped down from the counter. I hadn't come to talk about me. 'Well, watch out for Robert. Keep him at arm's length. Find another audience, Ivy. And maybe Maddie will go easier on you.'

'She should find someone else, he'll never go for her,' Ivy said. 'Doesn't matter what I do.'

'So that's what you think, is it?' said a voice behind us. I jumped. Maddie was standing in the doorway, hands on hips. Ivy and I looked at each other. We hadn't heard her come in. The red blotches came and went in her face. I felt my face go red, too.

'That's a matter of opinion. And I'd thank you, Jess, not to discuss my private life with the scullery maid, or distract her from her duties. She's easily enough distracted as it is. Out of my way, now. You may not have any work to do, but I have.' She pushed past me up to the counter, and dropped a pile of dirty pots on it. Her hands were trembling. I felt like a traitor. I'd meant to help, but I'd only made everything worse.

'Maddie,' I said weakly. 'You've got it all wrong.' But it was me who always seemed to get it wrong these days. I shouldn't have interfered. If I wasn't more careful, I'd have no friends left.

I left the two of them there. Sarah was coming downstairs

as I made my way along the passage. *Please, Sarah, don't you accuse me of anything now. I couldn't bear it.*

How I felt must have been written on my face for she slipped her arm through mine, and gave it a comforting squeeze. I felt as if a tiny ray of sun had managed to push its way through the clouds. That's what's best about old friends, I thought, they know you so well. They know when to talk and when you just want some silent comfort. And I didn't want to talk just then. I wanted some quiet. And I wanted to get as far away from the kitchen as I could. *If you can't stand the heat keep out of the kitchen*, Mam used to say to me.

Downstairs was my home – but it didn't feel like home just then.

Upstairs

'Hulloa!' George waved, stepping down from the motor's running board. He gave the metalwork a quick flick with a cloth. 'What do you think?' he said, proudly. Its pink carriage gleamed like a car in a showroom. I was astonished. There didn't seem to be a single dent in the metalwork. It was hard to believe what a battering it had taken only yesterday. I felt a bit sorry for George. He loved that car, and now it had to be sold.

'It looks as good as new,' I said.

'She's a beauty, isn't she,' George said lovingly.

I'd gone round to see the car as soon as breakfast was over. I was curious to see if it was roadworthy again. It was parked where Clemmie had said it would be – in one of the garages, next to Uncle's green motor and the carriage Aunt still liked to use when paying her afternoon calls. A vehicle that was unrecognizable had been hauled outside to make room for it. Clemmie had been to see the car. Arabella had shown no curiosity in it at all. She and George had barely spoken since Uncle's outburst. Her dwindling inheritance clearly rankled.

George tossed down the cloth. 'Fancy a spin?'

He had to be joking!

'I thought it was to be sold,' I said.

George shrugged. 'I'll bring Pater round.' He slapped the side of the motor. 'One spin in this girl and he'll change his mind.'

Did George always get what he wanted? His motor was a topic none of us had dared raise since the accident. Uncle had been icily polite to both of us since then. Did George really think he would thaw enough to let him keep the car?

George crouched down and peered under the chassis. 'Fred, how are you getting on?'

It was only then that I saw the pair of legs sticking out from under the car.

I felt as if a hand was squeezing my chest.

'All finished, sir,' a muffled voice said. He began to shimmy himself out.

'Do you need a hand?' offered George, reaching down.

'That's all right, I can manage, sir,' Fred said, sliding out from under the car, a spanner in his hand. He clambered to his feet and touched his cap to me. His hands were black and oily. 'Morning, miss.'

Are you all right? his eyes asked. They looked strained. He knew I'd been in the car then.

I tried to keep my tone as formal as his. 'Good morning, Fred.'

I'm all right, my eyes replied.

George tossed him a cloth. 'Here, take this.'

Fred put down the spanner and wiped his hands on the

cloth. There was a smudge of oil on his cheek. I wanted to touch it, wipe it away, run my hand down his face. I clenched my hands tightly behind my back.

'I've fixed the problem. You shouldn't have any more trouble, sir,' he said.

Sir! Sir! Sir! Each time Fred said that word, I felt as if a chasm was being driven between us.

'Good man!' said George. He smiled at me. 'Next to driving, tinkering with a motor is the best thing about having one,' he said – even though it was Fred who'd done the tinkering. 'Now how would my favourite cousin like another spin?'

'Aunt has forbidden it,' I said.

'I thought she might, but we don't need to worry about that, do we? It can be our secret.' When I didn't answer he gave me a quizzical look. 'I didn't think you were a girl who worried about little things like that. Or are you afraid I'll have another accident? I never have before.'

I was silent. I didn't like the way George was talking to me as if Fred wasn't there. And it didn't make any difference what he said. Nothing would tempt me to ride in that car again, even if I hadn't already promised Aunt.

'Well, maybe not today then,' George said. 'So what are your plans for this afternoon? How about a ride on horseback, Pen?'

Pen? No one had ever called me that before.

'Or is it Penny?' George smiled. 'Though I think Pen suits you better.'

'It's neither,' I said. I caught Fred's eye. He was trying not to smile.

'You haven't answered my question, Mistress Penelope?'

Which? It's none of your business.

'Let's go out together, shall we? Fred, would you saddle our horses for us?'

'Wait!' I said. If I wasn't quick, he'd have bullied me into riding with him, too. 'I can't. I hurt my shoulder – I banged it against the seat in the car yesterday. I won't be able to ride today – or tomorrow,' I added hastily.

'What a shame,' he said. 'You must take care of it, so it's better for the dance.'

'What dance?' I said blankly. No one had said anything about a dance to me.

'I'm having some friends over soon – for the Meet. They'll be staying for the weekend. We'll have some dancing.'

George seemed to have forgotten that Fred was still patiently waiting.

'Will that be all, sir?' he said now. 'I'd best be getting back.'

'Yes, sorry, Fred. Forgot you were still there,' George said.

'I'll get Jem to saddle up for you, sir.'

George nodded. 'Three o'clock please, Fred.'

I watched as Fred sauntered away, hands in pockets. He walked as if he didn't care how casually George had dismissed him. But I did. It made me uncomfortable. I had a sudden picture – me, ordering my kindly ayah about. Was that what I'd sounded like? I cringed, and felt my feet edge me away from the car. I didn't want to spend any more time with George. 'I must go,' I said. George nodded, before disappearing back into the garage again.

I made my way to the stables.

Fred was in the yard, rinsing his oily hands at the pump. 'Hello,' he said. 'You've not come to tell me you want to ride after all, have you? You shouldn't if you've hurt your shoulder.'

'Can I talk to you?' I said.

'I'd like to see how badly hurt that shoulder is,' he said. 'If you don't mind?'

Of course I didn't mind. The mere thought of him touching it made me tremble all over.

'We'd better go to Starshine's stall,' he said. 'You can pretend it's her you've come to see. Don't want people talking.'

'Are they?' I said, nervously.

'Not that I know. But there's always eyes about, people like to gossip.'

We walked together over to Starshine's stall. She lifted her head when she saw me, and I raised my hand to stroke it. A fiery pain shot up my shoulder. I winced and withdrew my hand hastily.

'It hurts, doesn't it?' Fred said. 'He should have taken more care.' He sounded angry. 'I don't trust Mr George.' He pushed open the door of the stall. 'Sorry,' he added quickly. 'I shouldn't have said that. It wasn't respectful.'

'You don't need to apologize,' I said, following him in. 'Anyway, I didn't like the way he talked to you.'

'I'm a servant,' Fred shrugged. *I'm used to it*, he might as well have said. 'Now I'd like to look at that shoulder.'

He came to my side. I felt his hand touch it gently. I could hardly breathe. 'Am I hurting?' he said. 'I don't want to hurt you.'

I leaned as close to him as I could. 'Fred,' I said, lowering my arm. 'It hurts less now. Just being here…'

Why was he looking at me like that? Was something wrong?

He walked away from me. He cleared his throat.

'Polly,' he said. 'I've something to say to you. Something I should have said before. Then today when Mr George mentioned that dance…' He shook his head. I felt that I knew what he was going to say, but I wouldn't let him say it. Fred and me – we were right together. I knew it. He knew it. What else mattered?

'Since knowing you. I—' He lifted his hand to stop me, to hold back the words he must have seen in my eyes.

'Come here,' he said. He took my uninjured arm and led me to the door. 'See that window up there?' He pointed to an upper window over the stable block on the other side of the yard. 'Well, that's where I sleep. Now see there.' He pointed to the manor. 'That's where you live. Can't you see that –

anything – between us … can't you see that it's impossible?' He shoved his hands into his pockets and looked at me stubbornly.

But if he was stubborn, so was I.

'No, I can't,' I said. 'You'll never change my mind.'

'Polly—'

'Don't do this,' I said. 'You're my only friend here.' But we were much more than that. I felt as if I'd always known that we belonged together – ever since the day we'd met. He was the first person I'd ever felt like this about, and I knew that I always would.

I clenched my hands into fists to stop myself from touching him. I wanted to raise them to him, so badly. A lock of his hair had fallen across his eyes. I wanted to push it back, feel it with my fingers, smooth away the little dent I could see growing between his eyes, run my fingers down his cheeks, all the way down to his lips. To touch them with mine. Just thinking about kissing him made me feel almost faint.

Could he truly say that he didn't feel the same?

I laid my head against Starshine. I felt her head come round, her wet nose nuzzle against me as if she was trying to comfort me. *She* understood how I felt.

'You're coming out soon, aren't you – you and Miss Arabella?'

In March – a month I'd like to erase from the calendar.

'I won't stand in your way.'

You already are. I can't turn off my feelings so easily, even if you can.

'Fred, my mother ran away to marry my father,' I said. 'He's a tea planter. He works for his living. And I'm proud that he does.'

'But he's a gentleman. I'm not and never will be,' Fred said bitterly.

'Gentlemen aren't born, they're made. You're more of a gentleman than cousin George will ever be,' I said stubbornly.

'Then there's money…'

'You have earnings…'

Fred threw back his head and laughed. 'Not enough to keep a gentleman's daughter on. Besides, most of it goes to my mam.'

'Surely you can find another job, one that's better paid?' Why did he put difficulties in our way? Besides, why were we talking about the future? What did that matter? All that mattered was now.

'Poll, don't make this hard for me.'

'It doesn't have to be.'

He stepped towards me, and raised his hands. I moved closer to him. I held mine up to clasp his. He stepped back. His hands fell back again to his side. I saw how he clenched them as if he was battling with himself. We looked at each other. I felt as if I could hardly breathe.

He'd change his mind. I knew he would.

'Leave me,' he said softly. 'Please.'

I left him, but as I always did, I left part of me behind.

Upstairs

'Wake up, Polly, it's snowing!' It was Clemmie not Baxter who was leaning over the bed. 'It's snowing!' she said again, impatiently. 'Don't you want to get up and see?'

'Snowing! Really and truly?' I didn't want to leave my warm bed.

'Yes, yes, come and look!' She tugged at the quilt I'd drawn up to my chin.

I had never seen snow before. Father had tried to describe it. Nasty wet stuff, he'd said. I had to see if he was right. I slipped out of bed drawing the quilt round me and ran to the window, feeling almost as excited as Clemmie. Clemmie got there first. She pulled open one of the curtains. 'Look!' We stood side by side, watching the thick flakes swirl, like feathers beaten out of an enormous pillow. Snow-covered trees were hunched under their burdens.

By the time we sat down to breakfast the snow had stopped falling, and the sun had poked a hole in the cloud. I was eager to go outside. I wanted to touch the stuff to see what it felt like. Would it stick to me as it did to the trees, or simply melt away in my hands? Clemmie was as eager as me.

'Mother,' she said, between mouthfuls. 'Please may we go outside? Polly has never seen snow before.'

Aunt was in an indulgent mood. 'Very well, but wrap up warmly. You must be careful, Clemmie.'

'I'm going to build a snowman. Will you help me?' asked Clemmie, as we pulled on coats and hats.

'Yes, if you show me how,' I said.

Clemmie smiled. 'I'm glad you've come to live with us,' she said. 'I couldn't ask Arabella. She thinks she's too grown up.'

Arabella was only six months older than me, but I knew what Clemmie meant. She was one of those girls who can't wait to grow up. I couldn't imagine her ever playing in the snow, or making a snowman; she'd think it was unladylike.

'Come on!' Clemmie said. Sam opened the door for us, and Clemmie took my hand. We stood on the step and gazed around. It was so quiet that I could hear myself breathe. The whole world seemed to be sleeping under a blanket of snow. 'We need shovels,' Clemmie said. 'We'll get them at the stables.' We trudged round to the side of the house, sinking into the snow up to our ankles. I wondered what Fred would say when he saw me. I hadn't seen him for days. I had made myself avoid the stables, telling myself that he would come after me. He would be bound to miss me, as much as I was missing him. He hadn't, but I'd hadn't given up. I knew that we were meant to be together.

We were nearly at the stable gate when I saw Fred emerge from one of the stalls. He didn't look up, but I felt myself blush. I had to hide my face somehow. I bent down hastily and scooped up a handful of snow. 'Clemmie!' I shouted, lifting the snowball, and taking aim. Clemmie laughed and ducked. The snowball flew through the air. I had just time to see a girl's startled expression before the snowball hit her full in the face. Where had she come from?

'You … you…' she sputtered, spitting snow out of her mouth. I ran up to her.

'I'm so sorry,' I said. 'Are you all right? I didn't see you there.'

'No,' she said bitterly, wiping snow off her face with her sleeve. There was a red mark on her cheek where the snowball had landed. 'You never do see us, do you, you young ladies.' I was taken aback. What had brought on such an outburst? I hadn't meant to hit her!

'I'm sorry,' I said again. 'I didn't mean it. Truly.'

The girl shrugged and stalked away. I stood there, staring after her. Clemmie ran up to my side.

'Sarah looked upset,' she said.

'Who's Sarah?' I asked.

'Sarah? Oh, she's one of the housemaids.' Clemmie knew all the servants.

'What's she doing out here then?' I said.

'She'll have come to see Fred,' Clemmie said casually.

'Fred?' I said stupidly.

'Fred. You know. The stable hand. They're sweethearts. They've known each other ever so long. It's supposed to be secret, but everyone knows.'

Everyone except me, Clemmie. The ground seemed to swim under my feet. I groped for the fence and held on to it.

'Let's build our snowman,' I heard Clemmie say. Her voice seemed to come from a long way off.

'You get the shovels, I'll wait here,' I said. I leaned back against the gate and tried to take some deep breaths to calm myself. Somewhere I heard Clemmie call to Fred, heard steps run across the yard, but I kept my back to them. I didn't turn round. I didn't want to see him. I never wanted to see him again.

'Here we are,' said Clemmie, breathlessly. 'I asked Fred to help us, but he says he's busy.' She had brought two shovels. 'One each,' she said. I took one from her and we walked back to the front of the house. 'We'll build it where everyone can see it,' Clemmie said cheerfully, digging her shovel into the soft snow. It felt odd to hear her cheerful chatter when I was feeling as if the world had exploded around me. My shoulder ached each time I drove the shovel into the snow, but it helped remind me that I was still alive. We patted the snow down with our hands. Then we rolled a giant snowball on top for its head. I chatted and laughed, but it didn't feel as if it was me. I felt as if I was watching myself, from somewhere far away, as if I was looking down at us, in the snow. Arabella and George were brought out to admire our snowman, Arabella in her slippers, squealing at the cold and tripping straight back in. George fetched a carrot for its nose, and coals for its eyes.

'Shoulder better now?' he asked as the three of us walked round to the stables to return the shovels.

'Quite better,' I lied. 'We will be able to ride together soon. I'm looking forward to the dance, too,' I added loudly to make sure that Fred would hear. I knew he was not far away – I'd heard him thank George for bringing the shovels back.

We went inside to take off our wet things. My feet felt so heavy – as if they'd hardly carry me up the stairs. I sat down on the bed. I wouldn't let him know how I felt. I'd never forgive him. Never! All the time he had had a girlfriend. All that stuff about a gulf between us when he'd just found it too awkward to cope with two girls at once. He had made his choice now. And he'd chosen her, that housemaid. That girl who had shouted at me. What a fool I had been. I felt my cheeks grow hot.

The snow-covered park had looked beautiful this morning. Now it just looked cold and bleak. Like I felt.

Fred and I would never be together.

I groped for comfort – and found none. I longed to be home in India, to feel Father's warm arms around me, to be with people who loved me. There was no one here I could tell how I felt. *No one. No one. No one.* I gulped – I could feel them come. I couldn't hold them back any longer. The tears began to trickle down my face.

Downstairs

'What's happened to you?' I said to Sarah, as I bumped into her on the stairs. Under her cap her hair looked damp, and there was a red mark on one cheek.

'Miss Penelope, that's what,' said Sarah. 'She threw a snowball and it caught me in the face.'

'She did what?' I exclaimed.

'She said she was sorry, but she should take more care,' Sarah sniffed.

'I'm sure she didn't mean it.' I'd meant to console, but Sarah rounded on me.

'Is that all you can say?'

I felt myself flinch at the anger I saw in her eyes. It wasn't my fault, was it?

'Sarah, I'm sorry, but she wouldn't have deliberately thrown a snowball at you. Why would she want to do that?'

'Search me. They don't care, do they? Posh girls like her. They do just what they like.'

Sarah was working herself up into a rage. This wasn't just about a badly thrown snowball.

'What is the matter, Sarah? You can tell me.'

'I was all right before she came here,' she said more to herself than to me. 'She's spoilt it all.' Her face creased and I knew she was trying not to cry.

Hurriedly I put down the carpet sweeper I'd been carrying, and put my arms around her. 'Don't be upset, Sarah. There's nothing to be upset about.'

'There is,' she wept. 'He's changed. He's not the same towards me.' She rubbed a hand across her eyes. 'It's ever since she came.'

'Has he said anything? He's not called it off?'

She shook her head. 'No, but there's something different about him. I know him so well, I can tell, Jess. I'm sure he's trying to avoid me. He's always making excuses why he can't spend time with me. He's too busy, he's got to look after a horse. He never was like that before. Never ever. He always found time somehow.'

I tried to think of something that would comfort her. 'I'm sure you're wrong, but Miss Penelope, she'll be coming out soon. Even if he does like her, she'll be busy going to parties and dances, and in a year or two she'll be married to some rich young man. You and he go way back, Sarah. Anyway, they'd never let her marry him. Can you imagine!' I laughed. The idea was preposterous. Surely Sarah could see that?

'She'll be going to London soon for the season. You'll have Fred to yourself,' I added. 'He won't be so busy then, once the family are away.'

I earned myself a watery smile. I gave her a quick hug before picking up the carpet sweeper and lugging it upstairs. I was behind with my chores, and still had the drawing room floor to sweep. I planned to nip in while it was empty. We had a lot of extra work to do now. Mr Barrett had told us after morning prayers that we'd be a full house soon. Mr George had invited some friends to stay for the Langdown Meet, and there'd be all the bedrooms to prepare for the guests and staff, on top of all the other cleaning. Then there was Miss P. As I pushed the carpet sweeper back and forth across the drawing room floor, I tried to forget what Sarah had said. Miss P hadn't been riding for days. Her shoulder still troubled her. I had never been on a horse and never wanted to. Great big brutes; one had nearly stepped on Sarah's toe once.

I was nearly done when I heard voices outside – Mr George's and Miss P's. I could hear some of what they were saying – they were talking about the dance. It was only an informal one, but Miss P sounded ever so enthusiastic. Well, I thought, who wouldn't be? Who wouldn't want to wear a beautiful gown and twirl round the room in the arms of a handsome young man? I'd tell Sarah that she had nothing to worry about. Even if Fred had developed a fancy for her, he'd soon get over it, once he grew up enough to realize that it was just a silly dream.

We servants were soon to have our own ball, too. I looked forward to it every year. This year maybe I'd meet the man of my dreams. I shut my eyes and tried to imagine myself in satin and diamonds. I'd have my hair done up differently, maybe a little rouge on my lips… I grasped the handle of the carpet sweeper, pretending it was my partner, and tried a few steps. I only knew a couple of dances, but Ivy was going to teach me some new ones. I was so caught up in my silly dream that I didn't hear the door open. And when at last I looked up again there was Mr George and Miss P standing there, staring at me. I stopped, the carpet sweeper still hugged in my arms. I could feel myself blush to my roots. I edged out of the room, muttering apologies, pulling the sweeper along behind me. Mr George was smiling. I saw Miss P smile, too, but there was a sadness deep in her eyes that I didn't expect.

I still had her room to finish, before beginning on the guest rooms. It should have been done while Miss P was at breakfast, but she'd burst in before I'd finished for gloves and hat before running out into the snow. It wasn't easy to find the right time to clean Miss P's room. She appeared and disappeared when you weren't expecting it. I opened the door. I could see her imprint on the bed I'd made earlier. It looked as if she had been sitting there for a long time. Smoothing it down again, I felt a moment's pity for her. It couldn't have been easy coming to live halfway across the world with relatives she didn't know. Fine gowns and a life of leisure seemed too high a price to pay.

I began on the dusting. There was a photograph of

her dead mother on the dressing table. I could see the resemblance to Miss P, even though it must have been taken when her mother was a lot older. But I'd dusted the photographs in the drawing room often enough to recognize that Miss P was the spitting image of her mother when she was the same age. I wondered how her ladyship felt about that – it must have felt like welcoming home a ghost.

I was on my way back to the basement when I saw that someone was creeping along the passage that led to the hall. Ivy! She looked shocked when she saw me – as she should.

'Ivy!' I demanded. 'What are you doing up here? You know it's forbidden.'

She looked sullen. 'I had to get out of that scullery. I can't stand it, Jess. Maddie gives me no peace.'

I gave her a sceptical look.

'You didn't have to come up here though, did you? You could have gone outside, or to your room. Hurry now – get back downstairs before anyone else sees you.' I took her by the shoulders and gave her a push. 'Come on, Ivy, don't dawdle, I haven't got all day.'

We reached the door that separated the upstairs world from the downstairs. 'Hurry up,' I said, throwing a nervous glance back into the hall.

'Even the door's different on our side.' Ivy touched the green baize that covered the door on the downstairs side. 'What's this for?' she asked.

'It's to help muffle the sound, so the family won't hear us.'

She snorted. 'They want to pretend we don't exist, don't they? What would they do without us, I wonder? One day they'll 'ave to. I wish I could see it. Them sweating over the range, washing up their own plates and cups, making their own beds—'

I didn't like that sort of talk. 'Enough of that,' I said. 'I'm not listening.' I put my hands over my ears.

'Well, I look forward to the day when they won't wipe their shoes on my back,' said Ivy. 'It's coming, Jess, whether you like it or not.'

'Until then you've got three meals a day – a lot better too than you got at home I don't doubt – and a roof over your head,' I said. 'But when this wonderful new world of yours comes, who knows? You might be on the streets – no job, no money, no home…'

Ivy snapped her fingers. 'I'm not afraid.'

But I was.

The future Ivy described didn't excite me; it frightened me. It was all very well, but what would we do – girls like me who'd only ever worked in service?

I put the carpet sweeper back where it should have been, in the store cupboard, then together we clattered down the stairs.

At the bottom I marched her into the scullery. I could see a heap of still unwashed pans sitting by the sink. A dirty rim ran round the sides. 'Ivy, get going with that lot before you get in more trouble and we'll talk.' As I perched up on the side again, I remembered the last time I'd sat there when Maddie had stormed in. I cast a glance into the kitchen. Maddie and Maisie were bent over the table, chopping up vegetables and I could hear Cook firing off orders. It was a busy time of day for the kitchen staff.

'So,' I began, 'what's up with you and Maddie this time, Ivy?'

'The usual. She makes my life really hard. She'd like to see me sacked, I'm sure. I'll sack myself when I'm ready.'

'You'll get yourself sacked if you're seen upstairs again. What made you go upstairs, Ivy? The truth, now.'

Ivy was scouring the scum out of the sink. 'I just wanted to see what it was like.'

'You see it at morning prayers.'

'I only see the hall,' she muttered.

'So you went exploring, did you?' She gave a giggle. 'Ivy,' I said, 'it's not funny. If anyone else had seen you you'd have been in real trouble.'

She turned round to me. 'You should see your face, Jess! But you needn't worry. No one saw me. I'd only got as far as the hall, before you came along.'

'Good thing I did,' I said. 'You might have come across the family.' I felt my cheeks go pink remembering how Mr George and Miss P had caught me dancing round the room with the carpet sweeper clasped to my chest.

'Don't ever go up there again,' I said. 'You might not be so lucky next time.'

'You'll not tell, will you, Jess?'

I felt annoyed. ''Course not. I don't split.'

'I'll return the favour one day. I'll...' She turned back to me and studied my face. I felt my cheeks grow hot as her eyes wandered over it from cap to chin. 'Tell you what; I'll help you get ready for the ball. You won't recognize yourself, Jess.'

She plunged her hands back into the water. 'Funny to think we'll 'ave our own ball,' she mused. She pulled a face. 'Only I'll 'ave to avoid young Robert, or Maddie will get the hump. That young stable hand's nice, but he's spoken for, isn't he?'

'Fred? Yes, he is. You keep your hands off him!' Goodness – what would our lives be like if Ivy took a fancy to Fred, too!

Upstairs

My partner's hand tightened on my waist. He was old – and nearly bald. I yearned to pull away, but I didn't dare. Aunt's eyes were on me. She gave me an approving smile. At least I was dancing… Arabella was standing by the wall, one of a gaggle of girls swooning over David Moore. Nearly all the girls had their eye on him – he was the handsomest man in the room. I'd no desire to join them. I'd caught him glancing over at me once or twice. I could see from his expression that he was used to attention and couldn't understand why I alone hadn't fallen at his feet. But I wasn't going to be another scalp on his belt.

I had my hair up. I'd asked Baxter to do it for me. I'd never had it up before. I wasn't sure what Aunt would think but she seemed pleased that I was showing some interest in my appearance. When Baxter held up a mirror for me I didn't recognize myself. I felt I was looking into the face of a stranger. Good. I wanted to be a stranger to myself. I didn't want anything to do with the girl who cried into her pillow at night. I'd kept away from the stables since the day I'd helped Clemmie build the snowman. I hadn't needed to find an excuse as the snow had made it impossible to ride. It still lay on the ground, like a dirty blanket, stubbornly refusing to melt, and the Meet had had to be cancelled. Each morning when I woke pain settled on my chest like a weight that I had to carry around with me. It was at its heaviest when the household staff joined us for morning prayers – I could not stop my eyes being drawn to Sarah's bowed head. I never saw her look at me, but just a glimpse of her fair head immediately brought Fred to my mind, and the wound I was trying to heal ached as badly as it had the day I'd learned about her and Fred.

Though the Meet had been cancelled there was still a houseful of guests at Langdown. George's friends had arrived yesterday. Some of the guests had been collected from the station, others had made their own way by motor, gleaming handsome vehicles that were now parked on the forecourt. When I'd heard cars drive up and horns toot I'd wanted to run away and hide. I didn't want to see them, I felt unfit for human company.

The dance came to an end and my partner deposited me among a group of girls – all friends of Arabella's. I stood with them, but they ignored me, so I wandered away and sat in an empty chair. I felt misery tug at me. The room was full of people, yet I had never felt more alone.

'Can I get you a drink?' I looked up to see that David Moore was standing before me. Was it the lack of interest I'd shown in him that had drawn him to me? I shook my head.

'Then may I sit down?' he asked. I nodded, not caring if he joined me or not. He pulled out a chair and sat down next to me. 'I feel that we've barely been introduced,' he said. 'How are you enjoying yourself?'

'All this – dancing…' I waved my hand. I tried to smile.

'You'd sooner be on horseback? Ah, the freedom it gives. George told me that you're a good rider,' he explained.

'George has never even seen me ride,' I said. He must have heard the abruptness in my voice, but he ignored it.

'Word has got around then. But wait till you come up in the plane. Did George tell you about that? I think you'll enjoy that just as much.' I turned my eyes to the window. The curtains had been drawn, so I couldn't see outside. It was dark now anyway. Fred would be up in his room, or talking to Sarah… I tried to push away the image of Fred's face that swam before me. It seemed to grow more vivid the more I wished it would fade. I tried to force it away by imagining what it would be like to sit in a plane, how I'd feel as it climbed higher and higher, into the clouds. But Fred's face remained obstinately before me.

'George told me you had a plane,' I said, in desperation turning back to David. 'But I'd thought he was joking.' Only a few brave men flew planes. I couldn't imagine even a rich young man owning one.

'I do indeed, I share it with some friends,' he said. 'Would you like a ride in it?'

'If you let me take the controls!' I said, simply for something to say.

'Ah! What spirit! We might be able to arrange it,' he said. He leaned forward. 'George told me that you lived all your life in India until a few months ago.'

'I did. I came here when Mother died. Aunt is trying to turn me into a lady,' I said, without thinking what I was saying. 'I don't think she'll succeed.' I shouldn't have said that either, but I was too miserable to care what I said. I'll have shocked him, I thought. But perhaps he'd see that he was wasting his time. Get up and leave me alone. And surely he could sense the aura of misery I carried around with me. But to my surprise I saw that he was listening attentively, a sympathetic expression on his face. I felt myself begin to relax. 'Dancing and parties, it's all very well,' I said, 'but...' I shrugged.

'It's not enough, is it? But things are changing, you know – even for women. One day women will get the vote, and then we men had better watch out.'

'The vote?' I said. In spite of myself I felt a flicker of life inside me.

David leaned back in his chair and studied me. 'You didn't know about the suffragettes?'

I shook my head, ashamed to be so ignorant. 'Who are they?' I asked.

He smiled. 'Well, of course,' he said, 'you have been in

India and missed the fun. Suffragettes are women who are fighting for the right to vote. They are a wild lot. They march on Parliament and do all sorts of unspeakable things for their cause like set fire to postboxes, and chain themselves to railings. But it's hard not to admire their spirit.'

In a few weeks' time I'd be presented at Court. I'd wear my hair up every day, not just on special occasions like this. But if things were really beginning to change for women then maybe my future wasn't as bleak as it seemed to me right now. I felt the weight on my chest shift a little. David was easy to talk to. And unlike most of my partners he had a view of the world that more nearly matched mine. But it was what he talked about, rather than the man himself, that interested me. A world in which anything was possible, even for young ladies like me. In which men took to the air and women marched on Parliament demanding their rights. I'd had a dream and it had been torn away from me; I'd felt as if my life was over even before it had begun. I'd almost let my feelings for Fred overwhelm everything else. But perhaps my life wasn't over, even if Fred wasn't part of it any more?

Downstairs

'Ow!'

'Stop wriggling, Jess!'

You stuck a pin in me!' I complained. I put my hand up to my head. Ivy swiped it away.

'There'll be another one if you don't sit still!'

I sat still and felt another pin slide into my hair. I was sitting on the bed, already dressed. I'd made the dress myself. I was very proud of it. It was a soft blue, my favourite colour, the colour of a midsummer sky, though Ivy said it was too pale for me. 'You'd look better in a darker blue,' she'd told me. 'It would make you stand out more.'

I didn't want to stand out more. Ivy would, whatever she wore. Ivy who only came up to my shoulder, but she'd long ago lost that half-starved look.

Tonight she was in green with gold trimming. In the candlelight the gold sparkled. She looked like a duchess.

Ivy had appointed herself our lady's maid. Sarah, already dressed, was pacing up and down the bedroom restlessly. I knew how she felt, but I wished she would sit down.

‘Sit down, Sarah, or you’ll wear out your dancing shoes before the ball’s even started!’ Ivy commanded.

Sarah ignored her. She was staring out of the tiny window. It was nearly time for the ball to begin. His lordship and her ladyship would open it, and we’d have to watch our p’s and q’s till they departed. Last year it had been near midnight before they had. By then my eyes were half shut. I’d crept up to bed long before the dancing had finished. We couldn’t lie in in the morning after our ball like they could.

Ivy stepped back and handed me the mirror. ‘Take a look.’ I almost gasped as I gazed into it. I didn’t recognize myself. ‘Shame it’s just for the staff,’ she complained. ‘It’s wasted on them.’

‘The family will be there, too,’ I reminded her.

‘Oh, them,’ said Ivy. ‘They’ll not dance with us, too stuck-up, that lot.’

‘Mr George might,’ I said. ‘He’s danced with some of us in the past.’ He danced with the pretty ones, anyway. I felt sure he’d dance with Ivy. She’d be fighting them off.

‘What? The young master – the one who has that posh car?’ Ivy’s eyes gleamed. ‘Maybe he’ll take us for a spin in it.’

‘I’d not go in that car with him,’ said Ellen, who was over by the window buffing her nails.

‘Nor me neither,’ I agreed.

Ivy snorted. ‘What a lot of cowards you are.’ She grinned. ‘Maybe he’d give me a driving lesson – if I asked him *very* nicely.’

She turned back to the bed, where she'd laid out little bottles and pots on a clean tea towel. She unscrewed one and stuck her finger in it.

'Head up!'

I felt something warm smear my lips. I jerked back. 'Where did you get that?'

'Sssh, or it'll smudge.' She wiped her finger on a tissue, then opened another pot. 'A bit of colour now … finishing touches, Jess.'

I put up my hands to shield my face. 'No, that's enough. I'll look like a … a harridan.'

'I'm wasted on you. Sarah?'

Sarah didn't answer.

'Ellen?'

Ellen shook her head.

'I'll do myself then,' Ivy said. She dabbed a bit of powder on her face, then drew a line around her lips.

I glanced at the clock. It was time we went. My stomach did a jig. I always felt nervous before one of these occasions.

Ivy put down the pot and picked up the mirror. She gave a satisfied smile. 'I think I'll do. Ready, ladies?' She held open the door. 'Jess,' she said. 'You look a picture. Those are lips that are meant to be kissed.'

I blushed. 'Ivy!'

'She's right,' Ellen said, admiringly.

I just hoped no one would ask where the rouge came from. Behind us Sarah had resumed her pacing. I grabbed her by the shoulder. 'Come on, Sarah, that's enough.'

'I feel sick, Jess,' she whispered.

'Nervous sick?'

She nodded.

'You look lovely. You'll be on your feet all night. He won't be able to keep his eyes off you. You'll see.'

Sarah nodded, but she looked unconvinced.

'And if he doesn't you'll make him jealous – all the partners you'll have.'

A tiny smile flitted across Sarah's face.

'Treat 'em mean, keep 'em keen, that's what I say, Sarah,' Ivy put in. I could hear voices and laughing in the corridor.

'After you, ladies,' Ivy said. 'We're going to knock 'em dead!'

We sashayed down the corridor.

'Excuse me, ladies.' Maddie elbowed past us.

'There goes old misery,' said Ivy.

'Ivy!' I said warningly.

'Well, it's not my fault Robert fancies me, is it? I don't do anything.'

'Don't dance with him tonight. Maybe things will settle down then,' I said.

Ivy didn't answer. She was smoothing down her gown. 'You know, Jess,' she said, 'it'll be the first time I'll be in those posh rooms upstairs.' She gave me a wink.

I pushed back the green baize door. I gasped. I felt as if I was stepping into wonderland. A whole team of waiters and lackeys had been hired for the night. The front door kept opening and shutting as staff and tenants from the estate were escorted inside – like they were posh lords and ladies. As they took off their cloaks you'd not know the difference. Over our heads the candelabra shimmered and sparkled.

Suddenly I felt Ivy dive behind me. 'What's up, Ivy?' I said.

'It's Robert,' she hissed. 'Crumbs, I think he wants to open the ball with me.'

The ballroom doors had been flung open and Robert was standing at the entrance. His eyes scanned each lady as she passed. It was clear enough who he was waiting for. 'Keep close by me, Ivy, I'll see what I can do,' I said.

We shuffled together up to the entrance. 'I didn't plan to enter the ballroom on my knees,' Ivy complained.

'What can I do about it?' I retorted. 'Keep down, or he'll see you.'

Robert hadn't, but someone else had, I saw – Mr George. He was leaning back against the wall – splitting his sides, he was laughing so hard. He strolled up to us, slipping on his white gloves. He bowed to Ivy, as if she was a gracious lady.

'May I have the honour, young lady?' He offered her his arm.

Ivy lowered her eyes. 'Thank you, sir,' she murmured. Even her voice was like a duchess's. How did she do it?

She was wearing proper gloves too – long white ones up over her elbow, like real ladies wore.

I watched as she glided into the ballroom on Mr George's arm. Robert must have seen, I thought. I felt a bit sorry for him – until I remembered how heartlessly he treated Maddie. Let him have a taste of his own medicine. Him the cock of the servants' hall!

I looked round for Sarah. I couldn't see her anywhere. I hoped she'd found Fred and they'd made it up.

My eyes picked out Miss Penelope. She was smiling, but the smile looked a bit strained, I thought. But she wasn't my problem tonight. This was our night, not theirs. Ellen and I took our places in our usual spot, over by the wall. My hands felt clammy. The small orchestra struck up a waltz. I felt like weeping as his lordship led her ladyship on to the floor. *Wouldn't anyone ask me to dance?* More and more couples were taking the floor now. Men walked past me, and turned away as if to say, it's not her I'm looking for. Ellen touched my arm. 'Over there,' she whispered.

'What?'

'It's Ivy, she's dancing with Mr George!'

We'd never seen Ivy dance a waltz, but she was dancing as if she was born to it. As they swept past us a second time, I saw Mr George's hand tighten on her waist. He bent his head closer to her. Ivy was laughing at something he was saying, not loudly, but like a lady would. Her cheeks were flushed and her eyes sparkled. I wondered what her ladyship would think, if she realized who her son was dancing with.

'May I have the honour?'

Cripes, someone was standing before me. Jem from the stables. 'Thank you, sir,' I said. He put his arm round my waist. I knew Jem only as one of the stable hands but he didn't look like a stable hand tonight. As he swept me into the dance, I felt relieved that Ivy had gone over the steps with me. I needn't be afraid I'd make a wrong move, or step on Jem's toes.

It was on my second turn round the floor that I saw Sarah. Fred was by her side, they weren't talking and both of them both looked tense and unhappy. When the dance finished I asked Jem to take me over to Sarah. Sarah looked as if she was trying not to cry. Fred had disappeared. 'It's no use, Jess, it's no use,' she kept saying.

'Sarah, have you danced with anyone yet?' I asked.

'They all think I'm Fred's girl. They won't ask me.'

'Smile, Sarah and maybe they will.'

'You're heartless, Jess.'

I nearly lost patience with her. 'I'm not. I'm trying to help. Forget him for tonight; let him see how popular you are. Look at young Ivy!'

'Her heart's not broken,' Sarah sniffed.

'Well, Maddie then. She's dancing.' I was amazed that anyone had asked her. Maddie had turned into a right sourpuss these last few weeks. But tonight at least she was getting something right. She was smiling, she ignored Robert, who was walking up and down, pretending he didn't care that Ivy was ignoring him.

Ivy swept across the floor towards us. 'He's a one, isn't he, that Mr George,' she said.

'Got your ride in his car then?' I was joking.

'Ahhha. That would be telling.' She gave a sly smile.

'You watch him,' Sarah said. 'He got young Emma into trouble.'

'That's just gossip,' I said. 'But you be careful, all the same. He's wild, Mr George.'

'Well, why did she leave so suddenly? You tell me!' Sarah said querulously. I shrugged. I felt that whatever I said now Sarah would object to, and I wanted to enjoy myself. It was our special night and not even my best friend was going to be allowed to spoil it for me.

But I wondered why Fred had shot off like that. He'd still not come back. Was he nervous of me because I was Sarah's best friend, or because I was Miss P's maid? Then I wondered what on earth had made me think that. What had Miss P to do with him? I reasoned with myself that Sarah had put the thought into my mind, with all her unreasonable and jealous suspicions, but as my eyes scanned the room again I realized that I hadn't seen her for a while either. I wasn't going to let my mind go down that path though. It didn't have a chance to either. Another young man came up to ask me to dance.

I was almost sorry when the gong sounded for supper. But I was proud that I had a partner to take me in. A grand buffet supper had been laid out in the dining room. I didn't know what half the food was, but it was all delicious. Behind us, the orchestra was still playing. So this was what it was like to be a lady. But would I want to spend all my days and nights like this? Tonight, I knew I would. I wanted it to go on for ever.

I was almost asleep when I heard the door creak open. Ellen was in bed, too – asleep, I judged from the snoring – but I hadn't seen Sarah since supper. Light steps tiptoed across the floor. I kept my eyes tight shut. *Please, Sarah, don't ask me to talk. Just get to bed. In a few hours' time I've got to get up.*

'Jess. Are you awake? Please, Jess.'

She sounded desperate.

Oh well. She was my best friend after all. I opened my eyes. Sarah was standing next to the bed. 'Do you want me to help you off with your gown?' I said as brightly as I could manage in the middle of the night.

Sarah sat down on the bed.

'It's over, Jess. Fred and me.'

'Oh Sarah.' I sat up. 'What happened?'

'I couldn't stand it. We danced only once, but he didn't seem to see me, he hardly spoke, I could feel he didn't feel as I did. So I asked him. He left when supper was over. I saw him go and followed him. He said we weren't right for each other.'

I could hear tears in Sarah's voice. I felt for her hand and squeezed it. 'He said … he said … we wanted different things. He knew that I just wanted to settle down, but he didn't. He told me he wants to leave service, make something of his life. He's never talked like that before, Jess. I don't believe it, I just don't.' Sarah laid her head down on my arm and cried.

I stroked her hair. I tried to think what to say. 'I should unpin your hair,' was what came out.

'Is that all you can say?' Sarah raised her head, and wiped her eyes with her sleeve.

'No, I'm really sorry, Sarah, but it's best you know now, isn't it?'

'It's that girl, that wretched girl, it's since she came here!' Sarah burst out.

I put a finger to my lips. 'Sssh. You'll wake Ellen.'

'Well?' Sarah said truculently, not even trying to lower her voice. 'Aren't I right?'

'Miss Penelope?' I said, uncomfortably.

'Yes, her. Who else?'

'I'm sure you're wrong,' I said.

'She's put ideas into his head. She's bewitched him.'

'Sarah, it's nonsense!' I exclaimed, forgetting to keep my voice down. 'She can't marry a stable hand. You know she can't.'

'She can make him forget his place.'

She had a point, but I wouldn't admit it.

'We were so happy till she came along.' She laid her head down on the bed and wept. I stroked her hair.

'Let me take those pins out,' I said. 'And maybe you'll see things differently in the morning.' I usually did. *A new day, a new beginning*, Mam always says to me.

Sarah raised her head. My eyes had adjusted well enough now to see the fury in her eyes. I could feel it too; she was looking at me almost as if she disliked me. Me, her oldest friend. 'You just don't understand, do you, Jess? Maybe if you'd ever cared about someone…'

I snatched back my hand. If she'd slapped me, she couldn't have hurt me more. How could she be so cruel? I wouldn't want any part of a love that made you so selfish and heedless of other people's feelings.

I lay down and shut my eyes.

'Jess.'

I didn't answer. I didn't want to talk to her.

I heard her get up off the bed and make her way to hers. Then a sob that sounded as if she was trying to stifle it. I felt like crying too but I wasn't going to get up and go to her. Light was creeping in at the window. It would soon be time to get up. Was it true what I'd said to Sarah? I thought bleakly. A new day, a new beginning? Or was our friendship over, too? I didn't know. I just didn't know. I buried my face in the pillow.

Downstairs

'Sit down, Jess.' Mrs Smithson was smiling, but she looked worried too. I couldn't think why. I'd been pleased when she'd summoned me to her parlour. I sat down behind the desk, smoothing my skirt. I was looking forward to hearing what she had to say. *Jess, we've found a lady's maid to replace you.* A proper lady's maid, who'll escort Miss P to London. Then perhaps Sarah and I could make up – it was bound to be easier once I was no longer at Miss P's beck and call.

'Jess, we've been very pleased with the way you've handled your duties. It can't have been easy...'

I looked up at her expectantly.

Mrs S drummed her fingers on the desk. 'As I told you, it was only ever a temporary position...'

I smiled. Here it came.

'...and a new lady's maid has been appointed. However, I have just had a letter from the woman's sister. It seems that she is seriously ill and will not be able to take up the appointment, at least for some weeks, or it may even be longer. As you can imagine this has put us in a very difficult position. The family is about to depart for London for the season, and there isn't time now to find a replacement.'

Mrs S was looking at me as if she was hoping that I'd jump up and say, I'll do the job. No, I'd let her say it.

'Her ladyship has suggested you remain in the post for now. Miss Penelope has been consulted and is happy for you to remain her maid.'

But what about me? Why weren't my wishes consulted?

'Of course in London you will not be expected to carry out any housemaid's duties,' Mrs Smithson added.

'It is just temporary then, Mrs Smithson?' I said, seeking confirmation. She must have seen how my face had fallen. It was the last thing I wanted.

'It is just temporary.'

'Very well.' I didn't seem to have any choice.

'It will be an excellent training for you.'

But I don't want to be a lady's maid. How many times do I have to spell it out?

'Everyone speaks very highly of you, and I know that Miss Penelope in particular will be pleased. London is unfamiliar to her and coming out is an important moment in a young lady's life. It will be a great help to her to have you looking after her.'

What about my life? I felt like crying. Why did no one ever bother about the lives of us downstairs? I wished I had the courage to tell them to stuff their stupid job. Ivy would have. She'd have got up and walked out, head held high. But I was no Ivy. And besides, what would I do? How would I support myself? I stood up, the interview over. As I walked back along the passage to the maids' sitting room, I thought about what I'd been offered. I didn't want to go on being Miss P's maid, but maybe it was as well that I'd be away from Langdown for a time. Ever since our row the night of the ball, Sarah and I had hardly spoken. Maybe things would have blown over by the time I got back.

I sat down, resting my head on my hand. London! At least that was something to look forward to. I'd never been there. It would be exciting to spend some weeks in a great city.

'Penny for them.' I looked up to see that Ivy had flopped down on the sofa beside me.

'I'm staying on as Miss P's maid for now,' I grumbled. 'The new lady's maid is ill and there's no one else.'

'Well that's a piece of good news,' said Ivy. 'Then you'll be going to London. So am I! It'll be fun. We can see the sights on our afternoons off.'

'I've never been to London,' I said.

Ivy was in a dream. 'And we'll take in a show or two.'

'I won't be able to do that,' I grumbled. 'I'll be waiting hand and foot on her ladyship.'

'Miss Penelope? She'll be out in the evenings, won't she?'

I shrugged.

'Oh, Jess, even a lady's maid has some time off! And we'll 'ave much more fun than she will!'

'Who will?' I looked up to see that Sarah was standing by the door. She didn't come in, of course, since I was sitting there. I let Ivy explain.

'We're going to London – Jess and me.'

'Oh, so Jess has persuaded her ladyship to let her stay on as Miss Penelope's personal maid,' Sarah said. She snorted.

Ivy looked embarrassed and I bridled. I didn't like the way Sarah aired our row in public.

'The new lady's maid is ill,' I said coldly. 'They gave me no choice.'

'So when are you leaving, Ivy?' Sarah said, ignoring me. 'The family go at the end of the week, don't they?'

I'd had enough. I got up and pushed past Sarah out of the room. One of us had to go, and I wasn't sorry it was me.

I'd only gone a few steps when I felt a hand on my shoulder. 'Sarah's got the hump, hasn't she?' Ivy said. 'What's up between you two?'

I decided to confide in her.

'She's angry with me,' I said in a low voice. 'She thinks I don't understand how she feels … about Fred finishing with her because I've never had a proper relationship.' I couldn't even look at Ivy when I said that. It felt shameful somehow – admitting that I'd never had a young man to walk out with – and all the hurt and anger I felt at Sarah welled up in me again.

Ivy squeezed my shoulder – just like Sarah used to. I felt my eyes fill.

'We've been friends so long,' I said, my voice trembling.

'Then you'll be friends again,' said Ivy. I looked at her. Had she grown older and wiser while I hadn't been watching? 'In the meantime, you've got me,' She said. She linked her arm through mine. 'It's our time off, isn't it?'

'If Miss Penelope doesn't ring for me.'

'Oh, let's not worry about them upstairs for a moment,' said Ivy. 'Trouble with you, Jess, is you're too conscientious. People put upon you. But that's at an end now. I'm going to look through your wardrobe. You're going to cut such a show in London town you'll be fighting them off!'

I managed a smile. 'Ivy, you're a tonic.'

'We'll be away from our enemies,' said Ivy. 'Maddie's staying here, I'm relieved to report. What larks we'll have, eh, Jess.'

'I won't have much time, Ivy. I'll be busier even than I am now.'

She clicked her fingers. 'We'll manage, don't you fret.'

Nothing was allowed to get in Ivy's way.

'They'll have the house to spring-clean,' I said. I wasn't sorry to be missing that.

'And the meals to cook. Mind, I'll still be doing the washing-up in London. But not,' she pulled my head down and whispered into my ear, 'for much longer. Not if I can help it.'

'Got enough saved up for that room yet?' I asked.

'Not yet,' said Ivy. 'But I will. Never you fear.' She said it very seriously, and I suddenly felt uneasy.

'You take care, Ivy,' I said.

'Oh, Jess, just worry about yourself for once, the rest of the world's not your problem.'

I'd never thought of it like that. But maybe it was time I did.

Upstairs

I leaned over Starshine's stall. 'Sorry, Starshine,' I murmured, feeling her wet nose push at my empty hand hopefully. I hadn't thought to bring her anything to eat. Behind me Uncle was talking to Fred and the head groom about the filly Uncle was hoping to race at Ascot. I didn't dare turn round. As soon as I'd heard Fred's voice my heart had seemed to fly from my chest. Soon he would come to saddle up Starshine and help me up on to her back. I'd feel the touch of his hand... I hadn't been able to think of anything else since Uncle had suggested the ride. I'd tried to find an excuse, but Uncle had brushed aside my excuses. 'You look pale,' he'd declared. 'You need fresh air. And so do I! It's time I had a good gallop with my niece.'

'But Penelope has a lot to do,' Aunt had objected. We were leaving for London in the morning. For once I agreed with her.

'Piffle!' Uncle said. 'The girl has a maid. She will pack for her. We want her to look her best for the season, don't we?' He'd smiled at me, a complicit smile. I'd smiled weakly back, but I'd felt uneasy. It was some weeks since I'd been to the stables. The pain I'd felt had almost gone. Even when I saw Sarah now it hardly ached at all, but I was terrified of destroying my new-found peace. I had tried so hard not to think about Fred, but now, stroking Starshine's nose, I could think of nothing else. I couldn't understand how I both longed to see him and never wanted to see him again.

I heard steps behind me. I knew whose they were, and I kept my eyes averted. I did not want Fred to see how I felt. My hands felt sticky. I clasped them behind my back.

'It's a long time since you were here, Miss Penelope,' Fred said.

So, he'd noticed then, had he?

I gave a brisk nod. I didn't look up, but I knew just where he was. I heard the door swing open, the creak of leather as the saddle was thrown over Starshine's back, the jangle of the harness as bridle and reins were tightened. The sound of hooves as Starshine was led out of her stall, a squeak as the door of the stall swung shut again.

Even then I kept my eyes to myself. I had my pride. I would not let him see how unhappy he had made me. How it hurt to know that he could be standing so near to me, and yet be so far away.

'How have you been, Miss Penelope?' he said.

'Never better,' I lied. 'I'm going to London for the season tomorrow.' I tried to make it sound as if it was my every dream rolled into one. 'So you will be away for some time then?'

Yes, so you can spend all the time you want with the girl you chose instead of me.

'Just help me up, Fred,' I said as haughtily as I could.

He nodded. I felt the touch of his hands as he helped me up on to Starshine's back. The warmth from them flowed through me. I tried to hide how I felt. He was standing very close.

'Poll, I've missed you so much,' he murmured.

It was as if he had dug a finger into the wound. I couldn't keep silent any longer. 'Isn't one girl enough for you, Fred?' I said angrily.

He looked confused. Did I really have to explain?

'I know all about Sarah, Fred, as does everyone else it seems. I'm not the trusting fool I was.'

'Sarah and I—'

I pulled on the rein to turn Starshine's head. I didn't have to listen to this.

'Poll, please let me explain.'

'I don't think there's anything more to say,' I said. Oh, if only he knew the effort it cost me to say that! In desperation, I looked across the yard. Uncle and the groom were still talking. How much longer was Uncle going to be?

'Please, Poll,' Fred pleaded.

'I'm only Polly to my friends,' I forced myself to say, as coldly as I could.

I saw him wince.

Oh Fred, don't look at me like that.

I pulled on the rein again to lead Starshine away. 'Come on, Starshine.'

He grabbed at the bridle.

'Poll—'

'Let go!' I said angrily, yanking it away from him.

'Won't you even let me explain?'

'You could have explained to me months ago. I have nothing to say to you, Fred.' He'd never know how much it hurt, how much I longed to fall off the horse into his arms. I looked away. Jem was attempting to heave Uncle's bulk up on to his splendid mount. 'I must go now, Fred,' I said.

'Please listen to me,' he pleaded. 'Sarah and I – I've known her since we were children. But there has been nothing between us since you and I…'

'I saw you together at the ball,' I said. 'I was there, too, remember. Perhaps you didn't notice.'

'Of course I did. I wanted to ask you to dance. I wanted to dance with you so much. I wanted everyone to see us together, but they can't, can they?'

'Please don't use that excuse again,' I said.

'Let me talk to you when you get back.'

I couldn't stand it any longer. Didn't he know how much he was hurting me?

'Come, Starshine!' I said. I urged her forward. We trotted over to Uncle's side. Uncle turned round in the saddle.

'Ready, Penelope?'

I nodded.

'I'm sorry to have been so long,' he said. 'I was talking to the head groom about the horse I'll be racing at Ascot. A splendid young filly!' He winked. I stretched my lips into a smile. Out of the corner of my eye I saw Fred walk over to the gate. I saw him open it. When I looked back again, he had gone. I felt a dull pain settle on my heart again.

'We'll go down to the copse,' Uncle declared. We trotted out of the yard together. If only I didn't feel so miserably wretched. Uncle swung round to me. 'Let's see you gallop then!' he said. I urged Starshine to a gallop. Her mane streamed behind her. The countryside flew past. I'd missed this. I felt the pain begin to slip away.

'You ride well,' Uncle called to me. 'You've been well taught.' We reached the end of the field. A low hedgerow impeded our path. 'If you're not sure about jumping it we'll go round,' my uncle said.

But I was eager to show my prowess.

'I'll follow you over,' I said, touching Starshine lightly with my cane. I felt her gather her haunches and then we were flying. With a thud we were over and galloping on to the next hedge. I took that easily too. Exhilaration filled me. I felt as if I had left the pain far behind me.

'Well done!' said Uncle admiringly, pulling on his reins and trotting over to me. 'You'll be the toast of the Meet.' We slowed to a trot and he told me about the meets that would be held at Langdown when the season began again, and the shooting parties that had been held there. 'The King came to one,' he said. 'That was in your great-uncle's time.' He shook his head. 'It nearly bankrupted him.'

The sun was low as we trotted back to the stables. The yard was empty. Empty and desolate.

'Where have the lads got to?' Uncle grumbled.

I saw a stall open. Expectation flooded through me. But it was Jem who was running up to us.

He touched his cap. 'Sorry, your lordship, trouble with a horse's shoe,' he said breathlessly. He helped us down and led the horses back to their stalls. There was still no sign of Fred. Where was he? I felt a gnawing anxiety. I'd felt sure I'd see him when we returned. The exhilaration I'd felt on the ride fizzled away. I realized I'd been deluding myself. How much of it had been due to thinking that I'd see him again, feel the touch of his hand?

'You'd better run along,' Uncle said to me. 'Your aunt will be worrying.' He smiled. 'The ladies, eh?' he jested to Jem. 'Must keep them happy. Now, Jem,' he said. He put a hand on Jem's shoulder. 'A word.' They walked away together.

I walked slowly over to Starshine's stall. She heard me and pushed her head out. I kissed her softly on the nose. 'Goodbye,' I murmured, putting all the feeling I had for Fred into that kiss. I made my way slowly to the gate. Fred was avoiding me; I wouldn't see him before I left in the morning. The weight had settled back on my heart again, even heavier than before. I could scarcely drag my feet to the gate. Why oh why had I not let him explain? Why had I let my temper get the better of me? As I reached the gate I looked back. The yard was empty again. Uncle had disappeared somewhere with Jem. I put out my hand for the latch, but instead of the latch my hand closed on something warm. I let it rest there. I felt someone's fingers entwine themselves with mine.

It was Fred. Fred who was standing there. Fred whose fingers were clasping mine.

'Polly,' he said softly. I couldn't speak. But everything I felt was in my eyes. Everything he felt I could see in his.

'You are the only girl for me,' he said earnestly. 'I knew that almost as soon as I met you. I didn't know what to do… I felt that you were too far above me, whereas Sarah … but I couldn't go on seeing her. I was lying to myself. And to her. I ended with her the night of the ball. You must be true to your heart.'

He gazed at me bleakly. 'But now you're going away. When will you be back, Polly?'

'I'm not sure,' I said. 'It may only be a few weeks. Or…' I didn't want to look further ahead. I didn't want to say that then there would be parties, and shoots, and trips to Goodwood, Henley and Ascot. I didn't want him to think about that. I didn't want to think about that. Many girls met their husbands in their first season. I didn't want to think about that either. I didn't like to think of the long weeks when we wouldn't be able to see or speak to each other.

'Can I write to you, Fred? And will you write to me?' I felt shy suddenly.

He nodded. He still looked miserable.

'I will come back,' I said. 'And when I do,' I said, 'we will ride together every day.'

'Even in the rain?'

'Even in the snow!'

He smiled. 'Aren't you afraid of anything, Poll?'

'Only of losing you,' I said.

We spoke in hurried whispers. There was so much to say and think and feel. If only we had more time. Fred kept glancing behind me into the yard. Suddenly I felt him withdraw his hand from mine.

'You must go,' he said urgently.

'My uncle?' I asked.

He nodded.

'If he asks why I'm still here, I'll say I had to talk to you about Starshine,' I said. 'Oh, Fred...' It was too soon. I couldn't leave him – not yet. My hand reached for his again.

'You must go,' he said. I withdrew my hand, but I kept my eyes on his face. I wanted to stamp it on my memory. His hair that shone like burnished copper when the sun caught it, the way it wouldn't lie flat, like mine, the way his brown eyes looked into mine, like now...

If only I had a picture of him. I'd pin it on the ceiling so that I could lie and look at it in bed, so that his face would be the first thing I'd see in the morning and the last thing I saw at night. He was gazing at me as if he wanted to imprint every tiny piece of me in his memory too. Our hands slid towards each other again. It was so hard letting go.

He stood back to let me through the gate. I didn't look back.

Upstairs

The train hissed to a stop. Doors banged. Voices shouted. Somewhere a whistle blew. I'd forgotten how noisy London was. As the cloud of steam outside the window began to fade I saw porters cluster round the carriages like flies. I'd only been in London once – the day I'd arrived in England. It had been winter then, and its glories had lain hidden from me under a foggy grey blanket that refused to lift.

A footman opened the door for us to descend and I stepped down carefully on to the platform. At once porters swarmed up to us, fighting for the right to take our luggage. Most of it had gone ahead of us. I heard Aunt's voice gently raised telling us to keep close by her. She had nothing to worry about. The crowd soon parted for us, first-class passengers, like the sea had for Moses.

We'd left Langdown soon after breakfast. I'd sat at one side of the carriage, Clemmie next to me, a bulwark against Arabella. As the carriage had bounced down the drive I'd tried not to think about Fred. Each clop of the horses' hooves was taking me further away from him. None of the stable hands were coming to London. Most of those servants who were coming had already left, to prepare the house for us. I was relieved that Sarah wouldn't be among them. I felt awkward whenever I saw her now. The housemaids always stayed behind to do the spring-cleaning.

I was thankful that the carriage only took us as far as the station. It always made me feel sick. I couldn't understand why Aunt didn't prefer the motor car – the motion was so much smoother. George's pink motor had departed with him to university. He'd said he'd see us in London. And in London too there'd be Flo – and David, who'd talked about things I'd never thought of before. Of learning to fly, and girls who went on marches, girls who refused to obey the rules of young ladydom. If they could, so could I.

We got back into a carriage for the last part of our journey – to Uncle's townhouse in Mayfair. I'd never heard of Mayfair before. The name conjured up something very different to the broad streets of imposing mansions I could see through the carriage window. We stopped in a street full of trees of waving blossom. A boy ran to open the courtyard gate and the carriage rolled into a gravelled forecourt. Above us towered several storeys of red brick.

Barrett stood on the step to greet us. I remembered the day I'd arrived at Langdown. I walked past him with more confidence now. Inside, I found myself in a large entrance hall. A wide staircase swept upwards. It was almost like a miniature version of Langdown, I thought. The servants had lined up to greet us. Most of the faces were unfamiliar.

I was shown to my chamber, a room at the front of the house. It felt strange to look out on to a street. To glimpse cars and carriages through the blossom. Baxter helped me change out of my travelling gown and into one of my new gowns. I'd had several new gowns made for me before we left Langdown. Even Aunt didn't expect me to appear in London society in Arabella's cast-offs.

While Baxter unpacked I put my photographs of Mother and Father on the dressing table. I remembered the one Aunt had shown me, of Mother when she was my age. It must have been taken just before she came out. How had she felt? I wondered. It hadn't been long after that that she had met my father. But where and how they had met, no one had ever told me. I knew so little of their past. I wished now that I had asked more questions, I wished she was here to advise me. A gong boomed from the floor below. I descended the staircase for tea. While one of the footmen served us with tea and cakes Barrett brought in a silver salver, stacked with calling cards.

'Ah, I see that many of our acquaintances are already in town,' Aunt smiled. Amongst the cards was a letter for me. Arabella of course was rudely surprised that anyone should want to write to me. I turned it over. It had a London postmark. I took a silver paper knife and slit open the envelope.

'Why, it's from Flo!' I exclaimed. 'She's in town.' I was delighted that she'd remembered me. 'She has invited me to tea. May I go, Aunt?' I asked eagerly.

'Well,' said Aunt, pursing up her lips. 'I need to know a little more about this … Flo, you say?'

I sighed impatiently.

'You may sigh, Penelope, but I must be sure that she is a suitable acquaintance for you,' Aunt said firmly.

What would she say if she knew about Fred?

Reluctantly I appealed to Arabella.

'Arabella, you remember Flo,' I said. 'She was a guest at Whichcombe Park when we went there for tea.'

Arabella shrugged. 'There were so many girls there, I hardly know.' A smile flickered across her face – a mean little smile. I yearned to say something to wipe it off. But I forced myself to keep my temper. I badly wanted to go to tea with Flo.

'Flo Waterlow,' I said.

'Waterlow?' enquired my aunt. 'Do you mean Countess Waterlow's daughter? Why didn't you say so before?'

Because I'm not a snob like you.

Aunt turned beaming to Arabella. 'Arabella, I didn't know you were friends with Lady Florence Waterlow? Why didn't you tell me?'

'I expect Arabella forgot, Aunt,' I put in. 'She was *surrounded* by friends.' I smiled sweetly at her. Arabella glowered.

'Well, we must call of course and leave our card,' Aunt said. 'Lady Florence's elder brother is the most eligible bachelor this season.'

I am planning for Arabella to marry him.

'And then may I go to tea?'

'As soon as we have observed the social niceties,' Aunt said. 'I will send round my card tomorrow.'

'But it's for *tea.* I'm not out yet. Surely—'

'Penelope!' Aunt raised her eyebrows.

I want Arabella to meet Lord Waterlow, too. And you, niece, will make sure that she does.

I drummed my fingers impatiently on the table. 'If you have finished tea, Penelope, perhaps you would like to retire to your chamber to rest. It has been a long and tiring day for you.'

Which must be why you seem to have forgotten all Madame's careful tutoring.

I had spent the day moving from one seat to another and was not tired at all. I longed to stretch my legs, and I was eager to explore the city. But I felt sure the nearest I would get to seeing anything *I* wanted to see would be from the interior of the carriage, and under the watchful eye of a chaperone.

I retired to my chamber, my letter in my hand. I held it as if it was a talisman. However awful the next few weeks would be, at least I had an ally now. Aunt had shown rare enthusiasm when she had learned that I knew the sister of one of the season's most eligible bachelors. And I knew why. Marriage to an eligible young man was the proper destination of all young ladies. It was the only reason we were here. But it was *not* the destination for me.

Downstairs

I lifted one of the heavy irons off the stove and pressed it down carefully. Steam billowed up. I lifted it up and then pressed down again, taking care to raise it before the delicate fabric scorched. I'd yards and yards to iron still and already my eyes were drooping with tiredness. It was my first day in London. Miss P was downstairs having tea. I'd got over the hurdle of having to eat dessert in the housekeeper's room. I told myself I'd get used to it, but I didn't really want to.

The others had chattered away like old friends, but I'd felt too shy to speak much. I knew that Barrett's eye was on me, judging me. And I was sure that the other ladies' maids looked down on me. But Mrs Barlow, the housekeeper in charge of the London house, spoke to me just as she did to all the other upper servants. I wondered how much Mrs Smithson had told her about me. Did she know that only a few months ago I'd been a lowly housemaid? Well, she'd find out soon enough. Miss Arabella's snooty maid would be bound to tell her.

My bedroom doubled as workroom. Here I'd tend to Miss P's gowns – brushing, washing, drying, ironing and mending them. I'd arrived ahead of the family, so that I'd have time to unpack and prepare myself before I was needed.

Mrs Barlow had shown me to my room. 'It is quite small,' she had said apologetically, opening the door, 'but you should find it adequate for your needs.' I'd looked round. To me it was a palace. It was furnished with a bed, a comfortable chair and cupboards. There was even a dressing table. I'd never had a dressing table before. I'd never even had a room of my own before. At Langdown I'd shared a room with the other housemaids and at home I'd had to share a bed with two of my sisters. 'It will do nicely,' I'd said, as if I was used to such grandeur. I felt as if I was acting a part. I still didn't feel like a proper lady's maid. It felt like wearing shoes that didn't fit. Mrs Barlow had smiled. 'I'll leave you to unpack,' she'd said. I'd made haste to put away my clothes and hang up my gowns. I'd written to Mam telling her about the job, and how much I was dreading it. But she'd written back saying what a lucky girl I was. *It's a real opportunity, Jess. So do your best.*

As I'd put my things away, I'd tried to tell myself she was right. There were privileges, too. I'd have a cup of tea brought to me in the mornings, a maid would clean my room, and I could have a proper bath when I wanted it. I'd laid out my brush and comb and my few toiletries on the dressing table, but it had still looked very bare. I had put on the gold chain Mam had sent me that had belonged to her mother, but the other ladies' maids were so much smarter than me.

After I'd unpacked I had to find out where everything was kept. I needed to get familiar with it before the carriage fetching the family arrived back from the station. It felt strange not to know my way around.

'Ah, there you are,' her ladyship's maid had said, as I wended my way along the corridor. 'Are you lost?'

I had taken a wrong turning!

'It's all new to me,' I'd said, making myself smile and trying to appear more confident than I felt.

'You'll soon get used to it,' she'd said, more kindly than I'd expected. 'I'll show you where the irons and sewing machine are kept.'

Ah, the ironing and mending. I told myself it was a change from being on my knees sweeping and polishing. I thought of them all at Langdown. Maddie was a good cook; she'd make them some nice sweet each day for their dinner – and they'd have much more time off. They'd have a lot of fun, too. But I wasn't sorry to be away. I felt sore remembering how cold Sarah had been. She hadn't even said goodbye! I wondered if Fred would make it up with her. I still found it hard to believe he'd broken with her. They'd been together for so long.

And then I found myself thinking of Miss P. I didn't like the way my mind jumped to Miss P whenever I thought of Sarah and Fred. If only Sarah hadn't been so jealous of Miss P. I couldn't understand why she had taken against her. It was absurd to think that there could ever be anything between them. She, a young lady. Fred, a mere stable hand. But Sarah was suspicious of anyone who even talked to Fred. It had made things awkward. I was bound to get to know Miss P better now, since I'd be with her so much more in London. I just had to pray that when we returned to Langdown I'd be returning to my old duties, and Sarah and I would get a chance to rebuild our friendship.

I put down the iron, and lifted up the gown. Miss P would be up from tea soon and I'd need to run her a bath. I'd unpacked for her already. The trunk had been closed when I'd gone to unpack it, but I'd seen from the disarray when I'd lifted up the lid that she'd taken care to remove certain precious possessions. I remembered how protective of her things she'd been the day she'd arrived at Langdown, how she had refused to let me touch anything before she'd removed what she wanted. I'd shown no interest in her possessions then, and I still didn't. She'd had several new gowns made. We were both relieved we could leave behind Arabella's pink gown. Neither of us had liked her in it.

Miss P was already in her room when I returned with the gown, pressed and ready. I laid it on the bed and went to close the curtains. 'Oh, please don't,' she said.

'It's getting dark!' I protested.

'I like to look out,' she said. 'And it's not dark yet.

Everything comes out earlier here, doesn't it? The leaves and the blossom.' She sounded sad. I felt sure that she was thinking of Langdown.

'What's it like at Langdown in the spring?' She was still gazing out of the window.

'Well, miss, you saw it only this morning,' I said.

'I could see blossom just starting in the hedgerows,' she said, more to herself than to me. 'What's it like when it's fully out?'

I was sorry she had asked. I hadn't wanted to talk about it, for it was the time of year I liked best at Langdown and I was sad to be missing it.

'In a few weeks' time the may will be out,' I said. 'The hedgerows will look as if they're covered in white lace. You've never seen anything so pretty. The tiny buds on the trees will unfurl into leaves. And the birds will be building their nests…' I smiled. Langdown was at its most beautiful in the spring.

'I wish I could see it.' She sounded mournful, not at all like a young lady looking forward to her coming out.

'Then you'd miss your coming out.'

'I'd rather be at Langdown,' she said.

'But you'll be back there soon enough,' I said as cheerily as I could manage. I was surprised that she minded. She hadn't seemed to care much for Langdown when she was there.

'You see I've never seen an English spring,' she said.

She was toying with her necklace. She seemed to have something on her mind.

'Baxter,' she said, turning from the window back to me. 'I wish you'd call me Polly.'

'Polly?' I said. 'Is it a nickname, miss?' She nodded, sitting down on a corner of the bed but then jumping up and going back to the window as if she couldn't make up her mind where she wanted to be. Her restlessness made her seem like a wild bird that had found its way in and now couldn't find its way out again. There was something of the wild about her, I thought. She wasn't like any of the other young ladies I'd seen at Langdown.

'Yes, that's what I was always called in India.'

'It's unusual,' I said. 'I mean Penelope is usually shortened to Penny, isn't it?' Was I being nosy? But she didn't seem to mind.

'Father gave me the name. He said it suited me better than Penelope. I only tell people I like – and Starshine, of course. Starshine is the horse I ride at Langdown,' she explained. 'Starshine was the first to know!' She smiled, wistfully I thought.

So – I came after a horse! But then I thought how imperiously she'd talked to me when she first came to Langdown. It seemed we'd come a long way since then.

'And I wish you'd stop calling me "miss", but I suppose I must put up with that.'

Yes, you had! I felt thoroughly confused. What had brought on this sudden burst of friendship? I hoped that Sarah would never find out.

'You see, if you're officially my maid now, I suppose I'll see you a lot more and it seems odd that you should call me anything else,' she explained.

She looked so in earnest that I nodded. 'Very good, miss – Polly, I'll try and remember.'

'Thank you – Baxter. And – could you not, could I not – call you Jess?'

I looked at her nonplussed. How had she found out my first name? I had never told her.

But I felt I knew where this was leading. Miss P felt alone and friendless here. She'd barely got used to one place when she was uprooted again, and planted somewhere else. But I shook my head. 'It wouldn't be proper, miss. Now,' I said quickly, in case she tried to argue, 'shall I run you a bath?'

'Yes, please,' she said, returning to her perch on the bed.

I wouldn't have minded one myself, I thought, as I went to run it for her. It had been a long day and I'd have felt better for a good soak. And even though tonight the family were at home for dinner, they seldom got to bed early. The long hours stretched ahead like a dark tunnel I had to struggle through. How would I ever manage to stay awake! And tomorrow the season began in earnest. This was just the dress rehearsal before the main performance. How was I ever going to cope?

UPSTAIRS

I took an immediate fancy to Flo's mother. She looked just like Flo when she smiled. And she made me feel welcome, which I never did at the houses of Arabella's friends.

'Flo has told me so much about you,' she said. She wanted to hear about India, too. She even asked about Father. But her questions never made me feel uncomfortable.

Arabella seemed eager to flaunt the connection that she had earlier seemed to despise. But she had to flaunt it at a distance. The invitation to tea was for me alone. After tea, when Flo's mother had kindly left us alone, I told Flo what a relief it was to escape from Arabella's company. 'She's resented me ever since I came,' I said. 'I don't know why.'

'She's jealous,' Flo said immediately.

'But why?' I said. What reason could Arabella have to be jealous of me? She – the eldest daughter of a wealthy lord!

'Oh, Polly, why do you think? Because you're ten times prettier and a hundred times nicer and more fun. My brother thinks so, too. I can tell.' She gave me an intent look.

I felt my cheeks go pink.

Flo pounced. 'You like him, too. I knew you would.'

Flo doted on her brother, and I was flattered that she cared what I thought.

'How could anyone not?' I laughed. My words seemed to disappoint her. I tried to think of something complimentary I could say about her brother. 'He has lovely eyes – so gentle,' I said. He did – they reminded me of Starshine's. But I couldn't tell Flo that her brother's eyes reminded me of a horse!

Lord Ferdinand Waterlow had come in while we were at tea. I was sure that Flo had arranged it. Ferdy Waterlow was shy and ungainly with long arms and legs that he didn't seem to know quite what to do with, and cursed with a stammering tongue he could not control. 'M-m-miss Penelope,' he had stammered, his face pink. Then he'd tripped over a footstool, and had retreated to a chair where he sat blushing. I had tried to draw him out but I could get hardly a word out of him. But I'd often caught him gazing at me, and I knew that Flo had, too. 'He is clumsy,' she'd said when he had stammered an excuse and left us. 'He stammers because he minds what people think of him. But he has the kindest heart in the world.'

'Can you curtsy now without falling over?' I said now to turn the conversation away from her brother.

Flo pulled a face. 'Just about. But I'm not sure if I'll manage when I have to curtsy to their majesties. Mother told me about her presentation. She said that she was so nervous that she thought she'd never get her knees to bend, but no one noticed. So I must not be afraid.' She laughed.

I was silent. My heart ached for my mother. Aunt was as vigilant as a mother, but made no attempt to try to understand me, and was too bewildered by me to show me any true affection. But Flo. She had a mother who loved her, who she could talk to, who could advise her how to behave in society. Not that I cared, truly cared, what society thought of me. But I had to survive the next few months somehow, I had to pretend… Fred had said it would be hard. And it was.

'Can you – curtsy without wobbling, I mean?' Flo asked.

'Sometimes,' I laughed.

Before I left Flo showed me her presentation gown. 'You'll look beautiful,' I said, admiring the little embroidered flowers that trimmed the cream satin.

'Will you show me yours?' Flo asked.

'When you come to tea,' I said. 'But I warn you Aunt has designs—' I stopped, feeling that I had said too much.

'On my brother, you mean?' said Flo. 'She is not alone. Half the ladies in town want him to marry their daughters. But I am determined that only a girl I approve of will be allowed to marry Ferdy. He has promised to ask my permission,' she said. 'And I will be firm on one point. She must care for him, as much as he does for her.'

I felt a rush of warm feeling for Flo. 'So money does not matter?'

'It does a bit,' she admitted. 'But more to Mother than to us. But isn't that beside the point? I don't expect he'll meet anyone who is not eligible in *that* sense.'

I thought of Fred and I knew then that I would never be able to wholly confide in Flo, sympathetic though she was. She would never understand how I could have feelings for a stable boy. The polite society in which Flo moved was her whole world, and she seemed content enough with it. But the world that contented her felt like a straitjacket to me. I longed to look beyond it. She had no desire to.

'I have two more cousins, neither at all like Arabella,' I said. 'I hope that you'll meet them, too. Clemmie is still a child. She's sweet. You'd never believe that Arabella could have such a nice sister. Then there's George, her brother. He's still at university, but will come down for our coming-out. He is rather wild.' I told her about our drive and how we'd nearly crashed into the carriage.

'That doesn't surprise me,' said Flo. 'I've not met him, but I've heard about him. Him and his friend – David Moore.'

'You know him – David, I mean?'

'By sight. I've never met him, but I've heard stories about him. His name has been linked with several ladies – if I can call them that,' she pursed her lips disapprovingly.

I remembered how David had promised to teach me to fly, and what he had told me about the suffragettes. But these were subjects I felt I could never share with Flo.

When the carriage was brought round, Lord Ferdy came to bid me farewell. 'I h-h-hope I will see you at Lady M-Montjoy's ball,' he said. I said I'd be pleased if he did. He went bright red, and Flo smiled at me warmly. I felt as if I were two girls – one leading the decorous life expected of me in society, the other – the real me – I had to try and conceal. Was this how Mother had felt? I felt sure that it was.

Upstairs

'Are you ready?' George smiled at me.

As ready as I'll ever be!

I took his arm and he led me out into the centre of the room. My heart was beating fast. Now now now, it was happening, the moment I'd dreaded for so long, my arrival into young ladydom, and there was nothing I could do about it. I tried to avoid the eyes that I knew were on me. Admiring? Criticizing? What were they thinking? How I wished I were back at Langdown.

I was one of several girls being hurried out before our presentation at Court. Uncle had already paraded Arabella to the room, their faces flushed with pride. Aunt I could see was watching me closely. *Behave – and I'll soon be rid of you.* I kept my eyes straight ahead. I was in white – a colour that didn't suit me – my hair rolled up on top of my head, flowers in my free hand. I curtsied – the deep Court curtsy I had practised at Langdown. I didn't feel like me at all. I felt like a doll. I told myself that the parade would soon be over.

My dance card was already nearly full. George had claimed the first as his privilege. 'It isn't seemly to dance with a cousin,' I'd said primly. I did not want to dance with Cousin George.

'Piffle!' he'd said. 'We'll show them how it's done, Pen. You've had enough lessons!' I didn't like the familiar way he spoke to me, nor the way he tightened his grip round my waist as he led me back out on to the dance floor. I wriggled uncomfortably. 'Sorry!' he said. I could smell wine on his breath and I turned away my head in distaste.

If I didn't look at him I could pretend that it was another who was whirling me around the room. If only I could shut my eyes ... it would be so much easier to pretend... I shut them and felt myself stumble. That was a mistake – George's hand immediately tightened on me. He said something, but I wasn't attending. I was thinking about Fred. I'd had a letter from Fred that morning. As soon as I could I'd rushed away to read it in private, reading it again and again until I knew it by heart. All three of my cousins had been with me when Barrett had brought me the letter. I shivered, remembering the unpleasant little scene that had occurred when it was delivered. Arabella had been waiting for a letter of her own, and had seized it off the salver. 'You must be mistaken, Barrett, it is for me,' she'd said rudely. Her face fell when she saw my name on the envelope, but she soon collected herself again. 'What's this?' she had said, staring at the envelope. 'I didn't know you had any friends living near Langdown?'

My heart gave a great thump. 'It's mine, Arabella, please

give it to me.' I held out my hand for it. Arabella smiled spitefully. She held it up above her head.

'Ask nicely, and I'll see,' she said.

'Give it to Polly,' Clemmie said.

'No, I don't think I will,' Arabella said.

'You're just horrid, Arabella,' Clemmie said furiously. 'It's not yours. Give it here now.' She lunged forward to grab it but Arabella whipped it behind her back.

George's head popped out from behind his paper. 'Can't a chap be allowed to read in peace!' he complained. 'For goodness' sake, Arabella, give Pen her letter.'

Arabella replied by dropping it on the floor behind her chair. I marched over and scooped it up. I saw George's eyes slide to me as I thrust it into my pocket. 'Aha. Secret, is it, Pen? A billet-doux from one of your many admirers?' Arabella's jealousy had got the better of her; she jumped up and, giving George a furious look, slammed out of the room.

Alone, I'd torn open the envelope, my eyes skimming the words on the page, before going back to read them slowly. For days I'd been expecting a letter from Fred. I had dreamed what he might write to me.

'*Darling Poll, I miss you so much. At night, I lie in bed thinking of you, dreaming of when I will hold you in my arms again. One day this torment will be over and we will be together for ever…*'

The words Fred had actually written barely covered one page.

'Dearest Poll,' he had written in black ink. *'I am thinking of you and missing you. I am not good at finding words for what I want to say, and there is so much I want to say, but I don't know how to, so I hope you will understand and not be disappointed. xxxxxxxxxxxx'* The kisses had filled up the rest of the line. I'd pressed my lips to them, wondering if he had done the same before he'd sealed the envelope.

'There is so much I want to say.' What did Fred want to tell me? As I was whirled around the ballroom I let myself dream of all the things he might want to say to me but found too hard to put into words. I came to myself to see that George was staring at me. The music had stopped. My feet had been dancing of their own accord. I had completely forgotten where I was. 'You were miles away,' George said. I hoped he wouldn't start teasing me again, but he simply led me over to the wall and deposited me among a bunch of girls who were waiting disconsolately for partners. He walked away at once. I felt that I had been rude, but if it meant that he'd leave me alone, I wasn't sorry.

I leaned back against the wall. The room was a blur of music and dancing feet and candlelight. The evening had hardly begun and I had partners for every dance. One after another boys came up to claim me – among them young Lord Ferdy Waterlow. If Flo hadn't gently nudged him I am sure he'd never have found the courage to ask me.

'Are you eng-g-gaged for this dance, Miss P-P-Penelope..?'

he had stuttered. His face was scarlet as he put an arm round me. We stumbled around the ballroom. I lost count of the number of times he stepped on my toes.

'I believe it is my turn to claim you, young lady,' a familiar voice said. I smiled as David Moore bowed before me. He led me on to the floor, his arm encircling my waist. David didn't step on my toes, or drag me round the floor as some of my partners had. 'You've changed,' he said. 'Is it the gown? Or the hair?' I felt myself blush as his eye travelled from my hair to my slippers. Pristine white when I had put them on, they were slightly stained now from the eager tramping of many boys' clumsy boots. 'The charming young girl has become an elegant young lady.' He smiled. 'But is that all?' he said, giving me a searching look. I felt my cheeks grow hot again. His eyes twinkled. 'I'll learn the truth one day; until then, how does it feel to be a young lady? Are you so much the young lady now that a ride in a plane will be frowned on? Or are you still a rebel?' he said as we circled the room again. I caught Aunt's eye. She smiled but her smile looked strained and her eye soon left me to wander the room – and I felt I knew why. Arabella had disappeared downstairs some time ago, and had not yet reappeared. I'd seen her when I went to check my hair and repair the hem of my dress that a boy had stepped on once too often. She had glared at me. Unlike me, her dancing slippers had barely begun to exercise themselves.

Like the other chaperones, Aunt had taken her seat in a gilt chair by the wall. The chaperones guarded us fiercely, their eyes roamed the ballroom constantly. Were their charges behaving properly? Why were they not dancing, or where had they disappeared to? Some of the girls hung about the door, their faces downcast, waiting for partners.

I turned back to David. 'Do you need to ask?' I said jestingly.

'So you've joined the ranks of the suffragettes?'

I shook my head.

'Why ever not?' he said. 'Many of our grandest society ladies are secret members of their set. Didn't you know?'

'What difference does that make to me? I'm never allowed out on my own.'

'Ah, the chaperone. I will have to introduce you to more suitable company.'

'Will any of them pass my aunt's scrutiny?' I asked.

'I see that word has got around. Yes, my reputation is not all that it should be, I admit. It would be wise not to be seen to dance with me too often – though no doubt the lady dowager, my mother, will be pleased to see me dance with a respectable young woman.' I felt his hand tighten slightly on my waist.

'If Lady Moore hopes that I will reform you, it is a poor hope,' I said.

'Ah, still a girl of spirit. So many of the girls here are so dull, they simper, they have nothing to say for themselves. They don't know how to dress, or conduct themselves. You, my dear Penelope, are most refreshing.'

I'd spoken in jest, but the warm look he turned on me made me feel uneasy. I pulled away slightly.

'Where shall I take you?' David said as the music stopped. I scanned the faces for one I knew. My eye fell on Arabella, who had emerged from her hiding place and was staring disconsolately at the dancers.

'Take me to my cousin.' *Let her see whom I have snared.* 'And why not ask her to dance, too.' I was joking but to my surprise I heard David's voice behind me, asking Arabella for a dance. I sat down in one of the gilt chairs to rest my feet before my next partner came to claim me.

While I waited, I gazed around me. I saw the mothers scrutinizing the room for eligible partners for their daughters, the girls competing for compliments, their eager desire to be married before their friends. If only they knew how I despised them, and the empty lives they led – their days spent dressing up, going to balls and parties. There had to be more to life than that. I was longing for the ball to be over. I had no shortage of partners but I was bored stiff. How dreary they were, these eligible young men. How little I wanted to dance with any of them. I yearned to be on my own, to think about my letter in peace.

Baxter plaited my hair for me before I went to bed. She asked me about the ball. I danced every dance, I told her. She seemed pleased. I thought of the girls who'd now be eagerly talking about their partners. I wished I had someone to confide in. I longed to talk about Fred. I thought about the letter he had written me. Even that had to be secret. I had to keep everything I felt about him secret. And I found myself wanting to talk about him all the time. But I couldn't. Sometimes I felt I'd explode with longing for him. How hard it was – even harder now that I was away from him. Did he feel the same? I wondered as I lay in bed trying to sleep. How much longer would we have to pretend? One day I was afraid I wouldn't be able to – everything I felt would simply burst out of me. But I had to try – for Fred's sake, if not for mine.

Downstairs

I patted my hair and surveyed myself in the mirror. I had put aside my housemaid's apron and cap along with my housemaid's duties. Now that I was Miss P's official lady's maid I was attired in a neat blouse and skirt. Ivy said I looked like a proper lady's maid. But I still didn't feel like one. I couldn't think what I'd have done without Ivy. She was my only friend here. I didn't seem to fit in anywhere. I didn't feel comfortable with the upper servants, but I couldn't relax with the lower ones either. They didn't trust us. I knew just how they felt because it was how I'd felt, too. I knew they waited till we'd left the room to chatter and gossip. I longed to be round the big table sharing my sweet with them, instead of perched on a high-backed chair in Mrs Barlow's parlour, making polite conversation. They talked about things I didn't know about. I felt a fraud – I didn't know what to say to them. Mrs Barlow tried to draw me out, but I still felt that the other upper servants looked down on me.

I looked at my watch. Where *was* Ivy? In about an hour the carriage would be back and then I'd need to dress Miss P again. When I was little I used to wish I was a young lady but I'd hate all the times I had to change my clothes. And that was another thing I didn't like about being a personal maid – all the gowns I had to look after. Then there was the hair to attend to. Miss P's hair needed a lot more attention than the daily one hundred brushes now that she was 'out'. I'd learned how to roll it up and dress it with flowers or jewels at Langdown. Her ladyship's maid had given me a few lessons.

I walked up and down the room impatiently.

Ivy had said she'd be here at three and now it was quarter past. I couldn't wait any longer. My free time was precious. I pulled on my coat and gloves. Ivy hadn't come to me, so I'd have to go to her. I made my way to the room Ivy shared with the kitchen maid. I knocked but there was no reply. So I popped into the kitchen. It was empty. Then I made my way along the corridor to the servants' hall. Robert was in there and Ivy's wasn't a name to be mentioned in front of him – hadn't been since the servants' ball. Next I nipped into the scullery. Ivy wasn't there either. I was beginning to feel upset. Ivy had let me down, and now my afternoon was spoilt. We'd planned to go out for tea together. Ivy had suggested a tea room, a Lyons corner house, but I couldn't go there on my own. It didn't seem a respectable thing to do. I was walking up and down, wondering what to do, when I saw Mrs Barlow emerge from her parlour, in hat and coat. She gave me a smile. 'Why, Miss Baxter,' she said, 'are you going out?'

That was another thing that took some getting used to – being called Miss Baxter. Here, only Ivy called me Jess. It felt peculiar.

'I thought I'd take the opportunity,' I said. 'I don't get much time off.' I didn't mention that I'd planned to have tea with Ivy. I didn't think the other upper servants would approve of us going about together.

She gave me a sympathetic look. 'It's a busy time for you, isn't it, the London season. If you haven't made any plans, why don't you have tea with me?'

Me – Jess Baxter – take tea with the housekeeper! What would they say at home when I wrote and told them!

'If it's convenient,' I said – as if I did this all the time.

'You'd be doing me a favour, Miss Baxter,' she said. 'I'd enjoy some company.' We made our way to the door.

'How well do you know the city?' Mrs Barlow asked me.

'Not at all. I've never been to London before,' I said shyly.

'Then you have a treat in store. I've lived in London all my life,' Mrs Barlow said. 'I wouldn't want to live anywhere else. Would you like to see the sights? I'll call a cab and we can have a proper drive round before tea.'

We walked outside and Mrs B hailed a cab. It pulled up straight away. The cabbie helped us in, treated us like we were proper ladies. It made a nice change.

'London is so busy,' I said, as the cab turned into a wide thoroughfare and joined a line of motors, cabs and wagons.

Our pace dropped to a crawl. I'd never seen so many vehicles in one place before.

'I expect it is, after the country,' Mrs Barlow said. 'But I like it. There's always so much going on. Take a look out of the window, Miss Baxter, or you'll miss the sights. Don't let my chatter distract you.'

I did. And I saw a sight all right. But it wasn't the kind of sight Mrs Barlow had in mind. Parked just ahead of us was a pink motor. For all I knew there were hundreds of pink motor cars in the city, but I'd have known this one even if Mr George hadn't been sitting behind the wheel. He wasn't alone either. There was a girl in the seat next to him. He was leaning close to her. I saw the girl's head nod. Then she turned away to climb out. As she did, she looked up and straight into my eyes. She looked away at once, but I could tell from the shock spread across her face that she knew who I was and I knew who she was, of course. Ivy!

Ivy had stood me up for Mr George? My mind was in a tumble. What was the stupid girl doing out with Mr George? Hadn't I warned her about him? Mrs Barlow wasn't looking out of the window so she couldn't have seen Ivy, but it would have served Ivy right if she had. All those plans Ivy had told me about. All those dreams. Had she thrown them all away – for him?

It was that fatal dance, I thought; she amused him, but he was just enjoying himself – Ivy the latest in a long string of idle fancies, easily picked up and just as easily tossed aside. I glanced out of the window again. I couldn't see either Ivy or the car now. I turned back to Mrs Barlow, and tried to compose myself while she pointed out the sights on our way to tea. *There is Rotten Row, where fine ladies and gentlemen ride. And that is the avenue that leads to some palace or other. Buckingham Palace.* I nodded and smiled, pretending interest, but I wasn't enjoying myself any more. I was too worried about Ivy. The stupid girl, the stupid stupid girl.

I didn't see her again until we sat down for supper. You'd never have known what she'd been up to – she looked as cool as the Langdown cat. I was still fuming, but I had to wait till the meal was over to confront her. As soon as we'd finished dessert I made my way back down to the servants' hall.

'Ivy,' I said, putting my head round the door. 'I'd like a word.'

I thought she might object but she got up at once – though she had the nerve to ask me what I wanted! 'You'll find out soon enough,' I said. The other servants glanced at each other. Robert smirked. Even if Ivy didn't realize she was in for a wigging, they did. I remembered how I used to feel when I was summoned by one of the upper servants. It felt odd to be at the other end of it for once. But Ivy was acting as if she hadn't a care in the world. I walked ahead of her down the passage. Once we were far enough away from the servants' hall, I turned and faced her.

'Well,' I said, folding my arms. 'You've got some explaining to do, Ivy.'

She looked puzzled. Then she clapped her hand to her head. 'We were meant to go out. I'm sorry, Jess. No wonder you're angry. I forgot.'

What a performance!

'I'll pass over that. As it happened Mrs Barlow invited me to join her, but I can't pass over what I saw from the cab. What were you doing in Mr George's car, Ivy? It's no good your pretending. I saw you. You know I did. And I know you saw me.' She couldn't wriggle out of this one.

She looked sullen. 'None of your business.'

'It's not respectable for a young girl to be out alone with a young man,' I said.

'Times are changing, Jess. How many times do I 'ave to tell you!'

'They're not changing that fast,' I retorted. 'Besides, he's wild, Mr George. You can't trust him.'

'You think I'm an idiot,' she flashed back. 'He says he can help me. He says I got real talent.'

'I believe you, Ivy, but I don't believe him. He doesn't care about us. We're just servants to him. He's using you, Ivy. He's having fun, and when he's bored he'll drop you.'

'You sound as if you think I can't take care of myself. But I can. What did I say to you, Jess? Look out for yourself and don't worry about everyone else.'

'If that's what you want.' I shrugged.

'You won't tell, will you?' She looked scared. Did she really think I would? Surely she knew me better than that?

'What do you think I am?' I said angrily. 'You know I won't say a word. But it's lucky for you Mrs Barlow didn't see you, or you'd have lost your place.'

'I'll be more careful,' she said. 'I promise.' She hesitated. 'Jess, I'm sorry about this afternoon. Really I am. I did forget. Please believe me. I just…' She smiled. 'Got a bit carried away, I suppose.'

I wanted to believe her. 'So what's he doing in town? I thought he wasn't expected back here yet.' Mr George seemed to spend precious little time at university. He'd come down for the young ladies' coming-out ball but had immediately left again.

'He's staying with friends,' Ivy said. She smiled. 'Friends he says he'll introduce me to. Friends who can help me.'

'No, Ivy.' I shook my head.

'What do you mean, "No, Ivy"?' she said truculently. 'Do you want to keep me down? So I always know my place? Always be in service? I'm not like you; it's not enough for me. His friends have contacts in the theatre. Jess, I can't go back to Langdown, I really can't. It's bad enough Robert glowering at me without Maddie making my life miserable, too.'

'Then look for another job in London,' I said.

'You mean a job in service? I've just told you what I think about that.'

'But you'll need a place to live, won't you? And in London at least you're in the right place, for when you're ready to launch yourself.'

It made sense to me.

'I'm ready now, Jess.'

'But where will you live?' I exclaimed.

'As I said, George has got friends…'

I noticed then that she'd dropped the 'Mr'. She really believed in him, but I felt like shaking her, to make her wake up and see Mr George for the scoundrel I knew he was.

'What, him – a young gentleman – know people in musical theatre?' I was sceptical.

'That's what he says. And I believe him.'

'What, you're giving in notice, are you?'

'Not yet, but soon.'

I prayed that she'd see sense before she took that step. But there didn't seem to be a lot more I could say.

'I wish you luck, Ivy,' I said.

'My life's about to change, Jess. I can't wait!' She flashed me a smile. 'I'll invite you to my first night.'

I smiled at her, but it was a wistful smile. I envied Ivy her self-belief even while I was afraid for her. But, I told myself, Ivy was a survivor. She'd come through whatever life threw at her. Beside hers, my ambitions seemed puny. All I asked for was a comfortable home and someone to share it with. But I was no nearer that now than I'd ever been.

UPSTAIRS

'You look a picture.' Baxter sounded almost as if she was in tears. 'Come and see.' I walked cautiously in my new slippers over to the long mirror and stared at myself. Three ostrich feathers had been wired into my veil. They bobbed up and down every time I moved my head. I didn't look a picture. I looked ridiculous. The sooner this pointless charade was over the better.

Baxter gathered up my train and I slowly descended the stairs. In the hall the servants had assembled to have a peep at Arabella and me decked out in our finery. I saw one or two of the older servants wipe their eyes with a hanky. Arabella looked as if she would faint with excitement.

A footman came to announce that our carriage was ready. As I climbed in, bending my head so that the ostrich feathers would not catch on the hood, I wished that the girl sitting facing me was a friend I could confide in; we could have chatted and giggled and given each other's hands a sympathetic squeeze before we alighted from the carriage.

At the palace we joined the line of carriages crawling up to the entrance. After we'd been helped down from ours, we made our way along the long, lit passages into an anteroom, where hundreds of girls in white were waiting, like us, to be presented, ostrich feathers waving from every head, like a flock of caged birds. If I could have run I would. Arabella had already abandoned me and plunged into a group of her friends. And then I saw Flo and squeezed over to her side.

'Nervous?' she whispered. I nodded, seeing the terror I felt reflected in her face.

Courtiers ran around us pushing us into an orderly line, and slowly we shuffled towards the throne room where we would make our curtsies one by one. As I advanced up the line of waiting girls I felt my hands inside my white kid gloves grow sticky. Once I crossed the threshold of that room I'd be a fully fledged young lady, and my life would never be the same again. A gentleman-in-waiting bent to spread out my train. There was no escape for me. My heart hammered as I moved forward to the edge of the throne room itself. I stood there swaying slightly, waiting for the command to proceed. The Lord Chamberlain held out his hand for my card. I fumbled for it. 'Miss Penelope Fitzsimmons,' he announced loudly. My gown whispered over the carpet as I glided slowly forward. I couldn't see anyone or anything clearly. I kept my eyes fixed on my destination – a raised dais at the far end of the room, where a portly bearded man sat on a throne under a crimson canopy, his breast covered with gold braid and medals. The King. By his side, in a gold dress, sparkling with jewels – his queen. Somehow I had to get from here to there. It seemed to take me for ever. Everyone's eyes were on me. Would I trip over my gown, drop my fan, or wobble as I bent my knees in my curtsy?

I reached the dais at last and swept downwards into my curtsy. I was hardly aware what I was doing but I had done this so often now. I lowered my eyes. Now it was time to raise myself. This was the moment we all dreaded – rising without wobbling. Slow. Slow. Slow. I was up. I took a deep breath, stepped to the side, three steps. Now I had to do it all over again, in front of the Queen. She smiled slightly, showing a row of bad teeth. I swept into another curtsy. Down, down, down. I felt as if I could hear Madame's voice in my head. 'Hold the pose. Now, rise.' I rose – the merest wobble – so slight, she couldn't have noticed, could she? – and I was up. I stepped back, my left arm outstretched to catch my train. *Please hurry!* I felt the train's weight bow my arm as it was flung over it. I walked backwards, curtsying until I was out of the room. I let out my breath in a deep sigh. The ordeal I'd dreaded for so long was over. I made my way into the green dining room where supper awaited us.

A gloved hand touched my arm. I swung round to see Flo. A huge smile of relief broke on both our faces.

'That's all over, thank goodness,' she said.

'I wobbled when I curtsied to the Queen.'

'I was watching, but I didn't notice,' Flo said loyally.

I'd been too far back in the line to see Flo's presentation. 'And you?'

'I didn't wobble.' Flo looked proud. 'How do you feel now it is all over?' she asked.

'Relieved,' I said with feeling. 'I'd been dreading it.'

'Do you feel any different though?'

'Not really,' I said. 'Do you?'

'I do. I feel that I really am a young lady now. I didn't feel like this at my coming-out ball. It's hard to explain…' Her voice tailed off. She smiled to herself. She seemed very far away.

It hadn't changed anything in me. I felt very lonely suddenly. Was there no one among this huge crowd of girls who hated this absurd charade as much as me? A girl came up to Flo and I listened as they talked – they were chattering happily, sharing their memories of their special day. I gave a deep sigh.

'It's all rather silly, don't you think?' Who was *that*! I turned round hastily. A sharp-featured pretty girl was smiling at me. 'I heard what your friend said, and I saw your face. And I thought, aha, a girl who feels like me – I hope you don't mind my saying so.'

Did I mind? In the hundreds of girls surrounding me I'd been lucky enough to find one who felt like me.

'Marjorie Lightfoot,' the girl said, holding out her hand.

'Penelope Fitzsimmons,' I said, taking it. 'But my friends call me Polly.'

'Then I'll call you Polly,' Marjorie said smiling. 'I didn't want to do this,' she went on, 'but Mother insisted.' She heaved a deep sigh. 'I can't think why,' she said. 'She wasn't presented.'

'She wasn't? Then…' I stopped. It was none of my business.

'No, my godmother sponsored me – she is very determined. She says it will improve my chances of making a good marriage. I fear they won't be happy until they've married me off to a duke and I end my days mouldering in some great damp castle. And then of course the King wished it. He winked at me, you know. I don't know how I kept a straight face.'

The King of England winked at the girl I, Polly, was talking to!

'Don't look so surprised!' Marjorie said. 'Even a king has friends. He dined at our house several times when Father was still alive. The first time he came I remember hanging over the banister to see him arrive. I was supposed to be in bed. But I wanted to see what he looked like. What child wouldn't? He winked at me then, too! If he hadn't been so amused I'd have been smacked for being disobedient.' A dimple appeared in her cheek. 'I was very disappointed that he wasn't wearing his crown.'

'Was he as fat then as he is now?' I asked.

Marjorie nodded. 'I think so. He likes a good table. Have you never seen the King before today?' she said carelessly, as if there was nothing unusual in it.

'Never,' I said.

'Who brought you here today? Your mother I suppose.'

'My aunt,' I told her.

'Your aunt?' She gave me a curious look.

'Mother's dead,' I said flatly.

'I'm sorry,' Marjorie murmured.

'Mother was presented at Court, too, I think,' I said, remembering the three ostrich feathers I'd found in the trunk, 'but she never talked to me about it. I think she probably hated it, too. I don't know if I'd have been presented if she were still alive. We lived in India, you see. I was born there. I'd never even visited England before I came to live here a few months ago. Father's still there.'

'How exciting!' Marjorie exclaimed. 'I'd love to visit India. I'm told the maharajahs are gorgeous! Will you go back there to live?'

I shrugged. 'Not before Aunt's succeeded in making a young lady out of me. So it will probably be a very long time – if ever,' I added.

Marjorie gave me a searching look, and I felt that there was something she wanted to tell me, but she merely smiled. 'All this business of being a young lady,' she agreed. 'All these balls, and parties. *So* wearisome. But,' she went on, 'as we have to go to them, I'd like to feel I had at least one friend to talk to. So tell me, will you be at Lady Gear-Warrington's ball next week?'

‘I expect so – Aunt is determined I will find an eligible husband as soon as may be.’

I felt a pang as I thought of Fred and the tender words he’d written to me. I had written back to him, but the letter still lay locked in my case. I had to find a way to post it without anyone seeing whom it was addressed to. I couldn’t very well give it to Baxter or Barrett. Nor would it be easy to post it myself – I was never on my own when we went out.

‘But you don’t want to marry, or perhaps you’d rather he wasn’t eligible?’ Marjorie said. Her eyes danced wickedly.

I felt a blush spread over my face. Marjorie pounced. ‘Ha! I thought so. Well, let me give you a word of advice. Make sure never to dance with a partner more than once in an evening – unless you mean to marry him, of course. Otherwise, dance as often as you like with whomever you like – it doesn’t matter how many admirers you have. There is safety in numbers.’

She assumed I had a fancy for a boy I’d met in society. I said nothing. It was safer to let her think so.

I felt sure that a girl as lively as Marjorie would have many admirers. ‘I can see what you’re thinking,’ she said. ‘Last week I turned down a prince. He was becoming a bore. It was fun at first, but then he started following me about – or rather, he got his minions to watch over me.’ She laughed. ‘I’d see these strange men pop out wherever I went. He wrote poems to me, too. But I knew I wouldn’t marry him. Who’d want to live in some barren desert, hidden away for ever in a silken tent among a prince's harem! But I kept the jewels,' she said. 'I'm wearing one of them now. Look!' She held out her hand. An enormous sapphire sparkled on the fourth finger of her left hand.

'You wear it on your fourth finger!' I gasped.

Marjorie smiled. 'It helps keep unwelcome suitors at bay. You should try it.'

I tried to imagine Aunt's face if she saw a ring on my fourth finger!

'I wish we could meet before the ball,' Marjorie said. 'Perhaps it could be arranged?' She looked at me questioningly.

'Aunt will never let me meet anyone without a formal introduction. She is very particular. Your mother will need to send round her card.'

'Who is your aunt?' Marjorie asked.

'Lady Langdown,' I told her.

'Oh, not the Awful Arabella's mother?' Marjorie exclaimed. 'Oh sorry,' she said, 'have I offended you?' A dimple came and went in her cheek.

'Not in the least. So you've met Arabella?'

'I have had that misfortune – yes. She looks down her nose at me. My family is not grand enough.'

'Even though you've had the King to dine?' I exclaimed.

'Well, perhaps we're not grand enough for your cousin.

We are rich, but not titled. It is an issue for some. But I will ask Mother to send round her card all the same. I promise.'

'Make it soon,' I said with feeling.

I'd have liked to have gone on talking to Marjorie, but I could see Flo searching for me among the crowd of girls pressed around us in the supper room. She caught my eye and raised her hand. Flo would never do anything so indecorous as wave.

'I'll have to go,' I said.

'Well now I know who you are, we will see each other. I'll make sure of that.' She gave a quick nod and I made my way towards Flo.

'I thought I'd lost you,' she said. 'I was searching for you everywhere. Who were you talking to?'

'Her name is Marjorie Lightfoot,' I told her.

'I don't think I know her,' Flo said.

'She knows my cousin Arabella,' I said. 'But she shares our opinion of her.'

'Then I'm sure I'd like her, too.'

I wonder, I thought, glancing into Flo's gentle face. Marjorie was a rebel, like me. No one could say that of sweet Flo.

As the carriage rolled back to the house, I lay back against the cushions and closed my eyes. Aunt and Arabella were busily picking over the evening. 'Did you see Lady Horley, what did she think she was wearing? And Lady Richenda nearly fell over, oh the shame of it! I could see what Her Majesty was thinking. And then her jewels…' I let their remarks wash over me. I'd made a new friend and I was determined to see her again soon. I could already feel my popularity soaring to new heights. If Aunt was impressed by an earl's daughter, what would she say when she learned that my new friend's family had had the King to dine! Surely that would satisfy Aunt, even if it wasn't enough for my cousin.

Downstairs

There it was again. I hadn't been mistaken – someone was tapping on my door. I huddled down in bed. Let them tap away. I wasn't opening my door in the middle of the night!

Tap tap tap. I didn't expect callers at this time of night.

Tap. Tap. Tap. Tap.

It was louder now.

Why wouldn't they go away? Then I froze. Someone was turning the door knob.

'Jess, it's me – Ivy.'

'Ivy?' I exclaimed. 'Don't you know what the time is?'

The door opened a crack. Ivy's head peered round. 'Jess, can I come in?'

'Ivy, it's one o'clock!' I was weary. I'd been up late waiting for Miss P to come home. It had been past twelve before the carriage rolled up. Then I'd had to help her get undressed. Only then could I think about getting to bed myself.

'I've something to tell you.'

'Can't it wait?'

'Please, Jess. I've got to talk to someone.'

And I would do. I was everyone's friend when it suited them. Thanks, Ivy.

Ivy opened the door fully, and tiptoed in. She was wearing her hat and coat.

That woke me up properly.

'Ivy, where have you been?' I gasped.

'I've been out.'

I remembered that I hadn't seen her since supper but then I saw less of the lower servants in the evening since I'd been banished upstairs.

'And you've only just got back?'

Ivy nodded.

'But it's past one!'

She shrugged.

'How did you get back in?' I said.

'How do you think?' Ivy said. 'I broke a downstairs window and climbed in.' She saw my expression. She rolled her eyes. 'Honestly, Jess. I'm not that stupid. George drove me back. He's got his own latchkey.'

'George?' I said stupidly.

'Yes, him.'

'Mr George? His lordship's son?'

'Who do you think?'

'Ivy, you don't know what you're doing!'

'You sound like me mam,' Ivy complained. 'Mind if I sit down?' she said, sitting down on the bed before I could answer.

I gave a deep sigh. 'All right then, let's hear it.'

'I've been to the theatre.'

'What?'

'To the theatre. I told you, Jess, he's got friends. And…' She gave me a huge smile, 'I've got an audition. Day after tomorrow for a part in a musical. It's on at the Gaiety. Jess, I'll be understudying the lead.' I saw a dreamy look come into her eyes.

'*If* you get the part,' I thought I'd better remind her. I still didn't think the stage was respectable, but I was impressed.

'I'll get it all right. Watch!' Ivy got off the bed, raised her skirts with both hands and did some high kicks. Her boots clattered on the wooden floor like thunder.

I grabbed her arm. 'Sit down, and be quiet, for goodness' sake. You'll wake up Mrs Barlow!'

Ivy lowered her skirts and sat down again. 'What do you think?'

'Very good,' I said grudgingly. 'But no more night flits, Ivy, it's too risky.'

'Well,' Ivy smoothed down her skirts and stood up. 'The audition's in the afternoon so you needn't worry. Honestly, Jess, you really are worse than me mam.'

She was very confident.

'If you get the job, will you hand in your notice?'

''Course.' She looked surprised that I'd even mentioned it.

'You've got somewhere to live, have you?'

'It's all arranged. Jess, stop fretting!' She got up and tiptoed to the door.

'I'll try,' I said.

'Nighty-night, Jess.'

The door closed softly. I lay back, pillowing my head on my arms. I glanced over at the clock on the table before turning down the light. Half past one! In a few hours' time Ivy would have to get up to light the range and sweep the kitchen. *If* she woke in time. I had a later start. At seven, after one of the housemaids had brought me a cup of tea, I'd get myself up and look over Miss P's gowns. She'd torn the hem of her favourite one, dancing. She'd said the boys were clumsy and I'd seen a faraway look come into her eyes. I'd seen a letter lying on the dressing table. She saw that I'd seen and picked it up and held it to her. From her father in India, no doubt. But she hadn't said and I didn't want to pry. We were on good terms, Miss P and I – she'd even told me she was pleased it was me looking after her, but sometimes I wondered. I felt that she was hiding something. I felt that she was on her guard. But I didn't mind. It suited me. I didn't want to be in her confidence. When we got back to Langdown, that new lady's maid would take over and it would be downstairs again for me. It couldn't come soon enough. I wondered if Ivy would be coming back with me. I didn't trust Mr George and his promises. But if that acting job was genuine and Ivy got the part, we'd soon be needing a new scullery maid, too. I felt sad – really sad. I'd miss her. In just a few months, she had brought a lot of fun into our lives, and now I couldn't imagine Langdown without her.

Upstairs

'My lady.' Barrett bowed as he held out the silver salver. Nearly every day it was piled high with invitations to balls, parties and teas – and calling cards. Some of these Aunt dropped straight into the waste-paper basket. Others were laid on one side and would be returned.

Aunt picked up the last card. She turned it over and considered it. She let it go, and I watched as it fluttered away into the basket, sharing the fate of one or two others received that morning. I looked at the pile Aunt had to answer. Amongst them must be the card from Mrs Lightfoot. Aunt was to expect her card today. Marjorie had promised it in a note she had already sent me.

I was too eager to wait for Aunt to enlighten me. I cleared my throat. Though my social success had made Aunt look more favourably upon me, I wasn't sure how to put what I wanted to say. 'Aunt,' I said, 'have you had a card from Mrs Lightfoot? I met her daughter at our presentation,' I explained. 'She told me that her mother would send round her card.'

There! What could be more proper than that?

I was surprised to see a smile flicker across Arabella's thin lips. Arabella had been sulking all morning. She had disliked all the attention I'd had at dinner yesterday and had come down late to breakfast. Ferdy and Flo had been among the dinner guests. Ferdy was as awkward as ever. But Flo had encouraged him to talk to me, which had infuriated Arabella. But what had upset her even more was that she could see that I did not care whether he talked to me or not.

Aunt rifled through the cards on the table. 'What did you say her name was, my dear?'

'Mrs Lightfoot,' I said.

'Ah yes,' said Aunt. 'I did receive that card. But I cannot receive that lady. She is unsuitable, quite unsuitable. I cannot accept her daughter as an acquaintance for you.'

I could not believe my ears.

'But how can she be unsuitable? She was presented at Court and her family knows the King!' I exclaimed. I appealed to Arabella, whose attention had been roused by the exchange. 'Marjorie told me she had met you,' I said. In vain. Ice not blood ran through Arabella's veins. I'd have had more success appealing to a statue. She fixed me with those cold grey eyes. 'We may have met, but we are not acquainted.' She gave me a pitying look. *It is a shame that you do not understand the difference.*

'I should hope not!' said Aunt tartly.

'But why?' I asked again.

'They are not suitable people for you to mix with. My dear, I owe it to your mother to protect you from unsuitable acquaintances.'

Why must she drag in Mother? It wasn't fair; Mother was not able to give an opinion.

'She is invited to the same balls as us. If they don't object, why should you?' I said stubbornly. Marjorie was the first girl I'd met who I could imagine becoming a true friend and I wasn't going to give up easily.

'I cannot be responsible for other ladies' decisions about their guest lists,' Aunt said firmly.

'But—'

Aunt put up a hand. 'I do not intend to discuss the matter further, Penelope.' She rose from her chair and swept from the room. How like Aunt to leave the room when she didn't know what to say.

But if Marjorie was unsuitable, I fumed, staring after Aunt's departing back, why wasn't David, or her precious son George? In society it seemed there was one rule for women, another for men. But I had no intention of letting the acquaintance drop. I would find a way to meet Marjorie, with or without Aunt's permission.

In the meantime I still had my letter to Fred to post. After I had got his I'd been in a dream, composing my reply in my mind. But when I'd sat down to write it I'd found it harder than I had expected. *'Dearest Fred, I think of you all the time,*

I dream of you every night, and ... and...' I'd screwed up that latest attempt into a ball and tossed it into the fire. I couldn't say that! Attempt after attempt had followed it into the fire. I couldn't throw the scraps of torn-up paper into the waste-paper basket in case someone found them and tried to piece them together, though I could only think of one person mean enough to do that, and Arabella had never yet dared come into my room. I'd have known if she had. The perfume she wore left a trail everywhere she went.

Now I had another letter to write – to Marjorie. In a fury, I scribbled, *'Dear Marjorie, Aunt is too mean to let me meet you. She is afraid that I might enjoy myself. But...'* I threw it away, disconsolately, resting my head on my hand. Surely I could find a way for us to meet. I was never alone, but... But we *can* meet, I thought suddenly. At least we could try. I had to return to the dressmaker for the final fitting for a new walking suit. Baxter was to accompany me. Baxter had never met Marjorie. But in any case we could pretend we'd met by chance. Baxter would never know. I pulled a fresh sheet of paper towards me and wrote: *'We are so busy that Aunt is afraid we won't have time to fit in any more engagements before we return to the country, but on Wednesday I have a fitting for a new suit at Harrods. If you can, meet me there, at three o'clock. I will only be accompanied by my maid. Please try, it may be our only opportunity to meet before I leave town.'*

There! I thought, smiling as I folded it up. I scribbled the address on the envelope. Then I rang for Baxter. 'Baxter,' I said, giving her the letter. 'Please make sure this is posted this afternoon.' I knew I could trust her to make sure it was delivered, and that she would ask no questions.

As I climbed into the carriage on Wednesday afternoon I wondered if Marjorie would be there, and what she'd say if she was. Would she have read the truth between the lines of my letter? Why, I wondered, did Aunt object to my friendship with Marjorie Lightfoot? What could her mother possibly have done to offend her? As the carriage rattled and bounced over the cobblestones I rested my gloved hand on the window ledge. A pink car careered past honking its horn impatiently. I glanced out. I knew only one car that shade of pink. George raised a hand and waved. I raised mine in return. He must have recognized the arms on the carriage, I thought. George had been a little stiff with me since my coming-out dance and maybe his salute was a sign that I was forgiven. The car pulled in to the kerb. A girl ran up to climb in. George leaned across and opened the door. It was then I realized that it was the girl, not me, who George had waved at. She looked very young, and I gave a gasp as he leaned across and kissed her. She rested her head on his shoulder as the car revved into life. As it moved away from the kerb, too fast, I remembered the afternoon I'd sat beside George in the car and how we'd nearly collided with the family carriage. He was as reckless a driver now as he'd been then. I'd never get into that car with him again, but then I felt sure he'd never ask me.

I looked over at Baxter. She couldn't have noticed. Her eyes were closed and she was leaning back against the cushions. Her face looked slightly green. 'Are you all right?' I asked.

She opened her eyes. 'It's the carriage, Miss Polly. It sways about that much.'

'I don't like it either,' I said. 'Oh, Baxter, I am looking forward to being in the country again.' I looked back out of the window. Wind had brought down what remained of the blossom, and the trees were now in full leaf. I yearned to be on horseback, to feel the country air blow across my face. The air smelt so much sweeter there. And...

I looked up to see that Baxter was watching me attentively. I felt myself blush, as if everything I was thinking was written on my face.

'Really, miss,' she said. 'You don't like London then?'

'It's been fun,' I said. 'But it doesn't feel like home.'

My letter to Fred was in my pocket. My plan was to post it in the nearest pillar box. But I had to do it when Baxter wasn't looking. That wasn't going to be easy. The carriage stopped and the footman came to the door to help me down. There was a pillar box a few feet away from where the carriage had parked but Baxter was practically hanging on to my skirts. The city made her nervous.

'Baxter,' I said desperately. 'I think I may have left my … a … a package in the carriage. Would you kindly go back and look for me?'

'Yes, miss.'

No time to lose. I fairly leapt for the pillar box and shoved in the letter. I'd just enough time before Baxter stepped back down from the carriage. She looked puzzled. 'I couldn't see any package, miss.'

'How odd,' I said. I pretended to search inside my handbag. 'No – oh, I must have made a mistake.' I kept my head down; my cheeks were burning.

'Polly!'

A hand waved at me. I saw Marjorie dart across the street towards me. Behind her trotted her maid, her arms full of bundles and boxes.

'Isn't this a surprise!' she exclaimed as she reached me.

'Isn't it!' We were both trying not to giggle.

'I don't need to ask what you've been doing,' I said, nodding at the hatboxes and bundles.

'We leave town, too, soon – and I've been doing some last-minute shopping before my banishment. To the country,' she added.

'I'm actually looking forward to leaving,' I said.

Marjorie linked her arm through mine. 'Maybe you are looking forward to seeing someone there again? I saw you post a letter,' she added in a low voice.

I felt myself blush.

'I'm sorry. It's wrong of me to pry. So,' she went on, 'your aunt objects to our friendship?' Her frankness made me blush again. 'It's all right, Polly,' she said. 'It was a sweet letter, but when no card arrived for Mother, I knew.'

I squeezed her arm. 'Aunt has an odd idea of who is suitable company for me.'

'Suitable young ladies and eligible young men,' Marjorie sighed. 'Why are they all so dull! You haven't forgotten my advice, have you?' she said. 'Safety in numbers.'

I shook my head. 'But I hope that when I am back in the country, I'll shake them off.'

'They are hard to shake off,' Marjorie said. 'Besides, there's the rest of the season to get through.' We reached the imposing front door of the shop. A doorman held open the door and we walked up the carpeted stairs. 'Royal Ascot. Glorious Goodwood. Will you be going?' she asked me.

I shrugged. Aunt hadn't said.

'Then the shoots begin again. At least that's more fun. But I'll miss London.'

'I thought you disliked the season as much as I do,' I said.

'Not that, but…' She bent her head and whispered: 'Promise you won't tell if I tell you a big big secret?'

'Of course not. You can trust me.'

Marjorie looked contrite. 'I'm sorry – but I have to be awfully careful. I've been longing to tell you, you can't think.' She gave me a smile and whispered: 'I've joined the suffragettes.'

'What!'

'So you've heard of them. I wasn't sure you'd know who they were,' Marjorie said, 'having lived in India all your life.'

'I hadn't – until David Moore told me about them. He said I should join them! But I think he was joking.'

'He's a bad boy, David,' said Marjorie. 'Watch out for him. But your cousin George is worse.'

'We passed him just now in the carriage,' I said. 'He was in his pink car. I saw him kiss a girl!'

'That sounds like George. He's a charmer, but heartless.'

We sat down while Baxter went to tell the assistant I'd arrived for my fitting. I pulled my chair close to Marjorie's. I was longing to hear how she'd come to join the suffragettes. 'Tell me all,' I said.

'No one in the family knows,' said Marjorie. 'I've managed to get to a meeting or two, but I don't feel I've won my spurs yet, and I won't until I've taken part in one of the rallies. Have you heard about them?' I shook my head. All I knew was the little David had told me. 'The suffragettes meet at Caxton Hall in Westminster and march to Parliament. The aim is to deliver a petition to the Prime Minister explaining why we feel we should have the right to vote. The difficulty is getting to the House. The police do their best to stop us. Some of the women get arrested and sent to prison.'

'Prison!' I exclaimed horrified.

Some of the shoppers turned round to stare at me.

'Keep your voice down,' Marjorie murmured. 'Yes, it is marvellous publicity for the cause.'

I stared at her. 'You mean they actually *try* to get themselves arrested?'

Marjorie nodded. I just stared at her.

'I don't want to marry in my first season,' she explained. 'I want to feel I've lived first. I want to make something of myself.'

She looked at me. 'Why don't you join us?'

I shook my head. 'It's too difficult. I'm well guarded. Besides I'll be back in the country next week.'

But until then... I pushed the thought away at once. It was impossible.

A shop assistant came up to us, her face a big apology. 'I am sorry to have kept you so long,' she purred. 'We are ready for the young lady now. If the young lady would like to try on the suit...' I made my way into one of the changing rooms.

The fitting didn't take long. Afterwards we dawdled through the shop, talking while pretending to admire the various fabrics laid out on the counters, the gloves, laces and scents. 'You'll have to write to me at Langdown Manor,' I said. 'If they let you write letters from prison,' I joked.

'I'll find a way to change your mind!' said Marjorie. She looked earnestly at me. 'Just think, if the suffragettes win the vote, it would be the beginning of a freer life for women. We would have more control over our lives. We'd be able to choose what we did and whom we married.' When she said that I thought about Fred and me. I tried to imagine what it would be like to live in a world where we didn't have to keep our relationship secret. Oh, I so wanted to confide in Marjorie, but I couldn't. It wasn't just my secret; it was Fred's, too. And it would be a million times worse for Fred than for me if Aunt ever found out.

I was sorry when we found ourselves back in the street. We stood there for a few minutes while the carriage was brought round.

'What are you going to do now?' I asked while the footman held open the carriage door for me.

'I am on – shall we say – other business.' She jerked her head at her maid. 'I can trust her. She won't talk.'

Our cheeks bumped together. 'Goodbye,' Marjorie murmured. 'I am so glad we met. I wish it had been sooner.'

'Write to me,' I reminded her.

'I will.' She raised her hand and I watched her walk away. I sat down in the carriage opposite Baxter, the walking suit on the seat beside her. I leaned back and thought about what Marjorie had told me. I admired her courage. But prison? I shuddered.

George's pink car was parked outside the front door when we got back. No doubt I'd see him at lunch. But what about his passenger? Would I find her sitting at table with us? Somehow I doubted it. A girl who kissed a young man in public would never pass as a lady. David was a bad boy, Marjorie had said, but your cousin George is worse.

DOWNSTAIRS

'Ta-ra-ra boom de-ay! Ta-ra-ra boom de-ay!' It was the middle of the afternoon, but it sounded like the lower servants were having a party. I stood for a minute outside the kitchen door, then slowly pushed it open. I could hardly believe my eyes. The servants were dancing round the table, arms clasping each other's waists, hands on shoulders. At the head of them all was Ivy, performing the high kicks she'd demonstrated to me in my bedroom. Her coat was unbuttoned, her hat askew. I stood still, mouth open. What had got in to them? What would Cook say if she walked in now? But I needn't have worried. There was Cook, hands on Maisie's shoulders, swaying from side to side as she followed the train of servants round the table. No one seemed to have seen me. They were too carried away to have heard the door open.

It was Ivy who saw me first.

'Jess!' she exclaimed. She stopped dancing and pushed through the servants to my side. They parted for her, as if she was a star. And they were right, she was. I felt myself enveloped in a huge hug.

'Jess, I got the part! And it's not just the one job either. They want me in the company!'

So that was what the excitement was all about.

I hugged her back. Her eyes were shining. I felt mine grow watery. I blinked them rapidly – it was selfish of me to think of myself but, oh, I'd miss her.

'No more dishes then,' I said.

'No more dishes, Jess.'

'Maddie will be pleased.'

'Wish I could see her face when you tell her I'm an actress!'

I laughed.

The other servants had stopped dancing now. Cook was mopping her hot face and shooting out orders as if she'd just remembered who she was. Maisie perched on the table next to me.

'So when do you start, Ivy?' she said.

'Almost at once. I won't be coming back to Langdown.' She flopped down in a chair and stretched out her legs. 'Oooh, I'm tired. I've been all morning on my feet in that scullery, and all afternoon prancing about on stage showing them what I could do.' But she laughed. I knew that today she didn't care how tired she was.

'Have you told Mrs Barlow?' I asked her.

'Not yet.'

Ivy unpinned her hat and tossed it on to the table. I looked at it lying there. It was as if in tossing away her hat, that symbol of respectability, Ivy was bidding farewell to a respectable life. Which was what I felt sure she was. Whatever Ivy liked to think, the stage wasn't a respectable occupation for a girl.

But what fun she'd have. If only I had talent like Ivy did. But I was a little mouse. I felt scared just going out into the town.

'So when's the opening night?' asked Maisie eagerly.

'It's after you go back to Langdown,' Ivy said. 'Sorry, Maisie.'

I was sorry, too. I'd liked to have seen Ivy perform on stage. I'd never even been inside a London theatre – or any theatre.

'But if the opening run's a success, we're going on tour,' Ivy said.

Maisie's eyes shone. 'Oooh, then I could come and watch.'

'You can all come,' Ivy said, grandly. 'Best stall seats for my friends.'

I sat down next to her. There was something I still needed to be reassured about. 'You do have somewhere to live, don't you, Ivy? Promise?'

'Of course I have. Told you, didn't I?' Ivy put her hands on my shoulders and looked into my face. 'What will you do when you don't have me to worry about, Jess?'

I gave a wry smile. 'I expect I'll find someone else to take under my wing.'

'I wish you were staying here, too. I'll miss you, Jess. Why don't you stay – you could find a job in the city?'

I shook my head. 'Don't like the city, Ivy. I'm not like you.'

'You don't know it. You've scarcely even seen it,' she said.

'I wish we'd had time to take in a show. But we'll do it one day, Jess, you have my word on it.'

'We will,' I said. 'Ivy, hadn't you better speak to Mrs Barlow now? Someone will need to let them know at Langdown. We're shutting up house here soon.'

'You're right. Best get it over with. They're bound to go on about the inconvenience. It's all that matters to them, isn't it? Their precious convenience. I can tell you, Jess, almost what's best is sticking up two fingers at them.'

'And Mr George?' I couldn't resist adding as we walked out of the kitchen together.

'Oh him, well he's been a good friend to me.'

I told her that I'd seen his car outside.

'He didn't run me to the theatre and back, if that's what you're thinking. He's got another little bird to look after now – name of Bessie.'

'So…?' I let the question hang in the air.

'So you needn't worry about me. I'm not an idiot, Jess. I can stand on my own two feet.' As if to prove it she planted both feet wide apart. We burst out laughing.

'Oh, Ivy, how I'm going to miss you,' I said. I put my hands on her shoulders and looked into her face. 'I want you to promise me something.'

'What is it, Jess? You look very serious.'

'I don't want to see you back here.'

'I think I can promise you that,' Ivy said.

UPSTAIRS

'Poll. My Poll.' He was holding my hands, as if he'd never let them go. My Poll, he'd said. My Poll. Now I knew what people meant when they said that they were so happy they wanted to cry.

'I was afraid you'd forget me,' I gulped when I was able to speak again. I'd dreamed about this moment so many times, but it was more wonderful than I could ever have imagined.

'I'll never do that. Oh, how I've missed you, Poll.'

He drew me slowly towards him. I could feel his breath warm on my cheek. He let go of my hands to draw me closer. I could feel his heart beating against mine. I felt dizzy.

I'd gone round to the stables as soon as we'd got back. I'd had a moment's panic when Clemmie said she would come too, but Aunt had ordered her up to the schoolroom. 'I'll be down as soon as I can, Polly,' she had called to me. Don't make it too soon, I'd thought. I was longing to have some precious moments alone with Fred.

He was in the yard, scrubbing his hands and arms under the tap. He must have felt me there because he turned round at once. Our eyes met. I felt that every fibre of him was as aware of me as I was of him. I struggled to hold back my tears. I hadn't thought I'd cry when I saw him. 'Hello, Fred,' I said, my voice husky. I walked towards him as calmly as I could, but my legs were trembling so that I could hardly stand. Jem came out of one of the stalls, a blanket in his hand. I gave him a cheery wave, wondering how I could be so natural with him in Fred's presence. *I must pretend and I don't want to. But I must – until...* 'Hello, Jem, I'm back.' Somehow I'd got my voice under control.

Jem gave me a grin. 'I saw the carriage. I expect you've come to see Starshine.'

'That's right. I've missed her.'

I talked on, hardly knowing what I was saying. Fred was drying himself with a towel. He tossed it aside and came towards me. 'Let's see how Starshine is.' He wasn't looking at me as he spoke. I followed him to the stall. He opened it for me to walk in first. I went straight to Starshine, and stroked her coat.

'Hello, Starshine,' I murmured. 'Do you remember me?' Her head came round to nuzzle my palm. I stroked her nose, but all I could think about was that Fred was standing there, a few feet away from me. *Don't disappoint me! Don't tell me you've forgotten me.* I remembered that he'd written that there were things he'd wanted to tell me but didn't know how to write. I had been away for weeks. How did he feel about me now? Had he and Sarah made it up? They had been together for a long time, whereas he and I... Doubts and fears seeped into me. I laid my head against Starshine's coat. Why was he still standing there? Why didn't he say something – anything – to show me that he still cared?

'Poll.' I could hear that he was close behind me. 'Poll, I...' He sounded uncertain, as if he felt the same fears as me. Slowly I turned to face him. We looked deep into each other's eyes. He reached uncertainly for my hands. I clung to them. All my fears fell away. The stall felt suddenly full of sunshine.

He glanced up at my hair. 'You're a proper young lady now,' he said. *So how was it?* his eyes asked. *Not forgotten me?*

How can you think that? my eyes replied.

I forgot everything then as he began to draw me towards him. I felt my hands tremble in his. 'So,' he said at last, 'are you still my girl?'

Did he need to ask? Couldn't he see how I felt in my eyes?

'Fred, I missed you so much,' I said. 'There will never be anyone but you!'

I thought of Ferdy and David, and I sighed. I felt uneasily certain that I'd not seen the last of them. Aunt was determined to marry me to Ferdy, or someone equally suitable. Someone suitable in her eyes – not mine.

But I couldn't marry him, or any of them. Even if there hadn't been Fred. I knew what sort of life I'd have with them. They'd want to wrap me up and display me. I'd never be able to be myself. They belonged to a world I didn't want to live in. Didn't belong in – and never could.

'I made one good friend in London,' I said. 'Her name is Marjorie.' I had promised Marjorie not to tell anyone that she'd joined the suffragettes, but I could still talk about them.

'Fred,' I said, 'have you heard of the suffragettes?'

'What made you say that?' he asked curiously.

'I heard someone talk about them,' I said.

'Well I have, and I'm for them. They want to change women's lives for the better.' He smiled. 'Are you trying to tell me that you've joined them?'

'No, but I admire them,' I said. 'Fred, if they succeed...'

He tipped my chin up to smile into my eyes. 'You think that you and I will be able to be together, no one in our way. If only it were that simple, Poll.'

'But...' I interrupted, then stopped myself. I didn't want to spoil our first day by going over all the tired old arguments again.

I looked at him. He was holding my hand, stroking it gently. I knew that there was something he wanted to say. Something that was troubling him. He couldn't hide from me any more than I could from him. Oh why had I said anything about the future? Now I'd spoilt everything.

'What is it, Fred?' I said. He was holding my hand tightly.

He raised his eyes to mine. They were full of pain. 'Mam has died,' he said. He turned his head away. 'Oh Poll, I missed you so badly. I wanted you so much. I can't tell you how much.'

I turned his head back to me. I took his face in my hands.

'Was that what you wanted to write?' I whispered. He couldn't look at me but he nodded. A tear slid down his cheek. I stroked it softly, wiping it away.

'His lordship gave me leave to go to Mam at once,' he said. 'After Mam died I stayed on until Uncle came to fetch my brother and sisters. My brother will be starting his apprenticeship soon, but they all need a home. It's a weight off me to know they will have one. He's a good man, my uncle; I don't have any fears for them with him. But they'll be a long way away. I won't be able to visit them often. I felt so alone when I got back here. I missed you so much.'

'I'm here now,' I said, putting my arms around him.

I comforted him as well as I could. I tried to shift some of the pain he felt to me. And as I held him I felt my own grief at Mother's death pour through me. For months I'd kept it in check but now I could hold it back no longer. It was as if his grief had touched something deep inside me.

At last we released each other. We wiped each other's eyes, and smiled. I'd never felt so close to him before. We talked then, of little things – about the filly that Uncle was to race at Ascot. Fred was looking after her.

'She's still a handful,' he said, with a sidelong glance at me. 'Reminds me of someone.' We burst out laughing.

I took his hand in mine and held it to my cheek. 'Clemmie said she'd be along soon. I'd better go back to the house in case she comes to find me.'

'Jem will be wondering where I am, too,' Fred said. 'You've been a long time greeting Starshine.' He smiled, squeezed my hand tight then let it go. 'You are such a comfort to me, Poll. I don't know what I'd do without you.' My heart felt as if it would burst with happiness.

Before I left him, Fred warned me that preparations for Ascot would keep him busy, but I was on air as I walked back to the house. Ascot would soon be over and then we'd go riding every day.

I was nearly there when I saw Clemmie. My heart gave a lurch. A few minutes more and she'd have been searching the stables for me. I gave her a beaming smile – I was so happy I felt that I loved the whole world and everything in it.

'I'm glad I've found you,' she said, running up to me. 'I was on my way to the stables. I told Mother you might be there. Mother says it is time for tea. You have been a long time.'

Her eyes were frank, but I felt a prick of unease. How long had I been then? I'd lost all sense of time. We walked up to the house together.

'I was talking to Starshine. I missed her,' I said. 'But she seems to have been happy enough without me.'

'Shall we ride together, tomorrow?' said Clemmie, looking up at me. 'I hardly saw you in London!'

'I know,' I said. 'We were so busy. But we'll have lots of time together now.'

'We're going to Ascot,' Clemmie said. 'I'm going, too. Father has a horse running. I expect you know. Isn't it exciting! Have you ever been to the races?'

'I did in India,' I told her.

'You never talk about India now,' said Clemmie curiously. 'Do you still miss it?'

'I miss Father,' I said.

'Perhaps he'll come and visit you. I'd like to meet him,' Clemmie said. I put an arm round her shoulder and gave her a squeeze. She was such a dear little girl.

'I wish you were my sister,' I said.

Her face went pink. 'Do you really? Really and truly?' I nodded. 'Well,' she said, 'I wish you were mine.'

We ran up the steps together.

I had to try and hide how happy I felt as I joined the family for tea. Aunt gave me a glance of surprise.

'Why – Penelope. Where have you been?' She looked me up and down. 'You haven't changed?'

I looked down at myself. I was still in my travelling gown.

'You surely haven't been at the stables all this time?'

I felt myself blush. 'I'm sorry, Aunt,' I said.

'Well, never mind for today. But remember, you are a young lady now.' To my surprise she did not chastise me further.

I sat down next to Clemmie.

Aunt smiled. 'Has Clementine told you about Ascot?'

I tried to sound interested, but my mind was still full of my meeting with Fred. 'She has.'

'Did she tell you that we have been invited to join the Waterlows?'

'Oh,' I said, unable to squeeze out any more enthusiasm.

Aunt's smile grew broader. 'Yes, young Lord Waterlow will be among the party. You have made a very favourable impression on that young man, my dear.'

I felt myself panic. The walls of the house seemed to be closing in on me. I had a desperate urge to get up and run from the room.

'Well?' Aunt seemed surprised by my lack of response.

'I will look forward to seeing Lord Waterlow again,' I forced myself to say.

'He is a most delightful young man. And his sister is so fond of you, too. A very desirable connection for you to have made, my dear.'

Even if I stood on my head and waved my legs in the air Aunt would smile on me now.

I was relieved when a knock on the door announced the arrival of tea. I had thought I was hungry but I could only pick at a scone. I crumbled it between my fingers. Arabella looked at me in distaste.

I escaped as soon as I could. Marjorie had warned me that eager suitors would pursue me to Langdown, but I hadn't thought it would be so soon. As I walked up the great staircase the eyes of Uncle's ancestors stared mockingly at me from behind their frames. *Ha! There is no escape for you.* In my room I went to the window and gazed out. I had looked forward to returning, but I had merely exchanged one prison for another. But at least Fred shared *this* prison, and as long as he was here I felt I could put up with anything.

Downstairs

'So Ivy won't be coming back?' Maddie said.

'No,' I said. 'She's got a job as an actress. Isn't it exciting?'

'Typical!' Maddie said. Her mouth shut in a tight line. 'Leaving us in the lurch!'

'I thought you'd be pleased,' I said.

'Pleased!' Maddie glared at me. 'Now I'm back doing two jobs again?'

'It's only for a few weeks,' I said weakly.

'Humph!'

Her temper hadn't improved in our absence.

The new scullery maid had been found very quickly, but wasn't yet ready to start. Me, I was wondering what my fate would be. I didn't want to wait until I was summoned. Leaving Maddie muttering to herself, I went to see Mrs Smithson. 'Ah, Jess, I was going to send for you,' she said. 'I wanted to give you time to settle back in first. From all I've been told you did very well, fitting in with the other upper servants very nicely.'

Is that what they'd told her? It's not what I'd felt.

Mrs Smithson was looking expectantly at me.

'Jess,' she said. She picked up a pen and fiddled with it. 'I have a favour to ask you.'

Oh no, not again.

I took a deep breath. I had to tell her how I felt. They couldn't keep demanding favours of me. I had to tell her that I did not want to go on being Miss P's maid. I had nothing against Miss P personally; I just didn't like the job.

'Begging your pardon, Mrs Smithson,' I said, 'I'm pleased that I've given satisfaction… But…' I cleared my throat. This was harder to say than I'd expected. 'I don't want to be a lady's maid any more.'

I could see that Mrs Smithson was disappointed. Had she hoped that a few weeks in London would help me change my mind? What about the other lady's maid? I wondered. The one I'd been standing in for. What had happened to her? Was she still sick? Couldn't they have advertised for someone else?

I was about to get my answer.

'You see, the woman we'd hoped to appoint will definitely not be well enough to take up this position,' Mrs Smithson said, twiddling her pen. 'And unfortunately there's not been time to advertise for a replacement. We've Ascot to look forward to and a houseful of guests.'

So yours truly has to pick up the pieces again. I see.

I looked up to meet Mrs Smithson's eye. At least she had the grace to look embarrassed.

She cleared her throat. 'I feel awkward asking this of you, Jess – especially in view of what you've just told me – but would you mind staying on for now – just until we find someone to replace you?'

I nodded. I didn't like it, but I didn't see that I had much choice. One day maybe I'd be back where I belonged.

'Very well, Mrs Smithson,' I said grudgingly. 'I'll stay on for now.'

'Thank you, Jess. Annie, who I appointed to take over your old duties, says she is happy to remain in post for now – and we'll need an extra pair of hands anyway.'

So yet again they'd talked to everyone except me. They'd even managed to appoint a new scullery maid. Ivy was right; I should stick up for myself more.

'And Jess, let me reassure you that you won't be expected to do any housemaid's duties until we find a replacement for you.' She gave me a long look. 'Are you really sure you want us to?'

I thought about the privileges I had as a lady's maid. I didn't wear uniform, I had my own bedroom, then there was the cup of tea brought to me in the morning, the luxury of bathing in a proper bathroom whenever I wanted – or when I had time.

'Miss Penelope will be sorry,' Mrs Smithson added smiling at me.

Thank you, Mrs Smithson; you've made up my mind for

me. Thinking about the privileges I'd enjoyed I'd almost begun to waver, but Mrs Smithson had used the one argument to persuade me that never would. All that ever seemed to matter was them upstairs. What I wanted didn't come into it. I'd always known that, but it really rankled now. I found myself envying Ivy. She'd had the sense to get out of service. I still had my dream – of a home of my own one day. But until that unlikely dream became reality there was only one place I wanted to be. Back downstairs with my friends.

'I am quite sure, Mrs Smithson,' I said as firmly as I could.

'Then that seems to be all.' Mrs Smithson smiled. 'Thank you, Jess.' I left her still twiddling her pen in her hands. I'd presented her with a problem, but I felt light-hearted for the first time since I'd taken on my new duties.

I went to collect my box. I'd hoped that I'd be relinquishing my duties as soon as I got back and had put it in the room I'd shared with Sarah and Ellen, but when I got there, I saw that it was sitting in the corridor outside. The bedroom door was closed. I tapped on it lightly. I could hear someone moving about inside. I hesitated. I didn't want to barge in. I hadn't seen Sarah since I'd got back, and I felt a bit nervous.

'Sarah? Are you there?'

No reply.

'Ellen?'

Still no reply.

I felt sure that Sarah was in that room. *Oh please don't say we can't make up, Sarah.*

'Sarah, it's me, Jess,' I tried again. 'Can I come in?' When no one answered I pushed the door open slightly. Sarah was sitting on the bed. She turned round when she heard me. She looked as nervous as I felt.

'So you're back, Jess.'

At least she was speaking to me.

I went over to sit beside her. I didn't ask why my box had been put outside in the landing. 'And very glad to be, too,' I said with feeling. 'Soon I'll be properly downstairs again, working with you and Ellen.' I smiled at her. Sarah looked awkward. *Oh no, Sarah, please say we can put the past behind us now.*

'So you aren't staying on as a lady's maid then? I thought you'd change your mind when you got to London.'

'It's not for me, Sarah. I missed you all. I even missed the cleaning!'

We both avoided mentioning Miss P.

'I've something to say to you, Jess.' Sarah plucked at the bedspread with her hand. 'I'm not sure how to say it, but I am really sorry – I was unkind,' she said in a low voice. 'I've been feeling so guilty. I was just so upset. I didn't know what I'd say to you when you got back.'

I took her hand and squeezed it. 'Let's just forget it, shall we?'

'You're my best friend, Jess,' Sarah said, squeezing my hand back. I just wished she looked happier.

'And now…' I let the words hang in the air. Sarah knew what I meant. Or rather, *who* I meant.

She shrugged. 'I never see him. I suppose I'm getting used to it.'

'I'm so sorry,' I murmured. Sarah moved up closer to me.

'Oh Jess, I wish he'd go actually. It would be easier, knowing I couldn't see him.' I could hear despair in her voice, but I didn't know what to say that wouldn't hurt. I gave her shoulders a squeeze. They felt thinner than I remembered. She'd lost weight, and she was paler, too. I hated Fred for hurting her so much. We stared out of the window. I tried to think of something to say, something that would banish the spectre of Fred I'd conjured up.

'Did you hear about Ivy?' I said at last.

'Going on stage, yes. Good for Ivy. Maybe we'll see her first night.'

'Maybe.' I smiled.

'Know what I heard?' said Sarah. She smiled – it was the first time I'd seen her smile like that at me for I didn't know how long.

'Tell me.'

'Lord and Lady Moorcroft are coming here – they're guests at the Ascot house party.'

Now it was my turn to toy with the bedspread. 'Really?' I mumbled. 'How do you know?'

'Ah,' said Sarah. She was still smiling. 'I heard Mrs S mention their names. She's in quite a flap. It'll be a full house soon.'

'So I heard,' I said.

'I expect a certain valet will be accompanying his lordship,' Sarah said. 'Don't you?'

I felt my face go pink. 'Oh.'

'Is that all you can say!' Sarah demanded. '"Oh".'

'It was a long time ago,' I said. 'He was nice, but he's just a friend, Sarah.'

He's probably married by now, I thought. Someone as nice as that wouldn't be allowed to stay single for long. He'd be snapped up.

'"Just a friend",' mocked Sarah. 'Really? Trouble with you, Jess, is you're shy. You don't think anyone will like you. He did. I know he did.'

This conversation had gone far enough. I got up. 'Must get my clothes unpacked.' I remembered that my box was outside. 'I put my box in here, but someone moved it,' I said.

'Ummm, yes,' said Sarah. 'That was me. Sorry. I only moved it because I thought you'd have your own room. Annie the temporary housemaid is in here with us,' she said. 'Just for now.' She smiled. 'I'll be glad when you're back with us, Jess.'

'I wasn't sure what I'd be doing. I was hoping I'd be back with you all now, but Mrs Smithson wants me to stay on until they've found a replacement.' Before I'd left for London I'd shared a room with the girls, but I hadn't been one thing or the other then.

'I think she was hoping you'd change your mind,' Sarah said.

'But I haven't,' I said.

I left Sarah and took my box to the small room that Mrs Smithson had told me would be mine until I returned to my old job. I put it down on the floor and hastily tipped the contents out on to the bed. I didn't have time to unpack properly now, I had to unpack for Miss Polly, press her gown for dinner and run her bath. Who'd want to be a lady's maid? Not me!

UPSTAIRS

'There,' he said. 'The bay. Can you see him now?' I raised my binoculars to where Ferdy was pointing. The gleaming thoroughbreds thundered past. Around me I could hear cheers as the horses pounded up to the finishing line. I was still trying to get the binoculars in focus. It all happened so fast. People leaned over to talk to Ferdy. George came up to shake his hand. 'Well done, old chap,' he said.

'He's won?' I said.

'Why yes,' said Flo, on my other side. 'Didn't you hear the announcement?' She sounded surprised. I glanced at the crumpled programme on my lap. I couldn't even remember the horse's name.

'Come.' She touched me lightly on the arm with her programme. 'We're going down to the winner's enclosure.' I stood up. I was thankful to get up and stretch my legs. It was too chilly to sit still for long. Flo had told me it was typical Ascot weather. Around us people were rising and moving away to talk to their friends, to drink champagne and to chatter idly about a horse's form. All of society was here, in the Royal Enclosure.

George and Ferdy were talking excitedly, laying bets on who would win the Gold Plate. George was for Bomba, but Ferdy was betting on Bayardo. Bayardo had already won the Buckenham and the Dewhurst Plate, I heard him say. I suddenly realized that I hadn't heard Ferdy stammer once, and it had been quite a speech. It was nervousness that made Ferdy trip over his words, and all his nervousness vanished when he was talking about his beloved horses.

Behind me, Aunt and Countess Waterlow had risen too, their huge hats a mass of bobbing plumes, but though her head was turned to Countess Waterlow Aunt's attention rarely left Ferdy and me. I wondered what fibs Aunt was spinning about me. It hadn't taken Aunt long to realize that Arabella would never be the next Countess Waterlow. Now her hopes were pinned on me. She was going to be disappointed. Even if I never saw Fred again, I knew I could never marry Ferdy. I couldn't think of a more unsuitable husband for me or wife for him. Nor could I understand why Flo was so determined to have me as a sister-in-law.

'My brother loves horses as much as you do, Polly,' she'd said to me earlier. Flo constantly pointed out anything Ferdy and I had in common. It was beginning to irritate me.

We began to make our way along the row, squashing past the eager spectators who hadn't moved from their seats.

The Waterlows owned a string of racehorses. I'd been down to the paddock once already to admire them. My eyes had searched in vain for Fred. He was here to tend Uncle's only entry, Donatella – the spirited young filly who had nearly trampled me soon after I'd arrived at Langdown. Uncle had high hopes for her. He'd taken me down to see her in the stables, a few days ago. While Uncle was talking to her trainer I'd managed a few words with Fred on his own. It was the first time I'd seen him since the day I'd returned from London. He had looked tired, I thought.

Ferdy caught up with us. He put out a protective arm to shield me from the crush of ladies and gentlemen who crowded the enclosure. I tried not to yawn. The excitement I'd felt earlier had begun to pall. I'd lost count how many times horses had galloped past me. They had all begun to look the same. We reached the railings that ran round the winner's enclosure. Inside I could see Ferdy's horse – The Troubadour. His red-brown coat shone with sweat. A man in a bowler held the halter. He doffed his hat when he saw Ferdy.

'Isn't he a beauty?' Ferdy breathed in my ear.

'Very,' I agreed, leaning away. I looked to Flo to rescue me, but she merely smiled.

I raised my binoculars and let them travel over the course. 'That's the royal box you're pointing at,' said Flo. 'Can you see the King?'

That wasn't who I was searching for. I lowered the binoculars hastily. We'd seen the royal party arrive earlier – sweeping along the course in open carriages. The King had looked fatter than ever, and I'd giggled to myself, remembering what Marjorie had said to me. I'd written to Marjorie, when I'd got back to Langdown, but she hadn't answered the letter. I'd begun to read Uncle's paper, scanning it furtively for news of the suffragettes' exploits. I didn't dare ask Aunt and Uncle – I had asked once and they had looked shocked that I even knew who they were.

I felt a heavy hand on my shoulder. 'Come along, Penelope. It's time to stop gazing at young Waterlow's horse,' Uncle said jovially. 'Our filly is racing next.' It was the only race I felt any interest in. Uncle's bulky form cleared a path for us through the spectators, like a steamer in full flow. We followed in his wake, reaching our seats just as the starting gun sounded.

I stood up and leaned forward eagerly, training my binoculars on the young fillies galloping around the track. Donatella was halfway back in the field but she was making good progress. If only that was me, flying around the course on her back.

'Come on, Donatella!' I shouted, not caring what anyone thought. 'Come *on*!' She was gaining ground, only just behind the little knot of horses leading the field. I clenched my hands into fists, and leaned forward as far as I could. She was drawing closer to the leaders. I could hear Uncle's hoarse voice behind me. We were all on our feet. She had caught up with them – she was fighting it out with a grey. They were running neck and neck. It was between the two of them now.

But a third horse was coming up behind them. One more spurt. That was all it needed. 'Come on!' They were galloping side by side. I heard a roar, and I sank down in my seat, feeling almost as exhausted as if I'd been running myself. The race was over. I swivelled round in my seat. It had been so close. Uncle was looking glum, but he forced a smile to his face when he caught my eye. 'Second!' I heard George say. 'Beaten by a hair's breath!' He sagged disconsolately.

Uncle shot a glance at him. 'Lost again, eh!' he said. 'How much have you squandered this time?' George was silent, sucking on his moustache. 'Come on, Penelope,' Uncle said. 'I'll take you down to the paddock. We'll leave the young cub to lick his wounds.' He snorted contemptuously. My heart leapt. I was bound to see Fred there.

'Let's all go,' said Ferdy, jumping up like an eager puppy. 'Miss P-P.' He offered me his arm. Uncle smiled, making way for him. If only he knew how reluctant I was to take the offered arm. Back we shuffled along the row of seats. I longed to shake Ferdy off. I was eager to see Fred, but not pinioned to the arm of this boy.

'So this is where you have been hiding yourself.' David was leaning towards me across the railing that penned us in. Unlike most of the men in the enclosure he was in a light summer suit, a panama perched jauntily on his head.

'I didn't know that I had,' I said.

'How long have you been here?' he asked me.

'All day,' I replied.

'Sitting here?' His eyebrows went up. 'I can show you a place where I promise you will get a much better view of the course. Look.' He pointed to where a line of carriages was drawn up. Several men and women had climbed up and were standing on top of them.

'Don't be ridiculous!' I snapped. 'I can hardly clamber about on a carriage. Anyway, I'm with a party.'

I threw a glance at Ferdy, who was regarding David warily.

'Ferdy,' I said, letting go of his arm. 'This is a – friend, David Moore. David, Lord Waterlow.' Ferdy bowed stiffly. David's eyes twinkled.

'Shame,' he said. 'It's the best view in town. But maybe you are right. Maybe it wouldn't be seemly for a *young lady* to clamber about on a carriage.' Was he mocking me? I felt myself flush. Ferdy took my arm again proprietorially.

'I am going to the paddock to see my uncle's horse,' I told David firmly.

'Very well.' The three of us wove our way through the crowds of ladies and gentlemen on to the course.

I saw people look speculatively at Ferdy and me. 'What a handsome couple,' I heard someone say. I dropped Ferdy's arm. Behind me Aunt and Countess Waterlow drifted along talking, but I could feel Aunt's eyes bore into my back. *How dare I drop Ferdy's arm. What an insult to the house of Waterlow!*

I saw Fred as soon as we reached the paddock. He had his

back to me, one arm draped over the filly, the halter wound round his hand. Donatella was tossing her head, trying to shake him off. It was extraordinary how everything seemed to vanish until there was just Fred and me.

'Penelope, I must talk to you,' said a low voice by my side. I came back from my happy dream to find that David was standing next to me. The intent look he gave me made my heart sink.

Oh, why won't they leave me alone? Can't they tell how little I care about any of them?

The look I gave him would have deflated anyone else. But nothing it seemed could dent David's self-confidence. 'Surely you don't like that puppy?' he murmured. He threw a contemptuous glance at Ferdy, who was hurrying up to claim my other side. They eyed each other suspiciously.

'We can talk here, can't we?' I said.

Does it not occur to you that I might not want to talk to either of you?

'No we can't,' he said. 'Come with me.'

What was he thinking? I could hardly walk off with him alone.

'David,' I said. 'I've come to see my uncle's filly. She's come second in her class. Please!' I left him and Ferdy and marched up to where Uncle stood, in the group around the filly. It took all my courage. Fred was standing only a few feet away from me now.

The jockey was talking to the horse's trainer. As I came up to them, Uncle smiled at me and put a hand on the jockey's shoulder. He could just as easily have tucked him under his arm. He was a small slight man who only came up to Uncle's shoulder.

'This is my niece. She is a fine horsewoman herself. Jumps like a man.' His eyes twinkled at me. I could feel myself blush as the men turned to me. Fred was still grappling with Donatella's bridle. I walked up to her and put out my hand to pat her back. Her head came round fast. Fred tugged on the bridle to pull her away.

'You be careful, miss, she's a nervous high-spirited creature. Remember?' I saw a smile glimmer on his lips. The jockey said something, but I didn't hear what it was. The men laughed. Fred's eyes were on mine. We were standing very close to each other now. If I'd put out my hand I could have touched his. I yearned to touch it, feel his fingers close round mine. We were so close, yet I might as well have been on the other side of the Channel. Fred looked glum as if the same thought was in his mind. *Please, Fred, don't look like that.* His hands were stroking the horse's nose. She had the same wild look in her eyes that I remembered. *You're like me. You want to be free. They're trying to tame you. But you don't want to be tamed. I know just how you feel.* I turned back to Uncle.

'The first time I saw Donatella,' I said loudly so that everyone could hear. 'I nearly walked under her hooves.

Luckily for me Fred saw and pulled me away.' Everyone laughed.

'She's a wild one,' said the jockey admiringly. 'Gave me some trouble, but I showed her who was boss. We'll win this race next year, won't we, girl.' He slapped the horse's side affectionately.

'She was a good purchase,' said Uncle proudly.

I could have stood there all afternoon, but Flo came up and took my arm. I let myself be led away. 'I hope you'll visit us soon,' she smiled. 'We have a fine stables and could find a lovely mount for you.'

'If you promise to ride with me, Flo,' I said.

She laughed. 'It would be a very dull ride. I can only manage a sedate trot. I don't enjoy it as much as Ferdy does. He will be so pleased to have a companion to ride with.' She looked fondly at her brother. Ferdy beamed. He was looking at Flo, but I knew that smile had nothing to do with Flo and everything to do with me, and I didn't like it. David had drifted away. But even if I managed to avoid a private conversation with him today he'd soon have another opportunity. He and the Waterlows would be amongst the guests at Langdown once the Royal Ascot meeting was over.

The crowd on the course had grown. The royal party was departing and spectators were hastening up to the railings to watch. I looked back to see that the seats that had been crammed with racegoers were nearly empty. People were slowly beginning to drift away. But we remained. Now that I couldn't see Fred, I was impatient to leave. The wind whipped my skirts around my legs. But Aunt, talking to Countess Waterlow, was standing her ground as if only a hurricane would uproot her.

She beckoned to me. 'The Countess has invited you to the Waterlow shoot.' That usually impassive face broke into a beaming smile. I had never seen Aunt smile as often as she had today.

'I'll look forward to it,' I lied. I looked round for a means of escape. Uncle was surrounded by a group of top-hatted racegoers. Ferdy was with him. 'Ah, I see you are looking for Ferdy,' said Countess Waterlow, smiling at me. *Oh no, I wasn't. Why must everyone so wilfully misunderstand me? Were they blind?* Countess Waterlow's skirt whispered over the grass as she went over to the group. The gentlemen bowed and began to disperse. Ferdy came up to bid me farewell.

'I will look forward to seeing you, Miss P-P-Penelope,' he said, battling with the words that would not come. 'At Langdown,' he got out at last. I nodded. He raised his hat to me. Poor Ferdy, I thought.

Like the royal family we rode back in an open landau. I pulled my wrap closer round me. Arabella sat on one side of me, Clemmie on the other. Arabella and I had hardly exchanged a word all day. She felt as rigid as stone. Disappointment turned her mouth down. Neither of us said a word to the other. We seemed to have fallen into an unspoken understanding – to have as little to do with each other as possible.

As soon as the carriage arrived back at Langdown, I hastened upstairs. I was nearly frozen, but Baxter thoughtfully ran me a bath, and I slipped in under the hot water gratefully. As I lay there, enveloped in the warm water, I thought about the day. I was dreading the house party. I felt uneasily certain that I knew what it was that David wanted to say to me. And then there was poor awkward Ferdy. Would he declare himself, too? I sighed to myself. I had a problem on my hands. Or was it two?

Downstairs

'I haven't got time for this!' I protested.

Sarah put down the brush and began to roll up my hair. 'Yes you have.'

I tried not to wriggle as she slipped pins into my hair to hold it in place.

'Now,' she said, handing me a mirror. 'Take a look at yourself.'

I gazed at the face staring back at me. I hardly recognized myself. Sarah had added a touch of make-up. 'You look like a real lady!' she said proudly, admiring her handiwork.

My eyes were shining. What had Sarah done to them to make them shine like that? Even Ivy hadn't managed that. My lips were fuller and redder, too.

What had Ivy said? *Those are lips that are meant to be kissed.*

I put the mirror down hastily.

'Your face changes when you smile,' said Sarah. 'You should smile more often.'

'I'd smile more if I had something to smile about,' I grumbled.

I was still Miss P's maid. Sometimes I thought they hadn't even begun to try and find a replacement for me.

'But look at you,' Sarah protested. 'That's a really pretty blouse. Last time he saw you you were just one of us housemaids, in uniform. Think what a surprise he's going to have when he sees you tonight. He won't be able to resist you.'

'He' was Daniel – Lord Moorcroft's valet. I'd been in a flutter ever since Sarah had told me that Lord and Lady Moorcroft would be amongst the guests arriving for dinner. They were staying for the whole weekend. It would be a big party. There was something to celebrate, too – his lordship's horse had come second in her race. I'd seen his lordship strut about triumphantly as if his horse had won the Gold Cup itself. Miss Polly had told me about it when I went to dress her earlier. It had taken us both a long time to decide what she should wear. I'd not have settled on the gown she chose, it didn't do her any favours, but she was determined to have her own way, and I had to let her have it.

'But I'll have to dine with him, and there will be all those haughty ladies' maids too,' I complained.

'Try, Jess. Just this weekend!' Sarah beseeched me.

'I don't know why you think he likes me,' I said. 'He won't even remember me. It must be at least a year since the Moorcrofts last stayed here.'

'He likes you, but he's as shy as you are,' Sarah said. 'You've got to be braver, Jess. Put yourself out.'

'I can't very well throw myself at him.'

'But you can at least *talk* to him.'

'All right, all right,' I grumbled.

'And one more thing,' said Sarah. 'I don't want you to go running yourself down. It's because you deserve it they asked you to be Miss P's maid.'

I nodded. 'Any more commands, Miss Sarah?'

We smiled at each other, like true friends do. And I felt that we were.

'Come on then.' Sarah opened the door, and curtsied as I swept past. 'You, Jess Baxter, *will* go to the ball.'

I laughed, and linked my arm through hers as we made our way along the passage that led to the stairs. It was going to be a long evening, and I felt tired just thinking about it. But this time, now, was mine. I told myself that I was going to enjoy myself.

A large crowd was already assembled when we reached the servants' hall. I hung back – at the sight of all those people my courage left me – but Sarah pulled me determinedly along behind her, past the visiting valets and ladies' maids. Some of them looked at me curiously. Robert gave a wolf whistle. Sarah squeezed my arm. 'See – they're noticing you.' But where was Daniel? I had a moment's panic. What if I was right and Sarah wrong? What if Daniel had left Lord Moorcroft's service? What if he was here, and ignored me? I couldn't think which would be worse.

'Hello, Jess.' A tall young man with sandy hair smiled shyly at me.

I swallowed. 'Daniel,' I said. He'd recognized me, seen through my disguise.

'I hear that you are now a lady's maid,' he said.

He had taken the trouble to find out about me. Maybe Sarah was right, after all.

'Only for now,' I said. I was anxious to put him right.

'Don't you like it then?'

'Well, your life's not your own,' I said.

'But is it ever in service?' Daniel said.

'I suppose not. But...' Oh, what was the use. I couldn't pretend, not with him. 'I don't feel I belong there.' I jerked my head up. 'With them. The other ladies' maids. I feel a fraud, to be honest.'

'You'd never be that, Jess.'

'And your life's not your own either,' I added – oh, I'd said that already. I stumbled on, hardly knowing what words were coming out of my mouth. *What had he said to me? 'You'd never be that.' Had he really said that? To me, Jess Baxter?*

'It's not for me,' I said when I'd found my tongue again. 'I'd like to settle down. I'm a homebird really.'

I blushed. Sarah had said to talk, but now I was talking too much. How did anyone ever get it right?

I thought he'd make an excuse to leave me, but he stood by me and gradually I felt myself relax. Sarah would be proud of me, I thought. My eyes wandered the room in search of her. I couldn't see her anywhere. The grooms and stable hands had come in. Fred was at the centre of them, but he didn't look as cheerful as you'd expect someone to be who'd looked after the horse that had come second in its race at Royal Ascot. But right then, I didn't want to think about him. Or even Sarah. I felt content, standing next to Daniel – as if I had come home. I didn't want anything to spoil the evening. When we sat down to eat I caught him glancing down the table at me, when someone said something funny, or silly, as if he knew we'd feel the same. For the first time since I'd become Miss P's maid I was looking forward to taking dessert with the other upper servants. I'd have someone to talk to, someone who wanted to talk to me. And suddenly I understood how Sarah had felt, it was as if you were soaring up above everyone else. One day I'd have to come down to earth. But not now. Not yet.

Upstairs

'Do you remember what I said to you, Miss Penelope?' I felt David press something into my hand. I looked down to see what it was. A pair of goggles. I stared at them, at him, at the plane a few feet behind him. I'd never even seen a plane until that morning, when the sound of its drone – like an enormous angry wasp hovering overhead – had driven all the guests from the breakfast table to the window. Aunt's nervous 'oh dear's' and Uncle's startled 'by Jove's' mingled with the oohs and aahs of the guests as the plane came into view above the trees before vanishing behind them again.

We had streamed eagerly into the hall, capes and cloaks hurriedly thrown over shoulders before hastening down the steps. George took Flo on one arm, me on the other. Ferdy stumbled along behind us.

Along with the other guests I had watched as the pilot had waved at us, before gently landing the plane on the lawn in front of the house. As the propeller had slowly whirred to a stop he had clambered out and jumped down, stripping off his goggles.

A disconsolate look crossed Ferdy's face when he saw who was striding up to us. David had informed us that he would be joining us on Sunday morning. No motor car or carriage had been requested to collect him from the railway station. George had explained that David was making his own way to the house. He had grinned, like a small boy with a secret.

'So, would you like a ride, Miss Penelope?'

Would I? I looked back. Aunt was standing among the onlookers. George was having to remind her that David was one of the guests. Aunt's normally expressionless face looked as bewildered as if she'd been told that he had flown down from the moon.

'I'll need my aunt's permission,' I said feeling woefully certain that she would never grant it. I couldn't imagine that Aunt would even allow me to sit in a plane, let alone be taken up in one. And I yearned to be in that plane, to feel what it was like to fly, wheeling and diving through the skies like a bird, touching the clouds – even if it had to be David who would be sitting beside me.

'Let me ask her,' said David. 'I can tell her about all the many hours' flying I've done.'

'Would you?' I said.

I knew Aunt wouldn't listen to me, but David could be very persuasive.

He left my side and strode through the admiring guests to where Aunt was standing. I saw him bow and smile. I watched my aunt's expression carefully. I couldn't tell what she thought, but David was persisting. He was still talking when Uncle joined them. I saw them confer together, and then David was striding back to me. He was smiling.

'I promised that it will be a very short flight,' he said, as he reached me. 'But it couldn't be anything else,' he grinned. 'These babies don't stay up for long.'

'She said yes?' I was almost incredulous.

'I laid it on a bit thick. Told her I was a flying instructor.'

I felt uneasy. What else had he lied about?

He must have seen doubt on my face.

'Don't you trust me?' he complained.

No, I do not. But…

I took a deep breath. I might never get another opportunity like this.

'Come on,' he urged. 'Let's not disappoint our audience.' He helped me to climb in.

'You'll find it's colder up there in the air,' he said, tucking a rug round my knees. I strapped on the goggles he'd given me and glanced at him. He had taken a piece of paper out from his pocket and was consulting it.

'What's that?' I exclaimed.

He laid it down on his lap and swivelled round to me.

'Let me tell you something, Miss Penelope. A good pilot makes certain checks before take-off. Surely you know I'd never risk your safety?'

Again, that look. I shifted my eyes away from his uncomfortably. I began to wonder if this had been a stunt laid on to impress me. Outside I could see Flo, eyes wide, Arabella, mouth turned down, and Ferdy, kicking like a disappointed schoolboy at the turf. Beyond all was a blur.

I tried not to flinch as David reached back to strap me in. 'Ready!' he said jubilantly. 'Prepare for take-off!' The blades of the propeller began to turn – slowly, then faster and faster, until I couldn't see them turn at all, and then I realized that we were moving, slowly at first and then we were running along the ground until – with a sudden lift that made my stomach lurch – we were airborne. I felt the plane sway slightly, as if it was being shaken by an invisible hand. I looked at the control panel. How much control did a pilot have? How much were we at the mercy of the wind? I gripped my seat tightly with both hands.

'You're quite safe,' David laughed, as if he could sense how I felt.

When I dared I looked down. Faces craned up at us, but they were getting smaller and smaller and further and further away the longer I looked. The whole of the estate lay below me. The manor looked like a doll's house. From so high up I could see it as I'd never seen it before, as a whole – like a jigsaw when all the pieces had been finally fitted together – the fields, the woods, the little estate cottages, the dairy farm, the stables.

I wondered if Fred would look up and see us. Had he seen the plane land earlier? Since Ascot I'd hadn't been able to see him on his own. I'd always been in the company of one or other guest – usually Ferdy. Ferdy had insisted I show him the stables. Fred must have noticed how he had clung to my side; how often he'd accompanied me there.

'So – how does it feel to be airborne?' David said.

'Wonderful,' I breathed. It was. When I shut my eyes I could almost feel as if I had grown my own pair of wings.

'One day I'll teach you to fly – if you'd like me to,' he said.

'Oh, would you?' I said eagerly.

'But there would be certain conditions,' David said. 'After all, it might be difficult to arrange, unless, of course, you were my wife. Then you'd be free to fly as much and as often as you liked.'

What had he said? Was he asking me to marry him?

'What do you say? I think we'd make a pretty good team. Wild rebels both of us. We belong together, don't you think?'

My head felt as if it was spinning. I couldn't think what to say. Though I'd half expected something like this, his proposal came as a complete surprise, and the manner of it – so brisk and matter of fact – took me aback.

'Are you really so surprised, Penelope?' David said. 'Surely you must have had an inkling what I wanted to say to you. Still silent?' – when I didn't speak – 'Oh dear, I'd rather hoped it was what you wanted.'

There was one important thing he had not said.

'You haven't said if you love me, David,' I said. 'And I don't believe that you do.'

'Ah, love,' said David. 'I should have mentioned it, I know. Well, you are the only girl for me. I knew that the first time I laid eyes on you. Will that do?' I could tell that he was smiling, though he was still looking straight ahead.

He didn't love me, any more than I loved him.

'I can't marry you, David,' I said. 'I don't love you, and I don't think you truly love me.'

'How can you say that?' he replied. Still that teasing note in his voice.

Because I know what it is to feel loved. But I can never ever tell you why.

'Are you sure you couldn't get to love me?' he said when I didn't reply.

'David, I can't marry you. Please – take me down.'

'Think about it?' he said. 'I won't take you down until you say you will.'

Couldn't he take anything seriously, not even a proposal of marriage?

I began to grow angry. 'Was that why you wanted to take me up? So that I'd be forced to listen to your proposal and forced to say that I might think about it?' I demanded.

'Not quite,' he said. 'I had thought you might say yes. Well, will you?'

'Take me down,' I said coldly. I felt the plane begin to

descend. The ground was coming closer. I was angry and upset and hardly noticed the bump of landing. David's hands leaned across me to unstrap my belt. 'I can manage,' I said coolly. 'Thank you for the flight, David. It was an experience I won't forget.'

He laughed. 'Please will you think about it?' he said. 'I promise that you wouldn't regret it. It would be fun – a lot of fun.'

He gave me his hand to help me out. I took it reluctantly, dropping it as soon as I could. I wanted to be on my own, to think about the extraordinary proposal I'd just had, but as soon as I'd climbed down from the plane I was surrounded by a horde of eager guests. *How did it feel, what could you see, would you do it again?* As I answered their questions, I found myself wondering what they would think if they knew I'd just had a proposal. If I'd accepted it, David would now be telling them I was to be his wife. What a way to announce it! The daring young pilot whom no girl could resist. I felt almost sure that that was what he'd planned – it would appeal to his sense of showmanship. He wouldn't have had the least idea I might turn him down.

David jumped down and the crowd that had surrounded me now surged over to him.

Flo touched my arm. 'You were very brave,' she said. 'What was it like?'

'Wonderful,' I said flatly. And it had been – until David

had spoilt it by proposing. I looked back – so many people were pressed around David that I could only just make out his dark head. Now that I had proved it was safe, no doubt he was being pestered to take others up, too. Arabella was gazing up at him adoringly. David would have more luck with her. She wouldn't care how he proposed. It would be a yes as soon as the words were out of his mouth.

Leaving them all crowded around the young pilot I stalked away. There was only one place I wanted to be. On my own. Flo hurried along by my side. 'Is anything wrong, Polly?'

We reached the house. On the steps I stopped. 'Flo, I just want to be alone.'

She looked hurt. 'I'm sorry, Flo,' I said. I hesitated. I hadn't intended to tell her about David's proposal, but maybe I should, and maybe she would tell her brother that he was wasting his time. 'Flo, I have something to tell you,' I said. 'Let's find somewhere quiet.' I opened the door to the drawing room, looking round it to make sure that we were alone. We were. All the guests were outside still, crowded round David's plane. David had caused a sensation. It was a party none of them were likely to forget. We sat down on a sofa, side by side.

'What do you want to tell me, Polly?' Flo asked.

'David proposed to me – in the plane,' I said.

'In the plane?' Flo repeated, as if she wasn't sure she'd heard what I'd said.

'Yes.'

'He proposed. He actually proposed?'

'Yes, Flo.'

She looked at me. *Please tell me you didn't accept him.*

'I didn't accept him, but he asked me to think about it. He was very determined.'

There. I had told her the truth, though I hadn't told her all of it. That I would never marry him, however long I thought about it, however many times he asked me.

She gazed at me. 'Polly, it is not my business, but you know what I think about David.'

'I do.'

'So?'

I shrugged.

'So you might marry him?' She looked at me in disbelief. It would be better for her if she did believe that I was considering David's proposal. Then perhaps the blind would drop from her eyes and she'd know me for what I was – a rebel. That I'd never be like her, or her brother. That she had made a mistake if she thought that I could ever grow to love Ferdy.

'Flo, how can I tell you what I might or might not do. David's proposal came as a surprise. I can't make decisions about my future just like that.'

'I'm glad that you told me, Polly,' Flo said earnestly. 'It means that we are friends – true friends.' She gave my arm a little squeeze. A big smile spread over her face. *Then there is still hope for my brother.* I gave up then. She could be as wilfully blind as she liked, I'd said all that I was going to say. I got up. I could see that some of the guests were making their way back to the house, and I could hear Uncle's loud voice outside the door.

'They're back. Flo, I don't want to talk to them. I'd like to be alone now for a while.'

She gave me a serious look. 'Will you tell me what you decide?'

'Of course I will.'

She gave me a little kiss. 'You know, I still hope that one day we may be sisters.'

I just smiled. I couldn't bring myself to tell her that we would never be that. And that it had nothing to do with what I said to David.

I opened the drawing room door and made a dash for the stairs before anyone saw me and tried to waylay me. I had told Flo the truth when I'd said I'd wanted to be on my own. It was still only eleven o'clock and lunch would not be served for another two hours. Surely no one would miss me if I kept to my chamber. And my chamber was almost the only place where I knew I'd be safe from David and Ferdy. I sat on the bed. I had a problem and I didn't know what to do. Two young men were eager to marry me. But I didn't want to marry either of them. There was only one person I did want, but he hadn't asked me.

I was so lost in my thoughts that I was surprised to hear Baxter's knock. My anger at David had subsided and I even felt a tiny flicker of pride. I'd had a proposal – in my very first season. And, whatever Flo thought, I knew that any number of girls would have been eager to accept David's proposal.

'Yes, what is it, Baxter?' I said.

'Didn't you hear it, Miss Polly? The gong has gone for lunch.'

Was it that time already? I leapt up.

'Sit down and let me do your hair, miss. It's a bit wild.'

I dabbed at it vaguely. 'Is it?'

'Yes, miss, sit down and I'll do it properly for you.'

I sat down obediently at the dressing table. I looked at myself in the mirror. Baxter was right. It was a bit wild. Flo was too well bred to have said anything, of course, but neither had anyone else. It was as if the morning's excitement had banished such important matters as appearance from our minds.

I felt Baxter's nimble fingers take out the pins that should have held my hair in place.

'What happened to it, miss?' she said.

'Did you see the plane, Baxter?' I asked.

She smiled. 'Yes, Miss Polly, I saw it come down and then go up again – more than once, too. Someone said that the pilot was one of the guests.'

'It was. He took me up. I got a bit windblown, I expect.'

'Miss Polly!' Baxter gasped.

'You should try it, Baxter,' I said, as if to fly in a plane was the sort of thing you did every day.

'You'd never get me up in one of those things, thank you, miss!' Baxter shuddered.

As soon as she had finished I hastened downstairs, slipping into the dining room just as the door was closing. I'd wanted to enter without anyone noticing but by being late I'd made myself conspicuous. Everyone looked up. There was one vacant place – next to Ferdy, of course. But beyond asking if I had everything I wanted, Ferdy was too nervous to say much to me. David, I was relieved to see, was at the far end of the table, on one side of Arabella. She shot me a triumphant glance, and I felt sure she had arranged for him to sit next to her. I amused myself wondering what she'd think if she knew that David had proposed to me. He was paying her a lot of attention. As we sipped our coffee afterwards I heard her say that she had enjoyed her flight enormously – and how she was longing to fly again. It had certainly added to her popularity. A group of guests not brave enough to fly had gathered round her. I wished I could think of an excuse to leave – I was weary of hearing her boast. But when a footman came to tell us that the horses were ready, if we'd like to make our way to the stables, I was in a quandary. I'd told Baxter to put out my riding clothes, but now I found I couldn't bear it if Fred saw Ferdy and me together again. When Ferdy came up to me, as I knew he would, I told him I was too weary to ride. He did his best to hide his disappointment. 'I'm sorry,' I said. 'Please make my excuses.'

'I wi-wi-will, of course, Miss Penelope,' he said.

As the party began to break up, I picked up a book. David had remained behind, too, and I prayed he wouldn't pester me again. But I needn't have worried. He had settled himself down near Arabella, leaning over the back of her chair and laughing at her remarks. If it was an attempt to pique me it failed.

I kept my head in my book, turning the pages as if I was very interested in it, but I could hardly focus on it at all. My boredom was intense, and I felt my resentment grow. If it weren't for them, I'd have been on Starshine now, riding across the fields, Fred by my side. I put the book down. After the big lunch I was beginning to feel sleepy. I felt my eyelids droop.

When I opened my eyes again, I saw that most of the guests had departed and the room was quiet except for the chatter of some of the older guests. I must have fallen asleep.

I glanced at the clock; it was almost time for tea. I still felt sleepy. A walk in the fresh air would wake me up. I had just time for a stroll before the riders returned.

Sam, the hall boy, opened the door for me and I walked down the steps. At the bottom I turned right, rather than left, to the ornamental gardens. There I ran no risk of running into returning riders, and I could avoid Ferdy's unwelcome attentions for a little while longer. I strolled along a winding gravel path that led to the Elizabethan knot garden. It was pleasant there, and there was a stone bench I could sit on and look out across the gardens to the rolling hills beyond.

I turned into the knot garden. The bench was already occupied. David and Arabella were sitting on it side by side. David was whispering something in Arabella's ear, then he took her face in both hands and gave her a kiss.

They couldn't have heard my gasp, but they must have felt my presence. They both looked up. David flushed red, but he quickly recovered himself. I saw a slow smile spread over Arabella's face. *So – you see that it is not just you who has admirers.* Let her savour this moment while she could; it wouldn't be for long. I walked up to them.

'You can forget your proposal of marriage, David,' I said.

I glanced at Arabella. She looked stunned, but nothing it seemed could disturb her composure for long. She gave a little laugh. 'Surely you don't think I care?' she said, but I saw her shift slightly away from David.

'No,' I said, 'I don't think you do. I don't think you care about anyone – either of you.'

I turned on my heel.

'Wait!' David said.

I turned back, expecting a plea for forgiveness, or at least some sign that he felt sorry. But he was smiling. How could he!

'Surely you don't object to a little harmless flirtation?'

What had he said? I shivered, as if a cold blast of air had suddenly swept through me. I felt as if I had seen into his heart, and I knew, as clearly as if he had told me, what marriage to him would truly be like.

'Do you really think I'd consider marrying you now!' We were talking to each other as if Arabella didn't exist. She looked at me with hate. I felt sure that she'd never forgive me.

'We'll see, shall we?' His eyes looked into mine. I felt as if he'd thrown down a challenge, but I had no intention of picking it up.

'Flirt with whom you like, David, it means nothing to me,' I said. I turned quickly away from them. I heard him laugh.

I walked on, hardly knowing where I was. I had to try to calm myself before I could go in to tea. At least I no longer needed to bother about David – heartless David. Flo had been right about him, and I had been right when I'd said that they didn't care about anyone but themselves. They suited each other.

I made my way into the drawing room. The footmen were laying out trays on tables with steaming teapots and china cups. Aunt saw me and beckoned me to her side. 'You haven't been riding, Penelope?'

I shook my head. 'I was too tired. But I've been out in the fresh air and I feel better now.' I sat down beside her. She gave me a searching look. Did the strain I still felt show on my face?

'How did you enjoy your flight?' she asked.

'Very much. He is a capable pilot, and I felt quite safe.'

Aunt gave me another thoughtful look. Was she trying to

draw me out? She must have observed David's attentions to me. But if she had she wasn't inclined to explore further.

'If I hadn't thought so, I'd never have let you up with him,' was all she said.

The footmen moved amongst us, handing out teacups and plates. David and Arabella had still not returned. A tiny frown settled on Aunt's face. 'Did you see Arabella while you were out?' she asked. 'She should be here to help me look after our guests. I wonder…' She glanced up at the clock. 'Yes, she should be here by now.'

'She may have forgotten the time,' I suggested. 'She was in the garden earlier.'

'It seems that she has,' Aunt said, dryly. She got up and tugged the bellrope. Barrett answered at once. I wondered what Aunt was saying to him. '*Be so good as to send a servant to the garden to inform Miss Arabella that it is time for tea.*' What would Aunt say if they were found together? I'd like to see Arabella attempt to explain herself. What sweet revenge that would be!

I finished my cup of tea. Aunt had drifted away to talk to Lady Waterlow, and Flo took her seat by my side. 'You didn't ride then?' she asked me.

'No,' I said, toying with my teacup. 'I didn't feel like riding this afternoon.'

I said it in such a way that she wouldn't say anything more. I looked around at the guests, idly chatting and gossiping as they sipped their cups of tea. Was this all that life was to hold for me? Just this – day after day? For ever? I felt panic rise inside me again. I felt trapped – a bird in a gilded cage. Was this how Mother had felt? No wonder she had fled.

'Doesn't all this bore you, Flo?' I found myself saying suddenly.

She looked bewildered. 'I don't understand.'

No, I thought, you don't. Marjorie would. She would understand how wrong I felt among these people. I gave Flo a rueful smile. 'I'm sorry, Flo, I'm not myself today.'

'Well, you had a proposal this morning, Polly. It would be surprising if you didn't feel ... well ... unsettled,' she said gently.

'I'm not going to marry him, Flo,' I said. *Oh, what made me say that?* Flo was beaming at me as if I'd handed her a present. Did she truly think that I'd turned David down for her brother? And here he was, sidling up to us, flushed and hopeful. I put my cup down. 'I ... I have something I have to do. Excuse me.' I made a dash for the door. I'd been rude, but I didn't care. I was halfway to the stairs when a door off the hall opened. Arabella was standing there. Her eyelids were red and swollen. I could see that she had been crying. I'd never seen Arabella cry before. I didn't think she knew how.

'You,' she said. 'How could you?'

'It is David you should blame, not me,' I said.

She dabbed at her eyes with a handkerchief. 'That wasn't what I meant. You told Mother where I was.'

Her moist eyes glared accusingly at me.

I felt a glimmer of guilt. But I banished it. I couldn't forget how often she'd gloated over me, the numerous petty unkindnesses. 'She asked if I had seen you,' I said coldly. I could feel my dislike of her increase with every second I stood there.

'Why did you come here?' she said. 'Why didn't you stay in – in India?' She spat out the word as if it tasted unpleasant.

'I didn't choose to come here,' I said, stepping back up the stairs. We were standing a good few yards apart, but it wasn't far enough for me. Her resentment seemed to breathe at me from every corner – to be woven into the very fabric of the house itself. I remembered how unwelcoming I'd always found it. So much of that was to do with Arabella. 'I'd leave today, if I could.'

'Oh you would, would you?' she said. 'I don't think so.' Her cold grey eyes glinted maliciously.

I fought down the panic that threatened to overcome me. She was guessing. She couldn't know about Fred and me. It was power Arabella sought, power over me. I kept my face as still as I could. I would not let her see how I felt.

'Arabella,' I said at last, 'if you have something to say, say it.'

She smiled – again, that cold reptilian smile. *The snake bites only when it is threatened or afraid.* We held each other's eyes. It was Arabella who dropped hers first. She gave a little laugh and walked away. I looked after her departing back. I wanted to go to the window, and fling it open to blow away the malice I felt all around me. I went slowly on up the stairs. I felt exhausted, as if I'd fought a battle. Arabella I knew would never forgive me. She stored up insults the way others stored compliments.

What was I to do? *If I married Ferdy…* I tried to imagine myself as Ferdy's wife. Ferdy was good and kind, and I would never have to see Arabella again. But it was hopeless. I just couldn't imagine it at all. I couldn't marry Ferdy, just to escape from Arabella. There was only one person I wanted to be with – but the prospect of that seemed further away than ever.

Upstairs

'Miss P-Penelope?'

I wheeled round at the sound of Ferdy's voice. 'Yes, what is it?' I said, trying to keep the impatience out of my voice. I was weary of the way he'd been following me about, like a puppy behind its master. How could I ever have thought I could marry him?

'I-I have something I want to say to you…' He looked almost as if he was in tears as he struggled for words. 'A-a-alone, please.'

It was coming. I felt sure of it. He was going to propose. I had hoped to spare him this. I'd said nothing to encourage him. He must know what my answer would be.

'Ferdy, I don't think you do,' I said. I wondered if Flo had told him that I had turned David down. She had looked so happy. I was afraid that she had, and that she had encouraged Ferdy to hope. Flo was so attached to her brother that she couldn't understand how anyone might not feel the same.

'Please,' he said, humbly.

I nodded. He opened the door to the morning room.

I walked in ahead of him, and sat down on a chair. He stood in front of me nervously.

'Miss P-Penelope. Penelope,' he said again.

'Yes, Ferdy.'

'Wou-wou-would you do me the honour of becoming my wife?' The words tumbled out as if he was hardly in control of them at all. I could hear how exasperated he was with himself as he struggled to express himself. Poor Ferdy, I thought.

'It's a great honour…' *What was I saying?* I looked up at him. He looked desperate. This was going to be harder than I'd thought. Forget the formal words, I thought. Just say it.

'Ferdy, I can't marry you.'

He looked at me as if I'd driven a knife into him. I'd wounded him cruelly, but I hadn't wanted to. I'd never thought that he'd mind so much. 'I'm so sorry, Ferdy.' I felt tears spring to my eyes.

'Ca-ca-.' Again he was struggling with the words. His face was flushed. 'Can't you … can't you think about it?' He looked at me pleadingly. 'Everyone wishes it. My sister. Your uncle and aunt.'

'Oh, Ferdy, this has nothing to do with them,' I said. 'This is about you and me.'

I just could not understand why he wanted to marry me.

'Ferdy,' I said, as gently as I could. 'We wouldn't be happy, you know. We're too different. I don't want to be a countess and spend the rest of my days being waited on, going to parties, to Ascot and Goodwood,' I said vaguely, hardly knowing what I was saying. 'You couldn't give me the life I want. I want to travel. I want to see the world – have adventures.'

'We could t-travel,' he pleaded. 'I am rich. We could go wherever you wanted.'

I shook my head. 'No, Ferdy.' He hadn't understood. I could never marry him. He was too young, too untried. And I felt he always would be. Birth and money would always protect him from adversity – from life itself.

'I love you,' he said. 'I loved you from the first moment I saw you.'

Oh, Ferdy. No, you don't. That's not love. You don't know me, you haven't even tried to get to know me. You'd grow to hate me, before you were ever able to love me.

'But I don't love you, Ferdy,' I said. 'I don't love you – at least not in the way I need to love you to marry you. I am so fond of you, Ferdy … but…' I sought for what to say, 'like a brother.'

'A little brother?' he muttered.

'A very dear brother.'

'There's someone else, isn't there?' He looked at me. I realized he was no longer stammering now that he was so much in earnest.

But why wouldn't he give up? Did he think that because he was rich he could have whomever he wanted?

'This is about us, Ferdy. You and me.' I couldn't think what else to say. I was getting weary. I stood up. 'I am very grateful to you, Ferdy. I hope that we will always be friends.' I held out my hand. He barely touched it.

I opened the door and quietly let myself out. In the hall I stopped. Aunt was standing there, an expectant smile on her face.

'Well,' she said. I felt sure she knew that Ferdy had proposed – and had no doubt about the outcome.

'I can't marry him, Aunt,' I said.

She looked astounded. I had turned down the future Earl Waterlow.

'I don't love him, Aunt. I can't marry someone I don't love.' I tried to walk past her but she came after me.

'Ferdy Waterlow could give you a very good home. What more do you want?' she said as if I hadn't told her.

'Someone I love,' I said defiantly.

'Love,' said Aunt half to herself. 'Just like her mother.'

How could she? How could she?

I burst into tears.

'Penelope,' she said gently. 'I am sorry. Let us talk about this quietly. Come!' She held out her hand. I wouldn't take it.

'Go away,' I sobbed. 'You don't care about me. You never have. You don't even try to understand me.'

Aunt looked dumbfounded. I didn't care. I ran up the stairs to my room. I couldn't stay there. I had to get away before they broke me – before the fate Mother had avoided became mine.

I hurried from door to chest to wardrobe, flinging a few things into a small dressing case, tears still running down my face. I unlocked the case where I kept Mother's things. There were the letters… I barely hesitated before tearing open the envelope of the oldest one. I recognized Aunt's handwriting. Some of the words were too faded for me to read. But the meaning was clear enough.

Dear Penelope, I read. *Your letter wounded me deeply. Surely you can see that we can never receive Alan here. The family was deeply insulted by your marriage. However, you are my sister and I love you as my sister. If ever you change your mind … that country is a dangerous unsafe place in which to bring up a child…*'

Even then Aunt could not bring herself to write the word – India. I sat with the letter in my lap. I looked at the date. It had been written about the time I was born. So Aunt had offered to have me brought up in England, or to be a home to Mother and me if she chose to leave Father. What sort of choice was that? I felt proud that Mother had spurned it. So what had made her change her mind? Why had she agreed in the end to send me here? Aunt had told me it was her dying wish. That Mother had regretted her decision to marry Father and run away with him to India. Let her think that if she wanted to. I hadn't believed her then, and I still didn't. I picked up another letter – the most recent one – and scanned it hastily.

I grieve to hear of your sickness and pray daily for your recovery. I have always regretted that you did not return to England…

There! She hated India. What other proof did I need?

My offer to take the girl remains open. Please will you consider it? What if sickness were to claim her, too?

'*What if sickness were to claim her, too?*' Was that why Mother had agreed to let me go? Had Aunt planted that fear in her? *A young lady needs a lady's example*, Father had said. But had that been the truth – the whole truth?

I'd probably never know, but deep down I felt certain it had never been Mother's dying wish to send me to England. At best she'd felt she had no choice.

But I did. I had a choice.

I stuffed the letters back into their envelopes and left them on the bed. When I'd gone, Aunt would find them and she would know why I had gone now, too. I didn't need to leave a note. Those letters were explanation enough.

I went to the door, and opened it. I almost fell into Baxter.

'Miss Polly?' She looked at my tear-stained face, at the dressing case in my hands. At the coat over my arm.

'Baxter,' I said. 'I'm going out.'

'What – with a case, miss?' she said. 'Oh no, Miss Polly.' She put a hand out to stop me.

I burst into tears again. 'Let me go! I must go.'

She took my arm. 'What's wrong? Where are you going? Please wait!'

'No.' I shook her off. 'No, I can't.'

I pushed past her and ran to the top of the stairs. I hurtled down them, not caring who saw me. One of the footmen opened the door for me. I don't know what he thought. I didn't stop to think.

I ran round to the stables.

Fred was there, but he wasn't alone. He was talking to the head groom. Did it matter now if anyone saw us together? But I made myself slip back out of sight until the groom had gone, then I called softly to Fred. He wheeled round. His eyes fell on me, on the dressing case, on the coat over my arm.

'What's happened?' he whispered. 'Are you going away? You look...' He shook his head bewilderedly.

I know. I look like a mad person. I feel like a mad person.

His eyes were anxious and strained.

'Are you going away?' he asked me again. 'Please – tell me.'

'Yes I am – with you.'

He looked startled. I'd thought he'd smile. I'd thought I'd said what he'd always wanted to hear. I was prepared to give up my life at Langdown Manor to be with him.

'No, look, something's happened, hasn't it? We'd better talk.'

'Yes,' I said urgently. 'I must talk to you.'

'It will have to be Starshine's stall,' he said. His calmness soothed me. I could feel that my hair was coming down in places, and I tucked some stray hairs back behind my ears.

'That's better,' he said. I could see that he was completely perplexed. Soon, soon I'd explain. He'd understand. He had to. I'd make him.

I followed him into Starshine's stall. He leaned back against the wall and looked at me, waiting for me to speak.

'Fred,' I said. 'I've had a proposal. I turned it down, but Aunt…' I turned my face away. 'She wants me to marry him. I can't marry him. He's like a boy. I feel as if they'll put me in a cage. I feel…'

Was anything I was saying making any sense to him? He still looked so bewildered.

'If it's because of me…' he said.

I felt cold creep through me from my toes to my head. Was he saying he didn't care? 'It's not just about you,' I said. 'It's about the life they want me to live. I can't marry him. I can't marry any of them. I can't stay here, Fred! They don't care about me. They don't understand me. My cousin Arabella hates me…' I began to weep.

'Oh, Polly,' he said.

I was still clinging to the dressing case. I felt Fred take it from me. His arms were about me. He stroked my hair. I wiped my eyes.

'Oh, Fred, can't we just leave? Now?' I looked at him beseechingly. 'What is there to keep us here anyway now?'

'We can't!' he exclaimed. 'You know that. How would we live?'

'I have some money. We could go to India,' I said eagerly. 'Father would help us.'

'Polly.' Fred took my hands in his. 'I'm not living off anyone. I want to make my own way in the world.'

'We can make it together,' I said. There had to be places where no one would care who we were or where we came from. Where hard work, energy and endeavour were respected more than social rank and wealth.

He shook his head. 'We can't leave – just like this.' I felt tears start to my eyes again. He stroked my cheek. I took his hand and kept it there. 'I know you're upset. But, Polly, they cannot make you marry anyone you don't want to. Really, they can't.' He shook my hand gently. 'You don't have to marry anyone ever, if you don't want to.'

'What am I to do? I can't stay here!'

'Polly,' he said, 'I've been thinking a lot about us. We're both so young.' I was beginning to feel as if I'd proposed and he'd turned me down. 'Now that Mam's dead...' He swallowed. I knew how painful it was for him to say those words, for I found it painful, too. '...and the children are at Uncle's, I'm free to make my own choices. I was going to tell you this soon anyway.' He hesitated. 'I'm leaving Langdown. I'm going away – far away.'

I'm going away. What was he saying? Couldn't he take me with him? How could he even think of leaving me behind?

‘On your own?’ I managed to whisper.

‘On my own. Polly, I’m going abroad – to Africa. I want to look about me, find a job…’

I was feeling almost as if I had stepped into the past, as if it was Mother and Father who were talking, not Fred and me. I pushed the thought away. That was the past – their past. Not us, not our future. That still lay ahead.

‘Can’t I come with you?’

Mother had run away with Father.

He shook his head. ‘No, Poll. It would be too dangerous. I don’t know where I’ll be sleeping, under a bush probably. Or if we’d even have enough to eat. Can’t you see that it’s impossible?’

Then why did he have to go away? Didn’t he love me? I could never leave him so easily.

I let go of his hand that I’d been clasping and rested my head against Starshine.

‘It’s for the best, Poll.’

For whose best? Yours, or mine?

‘We can never be together here,’ he said. ‘I can’t bear to see you, knowing that. It hurts too much. Always having to meet in secret. Never knowing when I’ll see you. Always having to pretend. I can’t go on like this, Poll. I can’t.’

‘So you do care, a bit.’ My voice was muffled against Starshine’s coat.

‘Oh, Poll, you know I do.’

But I felt as if I could already see the ocean separating us. Mile upon mile of water, as far as the eye could see. As if he was speaking to me from a long long way away. I swallowed.

'Why Africa? Why does it have to be so far away?'

'Because I could have a future there. There is a future there for young men like me. If I work hard…' He smiled, but he wasn't smiling at me, he was smiling at something far away, something I couldn't see, something I couldn't share.

Would I ever?

'Will you come back for me?' He would never know how hard it was to ask him that.

He stepped towards me, and took my hand in his.

'I've something I've been wanting to give you,' he said. He felt in his pocket and I saw him draw something out. He slid it on to the fourth finger of my left hand. I gazed at the simple band of gold on my finger. 'It was Mam's,' he said. 'Will you keep it safe for me…?'

'Then?'

'Yes, Poll. I will come back.'

He leaned his head close to mine. I studied his features one by one. Then I kissed the ring and entwined my fingers with his. 'I will never take it off,' I said.

I picked up the dressing case. If I was careful, I'd get back to the house before anyone else saw me. Baxter would say nothing, some of the other servants might gossip, but it would blow over. And Aunt? Arabella? As I looked at the ring on my finger they seemed to dwindle. I could face them even now.

'When will you leave?' I said. I felt sick just asking that. I dreaded what he might say. But I had to know.

'I've to ask his lordship.'

'So, not yet?'

'Not yet.'

We smiled at each other. We squeezed each other's hands. Then we let them go.

I'd see him tomorrow. He'd be here in the morning. And the morning after that. It wasn't goodbye. Not yet. And I had his promise. It shone on my finger. He would come back for me.

'I'll see you tomorrow,' I said.